Praise f   y

"I've been telling   the moment
I read the first sho.   , 'Intertropical
Convergence Zone,' and apparently, ...   irt from exactly
no one. Which is only as it should be—Nadia is the coming storm,
a 21st-century baby whose particular brand of politicalpunk witchcraft should determine the way the wind blows over horror's next
few decades. She's exactly the sort of fabulist we most deserve, especially in this potentially catastrophic era… one who casts a cold,
assessing eye over the wreckage before cobbling it together into the
image of some loathsome new god, the kind that runs on blood
worship and drunken karmic nihilism. And when we're all down
in the mud crying and cutting each other like good little cultists,
pinned flat by the weight of her shadow, I can only aspire to be the
first to admit we did this to ourselves."

—Gemma Files, author of *Experimental Film*

"Weird fiction has been stuck in the era of new-fangled radio sets
and fifteen-cent pulp magazines for ninety years. Finally, Nadia
Bulkin has come to drag us kicking and screaming into the horrors
of The Endless Now with a collection of hip, ultracontemporary,
politically astute, and chilling stories."

—Nick Mamatas, author of *I Am Providence*
and *The Last Weekend*

"Bulkin delivers a dose of delicious darkness with her debut
collection."

—World Fantasy Award-winning editor Silvia Moreno-Garcia

"An expert balance of the fantastic and horrific, *She Said Destroy* is
a prime example of how modern fabulism continues to reinvigorate
and reinvent all modes of speculative fiction. This book is inven-
tive, insightful, and inspiring, not to mention unnerving. The stories inside deftly blend the horrors of the cosmic with those of the
personal, evoking awe both terrifying and sublime. Nadia Bulkin's
writing is beautiful, exciting, and a stellar contribution to the field
of fantastic literature."

—Simon Strantzas, author of *Burnt Black Suns*

Praise for Nadia Bulkin's *She Said Destroy*

"Horror is a tough act to perfect, but time after time, piece after piece, Nadia Bulkin shows us how it's fucking done. Her fiction dances along a razorwire tightrope, juggling the horrific and the grotesque with flourishes of pitch black humor, the darkly fantastical with the achingly real, and more original monsters than a medieval bestiary. This sharp, sinister, and stylish collection encapsulates why Bulkin is one of my favorite contemporary short story writers."
  —Jesse Bullington, author of *The Enterprise of Death*

"The dark stories of *She Said Destroy* are harrowing, astute tales of horror and the fantastic, vagabond journeys through the regions and classes of today's world, alongside the forgotten and the monstrous. Bulkin's craft is an enlivening, challenging, and distinctive voice that lingers long after reading, and reshapes weird fiction each time."
  —Andrew S. Fuller, author, editor *Three-lobed Burning Eye* magazine

"Nadia Bulkin's unique, intelligent voice captured me the first time I read one of her stories. She's never let me down since!"
  —Paula Guran, editor of *The Year's Best Dark Fantasy & Horror*

"Nadia Bulkin writes prose like a scalpel, deftly slicing to the beating hearts of her characters and the dilemmas they confront. Impressive in subject and setting, these stories range far and wide through literary and cultural history to find the darkness that threads through the (post) modern world. As substantial a debut as I've seen, and highly recommended."
  —John Langan, author of *The Fisherman*

SHE SAID DESTROY

SHE SAID DESTROY

NADIA BULKIN

WORD HORDE
PETALUMA, CA

She Said Destroy © 2017 by Nadia Bulkin
This edition of *She Said Destroy* © 2017 by Word Horde

Introduction © 2017 by Paul Tremblay

Cover art © 2017 by Kathrin Longhurst
Cover design by Scott R Jones

Edited by Ross E. Lockhart

An extension of this copyright page appears on page 241

First Edition

ISBN: 978-1-939905-33-8

A Word Horde Book
www.wordhorde.com

TABLE OF CONTENTS

To my mother Jan and my best friend Lindsey, for everything.

INTRODUCTION BY PAUL TREMBLAY

"At the beginning, at the very very beginning of time, the General ate a bullet."

I f I could be allowed to intro the intro with a small bit of fannish, personal indulgence...

The opening story to this collection, "Intertropical Convergence Zone," isn't the first story Nadia published, but it is the first story of hers I read. It was published summer of 2008 by the venerable *Chizine*, a now defunct webzine that remains near and dear to my heart. My winning their 2003 fiction contest (Nadia won their 2010 contest with "Pugelbone") was the first hey-maybe-I-can-do-this boost to my fledgling career, and I then spent a few years as one of *Chizine*'s fiction editors.

I was no longer an editor at the zine at the time of her story's publication, but oh I was jealous of all who got to read it before me. I read it late one summer night (cursing the white letters on black background that had me blinking and blurry afterwards) and if I didn't actually say the following out loud (I'm willing to bet I did), I thought, *Holy shit! Who wrote this?* She had me hooked from the opening sentence (quoted above).

Being an inveterate music geek I compare the excitement of finding a new-to-me author to discovering a new band. At first

I selfishly hoard the music and lyrics to myself (Look what I found! It's mine, all mine!), but that stage rapidly morphs into obsessive proselytizing, telling everyone I know about my new favorite band and making them listen and then judging them if they do or don't get it.

Yeah, that's how I felt after reading "Intertropical Convergence Zone," Nadia's blistering and gut-wrenching reimagining of the Suharto presidency in Indonesia. I was a juror for the Shirley Jackson Awards the year her story was published and I took a fan's unearned and obnoxious pride in my fellow jurors' joy at reading, discussing, and then nominating the story for the award.

It was as fans first (clumsy editors second) that John Langan and I asked Nadia if she would write a story for our *Creatures: Thirty Years of Monsters* anthology. Most of that book is comprised of reprints and we only had the budget for two original stories. Nadia was at the top of our wish list. "Absolute Zero," the brilliantly weird and melancholy inversion of *Frankenstein* in which a lonely Nebraskan teen's deadbeat dad is a stag-headed monster, is included in this collection.

She Said Destroy will infect you and then you'll be pressing this book into other people's hands like you once forced your friends to listen to mix tapes (sorry, I'm old) or mix CD's (see previous paranethical) of your favorite bands. I'll try not to beat the music metaphors to death (too late, but I don't feel too bad about it as Nadia has lyric quotes and song references on her website, so there!), but Nadia is a punk rocker.

"…because I will always be your General."

Nadia has a clear personal, academic, and professional interest in politics, and the politics of Southeast Asia specifically. She grew up in Indonesia and lived through the turmoil and chaos prior-and-post fall of President Suharto. She later earned advanced degrees in Political Science and International Politics; her M.A. thesis was titled "Constructing the National Project: Toward Democratic Nationalism in Indonesia."

Part of the magic of Nadia's fiction is that her stories are rooted in the complexity and nuance of socio-politics without ever being didactic or staid. Nadia has a fierce sense of justice—particularly when it comes to how politics affects the ordinary citizens and the forgotten people who live at society's edges—and righteous outrage at the broken compact of the social order. These incredibly taut stories are alive, intelligent, humane, so of our time as to be prophetic, and unlike the work of anyone else writing contemporary horror fiction. Within her integrity of vision she manages a delicate balance of anger, empathy, and melancholy so resonant and recognizable to those who dare pay attention to what's happening around them and within the wider world. In Nadia's fictional universe, regional myth and brutal realism are as blurred as betrayal and loyalty and her expertly wrought characters perform or attempt to survive horrific acts in the name of one or both. (*"We're not turning into better people, but our retribution is getting closer."*) We are made to see and to be able to identify the lasting stain of violence perpetrated by individuals and by the state. The body politic is itself the monster here (*"You live in a monster's empire"*), a ravenous entity that consumes its downtrodden constituents, the ones who can see their own end coming, just as it eventually consumes the queens and kings who are willing feed it whatever and whomever it demands.

Within the pages of *She Said Destroy* you'll find a man willing to do anything to be a forever president and another man who must painfully supply the grease to those grinding political gears; a rage-fueled final girl batters and bests an all-too-familiar, murderous monster (*"dumb beasts can't help it and we can't help them"*); a dystopic underground nightmare built on the broken backs of ancestry and class; a poor babysitter is charged with watching the cursed children of a well-to-do family who were "born lucky"; a hotel that once hosted a notorious war criminal now houses an unexpected ghost; and a tour de force reimagining of Innsmouth via Indonesia.

> *"…a final signal of Truth emitted from some deep crevasse of the world. Listen."*

Not every story here is overtly political. What is also startling about *She Said Destroy* is its range of subjects and characters, including the lost Midwest small-town teens of "Only Unity Saves the Damned" who yearn to escape their depressed fiscal destiny through a faked viral video about a local legend, another Midwest small town haunted by the ghost town next door with "Seven Minutes in Heaven," and the bullied school girls bent on otherworldly revenge of "Girl, I Love You."

However, Nadia knows politics are impossible to avoid in fiction, especially, I would argue, in horror fiction. And she knows refusing to choose a side is in fact making a choice. Nadia chooses to tell the stories of the outcasts and disenfranchised. Her stories are transgressive and progressive like most of the best horror stories are. The best horror stories, the ones that stay with you long past the reveal or the affect, are the ones that expose their characters to a calamitous, horrific truth that changes everyone and everything irreparably. There is no restoration for the status quo. Change is forever. The reader is of course changed too.

In the "socio-political horror" stories (Nadia's apt self-description) of *She Said Destroy*, we're confronted with uncomfortable truths about family, religion, politics, and our place within all three we cannot ignore or avoid. Nadia dares ask her characters, and by proxy us her readers, the most difficult questions in art and literature: Why is the world like this now? Will it always be like this? What are we going to do now? How does anybody live through this? How are you going to live through this?

The answers in *She Said Destroy* are a defiant call and they are as boundless and as terrifying as the collective hope and horror of us.

"And last the darkness"

Paul Tremblay
5/29/2017

INTERTROPICAL CONVERGENCE ZONE

At the beginning, at the very very beginning of time, the General ate a bullet. Those of us who weren't sure about the dukun were worried, and we sat with our elbows on our knees and our chins on our fists around the table, under the single naked bulb with the dangling string. The dukun, who said his name was Kurang, had already washed the bullet in holy water that he said came from the very north-of-the-equator springs the Sultans of Sriwijaya bathed in. He said some incantations and then told the General to eat it.

"There. Eat. Eat it. It will make you know things about people, so you know where to aim when you shoot them."

The General stared at the bullet until sweat dropped onto the plate.

Kurang bent over. "Mister General," he said, "I promise, good things will happen. You'll see like a garuda, Mister General." He always mocked us. Kurang was one of those villagers who doesn't really give a shit about national unity. They're godless men and that's another thing that bothered me, because the General was devout as all hell. "And then you lift your gun, or they lift their guns..." He looked at us, the uncomfortable posse. "And you

1

know exactly where to aim. This bullet has the gift, Mister General. It will give you the gift too."

We'd pulled it out of a dead man two days earlier. A clean heart wound that had punctured a major artery—he died immediately. It was perfect, we thought as we smoked our Marlboros and sat on our folding chairs, watching the corpse. Of course we bound him up first and put him against the chalk sketch lines on the basement wall so he wouldn't squirm and so we knew where to nuzzle the barrel. What Kurang told us was this: the dead man has to be the right man, the bullet has to go through the heart, and the bullet has to kill right away.

He was someone who'd been in on our list for a while. A Communist, of course, a party pusher who carried around paperback Mao and mingled with pushcart-peddlers and pretended to be one of them. He was going to go eventually, so we figured, may as well be now.

"Eat it, Mister General. Don't you want to be a great man?"

He took it like a pill. He started choking. We pushed our chairs back and got up and cursed at Kurang but Kurang was already right at the General's side, helping him swallow the tea. "There, there," said Kurang. "Hush hush, it's okay, Mister General."

We waited for something to change. Nothing did at first. The General made a joke, we laughed; he announced he was going to bed to sleep, and Kurang said that was a good idea. The General walked out of the room rubbing his ribcage, looking puzzled. We said to ourselves: okay, if he's dead tomorrow morning, so is that dukun.

But he wasn't dead. He was up bright and early and he wasn't wearing his glasses when we had our morning meeting in his office. He doled us out assignments. They had schedules on them and everything. We asked him why he wasn't wearing his glasses and he said, "Don't need them. I feel so sharp today. It's like looking through a submarine periscope, you know?" And he made this pantomime motion of a navy admiral looking through a periscope and adjusting the lens and then laughed. We all laughed. He laughed until he coughed out a tiny pellet of a bullet that burned one of his memos. We asked the dukun but he said that was a normal side effect.

So that was how it started. Nothing very strange. My daughter was drawing people's faces back then, which was also not very strange, except she never filled them in. Whole families without faces.

***

A week later the General had indirectly sent ten of the most dangerous Communist strategists into the next world. I assume they went to hell, but I've never been to check. They were hidden ones with inconspicuous day jobs—moonlighters. One was a doctor, one taught mathematics. The Communists were squabbling now like hens without a rooster, and they went looking for new warmth. They went for navymen. I don't know what's wrong with the navy, if it's from fighting pirates in the Sunda Strait or if it's just being seaborne that fucks with your head, but they had too many dinners with Communists. I have always thought this.

I was getting out of the lounge when I saw Kurang on the street corner in this horrible fake trenchcoat with buttons hanging like eyes out of sockets. He wasn't even smoking, he was just there.

"What? Looking for a hooker?"

"You want to help Mister General, right, Lieutenant?"

I looked around for any President's men. Just zombies and

shapeshifters, hanging around in rags and eating noodles, probably infected with hookworm eggs. I looked at Kurang. "Are you
following me?"

"You're the best Lieutenant. Mister General needs to get those
sea-men to see his way, see?"

There were all these prickly red, bulging spots on his face.
Sometimes I thought they were moving, but then I'd think, no,
trick of the light.

"There's this knife, a kris. It's on one of the outer islands.
Right now a fisherman's son has it. If the General eats it he will
be able to draw people to him and command them, you know,
make them see like he sees. You go get it and bring it here, we'll
dress it up nice."

It was for the General, so, okay. I love this country, and Com-
munism's a Satan and the President's its lackey. Leave it to them
and we'll all be starving and dying in shrapnel and colorful
bombs. No, no. We need a man like the General, an honest
man. He's one of us.

Before I left I went home. My daughter had begun to draw
deep-sea creatures by then. She gave them all to me, slips of paper that she folded into infinite squares and I put in my wallet.
"To protect Daddy," she said, and then went back in the house.
I hated the pictures. Curling, coiling beasts. I didn't want their
protection, but I kept them anyway.

***

I stood on the sand, shifting. The waves there came from Australia. The dukun told me the name of the island and village and
the man, and I asked the locals to fill in the rest. When they saw
my credentials and I said that the General needed their help,
they helped me. Sometimes I had to show them my gun.

I got to the beach by motorbike. That was our last frontier, those eastern islands. They were populated by people but I think those people were a different species. It was in their eyes. I could tell. Even the children had that look. They all had filariasis, and maybe that was why—microscopic worms sleeping in their veins. It's a horrible disease. They're the only people in this heat-soaked country who shiver in the sun.

At the beach there was no one. There was a limping half-wild dog, and there was a kite. I thought the men at the convenience store had lied to me, it wouldn't be too surprising, but then I saw him—seventeen years old, curly black hair, standing by his father's boat. He had the kris sticking out of his backpocket. He didn't know what to do with either. I went toward him and stood on the shifting sand and called to him to give me the knife, I worked for the General and I needed it.

His lips moved and his head shook to say no, but I didn't hear any words. All I heard was the sound of a low motor, not the Pacific, but a real low motor that opened up with a chainsaw sound into a voice—like jaws being torn open and held there. It was the knife. I saw its handle swivel in the backpocket of his trousers—it turned to look at me.

It said, "Eat me, Lieutenant."

I didn't dare look at it even though its booming voice pounded in my ears. I held out my hand to the fisherman's son, and said something to him—I don't remember what because I never heard it. All I heard was:

"Eat me and be great. I will live between your lungs and I will give your voice a resonance you have never known. Eat me, Lieutenant."

The boy backed onto the damp, dark parts of the sand. The knife was thunderous and the waves were rocking. He shook his head no no no, and then he reached behind his back and grabbed the screaming knife and yelled.

When I shot him he was flying toward me with the kris quivering in the sun. I saw all the way into the back of his mouth. His body went sloshing to Australia on a bed of foam but the knife stayed, stuck in the sand. Hermit crabs came out of the spot in droves where it burrowed. All up and down the beach it called and called. And I was all alone to listen to the beached monster. I thought this was the end of the world. All I saw was ocean, the color of sky, and all I heard was the dark sound of power being born. I wrapped my hand in cloth and I pulled it out of the sand. There was my face in the blade. By then the knife was no longer articulate. It was just the sound of the great furnace, the great God, roaring in want. The kind of sound caves make when you are alone inside them. But I did not touch it, I kept my mouth shut, and I put it in a plastic bag.

Then a plane passed overhead. The wolf-dog came lolling over the dunes and I saw the fisherman's son rising and falling. He was about the size of a shark fin by then. I climbed back to the palm trees, where the motorbike was.

***

Kurang broke the kris into manageable pieces. This surprised us, because he was a feeble man, all bones and no taller than a pony's shoulder. But he split it with his bare hands and then, panting, told the General to eat.

What if the pieces caught in his throat?

"They want to be with you," said Kurang. He leaned over into the light—turned out he had a lazy eye that I hadn't seen before. "Mister General, the knife wants to help you."

The General, who now accidentally spit tiny burning bullets at foot-soldiers when he yelled at them during drills and had already blinded one, agreed to partake of the knife with less coaxing than Kurang needed to get him to swallow the bullet. He had been paranoid, the past few days, that his chance to rescue the country was slipping by. He thought the President was in talks with Communists and that it would end for all of us. Our jobs, our lives, the bright new tomorrow.

According to the servants he had some coughing fits the night after he ate the knife. But the very next day he made a statement condemning Communists as heathens and urging people not to forget what made this baby country of ours so great: unity, justice, development, democracy, and deference to God. And the everymen said yes. That's all I heard in the warung over sweet black coffee and kretek, wow, what a smart man he is. He's got the right idea. I agree completely. The General also slashed the sheets getting out of bed as well as the morning paper, and there was some accident with the family cat—nothing fatal, just a peculiarity.

When I got out of the warung it was like I knew Kurang would be there, and he was, with a smile.

"What does he need now?"

"He needs protection from death. He needs to be able to survive his enemies' bang-bangs." He cocked his head. "He wants to be Forever President, Lieutenant. So he can fix everything." Then Kurang winked. It was insulting and cheap and I tried to hit him, I don't know why. He was a dukun, I should have known he wouldn't let me. A blast wave blew up from behind his left ear and threw me back.

"But the General *does* want to fix everything," I said after I got my breath back. "People are tired of being poor and they're tired of seeing the President blow it on whores and private—"

"Oh yes, monies. They'll come too. But first things first, Lieutenant, and first he needs longevity." There were definitely things under his skin, no doubt now—long tape worms pressed up around his cheeks. Almost like burn-scars but these wobbled, and tonight his hair was churning too, filled with what looked like fingers. "There is a very old goat that lives in Jogja. Mister General will need its liver."

Before I walked off I looked back at Kurang, still standing with his back to me, still wriggling with all the things inside him. "Maybe you should see a doctor about that," I said.

He turned around but I can't say what happened then because I just started to run. I remember for the next week I didn't look in mirrors and I might as well have been shaving blind. My daughter saw all the cuts on my face and asked if I had been in a fight with witches. I thought about what to say and finally I said yes. I said yes, I had, I was fighting to protect her. Then I kissed her earlobe and her tiny golden earring, and she gave me another picture. I tried to be proud like when her brother brought home perfect math scores but it was just so horrible. I asked her what it was. "It's to protect Daddy," she said stubbornly. So I don't know what it was. There were yellow eyes but there was also an uncooked darkness, and something like a mouth, if those were fangs. I wondered if I should have been grateful. At least she was drawing faces now.

***

I went by plane. It was not quite Jogja, but a subvillage. I put my hands in my pockets and said I was looking for a very old goat. They thought I wanted to buy it and so they all claimed to own it—or if not a goat, a cow with three horns or a chicken with no head. But then there were the school children. "Is there a very old goat in this village anywhere?" With big malnourished eyes they stared. I gave them money and where they pointed I went.

At a little house, under a spirit-willow, sat a man half-blind with age and chemicals, who sang to himself. He took me to the orange orchard to see the goat, and then stood there whistling by the roadside. The creature hobbled in the grass, gnawing on orange rinds. It was clearly weak but still it wore a loose rope that tied it to a tree.

"You can't buy it, you know," said the old man, swaying with his cane. "It's one with me. It was born the same day I was and I can't part with it." It was true, they both had eyes the color of haze, and hair the color of smoked bone. The same awkward gait from back legs that were too long. Maybe they were congenital twins. I took out a cigarette.

"I don't want to buy it. What do you think would happen if it died?"

"Oh, I don't think it will. It's one hundred and two."

The goat lifted its head and after a search its cataract eyes fell upon me. It was older than my father. I couldn't even imagine a world that old. That was far far before the beginning of time. It outlived the Dutch and the Japanese and the Dutch again. It probably never thought a native son would harm it. For a moment the cigarette just sat between my lips, dumb and silent. The goat bleated wretchedly. It started stumbling our way, on furbare legs and cracked hooves.

"Maybe it's tired of life," I suggested.

"Nonsense," said the old man. "It will live forever."

I thought about luring it to me with a salty hand and giving it a deceptive calming squeeze before gutting it, but in the end I just grabbed it by the neck, rough and unceremonious, and slit its jugular. Of course I watched sacrifices when I was a boy but this was profane. I wiped my hands on its fur—sick old blood, it's the sickest thing—and looked back at the old blind man. I already knew he was going to die. When the last pumps of life gave from the goat and onto my shoes, the old blind man started to bleed. Just then. In the neck. The only body I could drag back was the goat's and even though it was in a burlap sack the village knew and was silent. I never lit that fucking cigarette.

***

No persuasion was necessary to make the General eat the goat's well-aged liver. He gobbled it down and, when the raw slab went slipping down his throat, looked up in eagerness. Kurang patted him on the head—no choking this time, it went down easy besides giving him a drugged look—and said, "You're going to be President for a long time, Mister General. Maybe fifty years."

"Fifty?" said the General, and snapped his fingerblades. A bullet coalesced on his tongue and Kurang had to duck to avoid it. "You said I would be President forever!"

"Well, no one can be President for*ever*," said his dukun, and gave him the glass of tea. "But I promise that you will live forever in their hearts and their history books. You will have the biggest chapter, Mister General. Your shadow will loom forever, on monuments, on boulevards. Like Mount Bromo, you will be like Mount Bromo, okay?"

The man himself had not grown but by dawn he'd become impermeable. He was a monolith, an impenetrable fortress that was sharp to the touch and spat bullets. He fired his bodyguards. And his hair turned gray overnight and he walked with a strange limp, so he put on his army cap and sat in leather chairs with golden curlicues for feet and looked majestic.

Kurang was waiting for me when I got home. He'd gotten through the peeling front gates somehow and was leaning against an outer wall of the house, just barely out of sight. I threw up my hands.

"There is nothing more he needs!"

"He wants to be loved."

I blinked. The sun had turned our garden purple. Everywhere were rainbows. "He *is* loved," I said. "We love the General. We'll follow him anywhere, to the end of time if we have to."

"He wants to be loved by the people. He wants them to look at his portrait after he is gone and think, oh, my father, my dead father, how your children miss you." He rubbed his feet together. Something came slithering out from under his pant leg and it swam through the tiles of our veranda and then dove into a bed of bougainvillea. "Or something like that. He wants to have that statue in the center square, with little children on his arms, like parrots. He wants to be shown all smiles. You understand?"

"What is it then that he needs to be loved?"

"He needs your daughter's heart."

I walked for hours in the city after he told me that. Of course I said no. But Kurang said, if you don't do it we'll find someone else who will, and to have it to headquarters by the beginning of the coup. Three days, he'd said and lifted his fingers with a smile. I walked for hours, me and the legless beggars and the eyeless cats. They reached their limbs out to me and begged me to help them in a way only the General could. And now and then under street lamps, behind minivans, I would see Kurang. with his fingers raised in a salute. At the end of the first day one of his fingers fell off, and then there were only two.

Please know this—I loved my daughter, love her still. Please never doubt this. But I did not know what else to do. Yes, I thought about hiding her away in the mountains, with her grandparents, in that village washed up against the Australian sea. But he would have found her. And when I pointed my gun at Kurang and said leave her alone or I will shoot, of course my gun jammed. And then I said take my heart instead, but Kurang said mine was a murderer's. It wasn't good enough.

"You can keep your son," said Kurang, "and your wife. Aren't you willing to sacrifice just this one thing of yours for the good of your people? Selfish selfish, Lieutenant. Men like you are the reason this country is going to shit."

I was curled up on the sidewalk beating my head against the concrete and crying, "I can't, dear God, I can't."

"Then just bring her to headquarters. Someone else will do it. You can hold her hand."

When I came home at the end of the second day my daughter ran to me and wrapped her little arms around my legs. "Don't you have a picture for me today?" I asked; she said, "I've hidden it, Daddy. You'll find it later."

I said we had to go to Daddy's office and I held her very close, close enough to feel that precious heart of hers rejoicing while mine wept. She had a strong beat, my little girl. I knew that before she was born, when I listened to her drumming in her mother's belly. Stronger than mine. And despite the monsters in her drawings she was all smiles, all the time—even that night, as her long lashes closed in contentment and she waited. Dear God, Dear God. Every day I ask her to forgive me, and every day I pray she doesn't.

***

The General became our paterfamilias. He was painted on billboards with children on his lap, all of them pointing at some new horizon just over that swath of development projects. People do greet him with jubilation, they kiss the rings on his fingers and thank him for all the good he's done. His birthday celebrations at the palace are something else, or so I've heard.

He sends me pictures in manila envelopes. I suspect Kurang would have advised him against it, but Kurang is dead now. His head fell off a couple years back, and it turned out there was nothing inside of him but snakes and grubs and centipedes. The General says he draws these things late at night and he doesn't know why he feels that he should send them to me or why they come racing out of his fingers, but I do, and I tape the monsters up all over the house, over family portraits, over the clock, over the calendar.

And I wait for him to die. I know he's a good man who's done good things. God only knows he's a better President than that Communist. I just think, maybe when he's dead, he'll give me back her heart.

THE FIVE STAGES OF GRIEF

Matilda died on Saint Agatha's Day, even though she is my patron saint. When Matilda took a bad turn and the doctors said it was time to make preparations, Mother and Father gave Saint Agatha to Matilda, just because of the date. She was too young to be confirmed and they couldn't let her cross over without a patron saint.

But Saint Agatha was mine, and I thought that Matilda could have chosen her own, because she came home the morning after feast day in her hospital gown. Father was carrying her. I remember—I was sitting on the chair with Lelacey on my lap facing the locks and bolts on the door. Mother was carrying all of Matilda's things, the stuffed rabbit and the picture books and the little yellow duck that clapped. The three of them went up the stairs in a flurry, with Mother singing nursery rhymes. I watched Matilda during their ascent and she had a strangeness in her eyes, a distance. They'd get darker later, as weeks passed.

She sat at the table and watched us eat for the first of many times that night. Mother talked to her continuously, but the rest of us couldn't. For all of Mother's prodding Matilda would only stare at the food. She didn't have silverware or a plate set out for her but she still reached over to the potatoes with her pale baby arms.

"Matilda," said Mother, but she put them in her mouth anyway. Then her face puckered.

"I can't taste it!" said Matilda. She shoveled in more and her tantrum became an alarm because she couldn't taste any of it, she said. Father said that she wasn't really hungry, this was just out of habit, and Mother just said her name: Matilda, Matilda.

I sent myself to bed early, and took Lelacey with me. Her screaming went on for another hour before quiet overcame, and then our bedroom door opened and Father brought Matilda in. She was a still heap by then—it looked like he was carrying a stack of fire logs. He tucked her in and took a step back as if he was making sure that the sheets weren't moving with her breathing. I called him and he came.

"Why is Matilda still here?" I was whispering so she wouldn't hear even though her bed, aside from the lump in the middle that was her, looked unlived in. It was no change for me—it was lifeless and bare all through her hospital stay too. "Grandma and Grandpa went to Zurichia."

He stroked my arm. He squinted but it was dark. When he smiled his teeth didn't show, they didn't glimmer—they were hiding behind his workman lips. "Because we're not ready for her to go yet."

I looked at the unmoving piece of driftwood in her bed, and I nodded, because Father looked like he needed me to understand. And after he left I did sleep for a bit with Lelacey in the crook of my knees, but I woke up sometime before light when Lelacey started bristling and hissing, with Matilda standing over me all pale-faced and dead. I only came to the hospital a few times and I never got very close—there was concern about a contagion, and I hadn't had all my shots—but even then I never remembered her smelling like sulphur: just antiseptic and the lilies Mother always brought. She was so pale, so sunken in. I wanted to hide but I knew if I pulled the covers over my head, she'd still be there, this dark amorphous blur behind the cotton.

"Go back to sleep," I said, without looking at her.

"Nothing happens when I close my eyes."

Grandpa was only with us for a week after he died, and he spent most of that time while he was waiting for Grandma in the big rocking chair—not rocking, really, just resting his eyes like he said. I suppose he didn't sleep since he could no longer wake. He didn't go to bed and he didn't try to eat, and he was fine. Quiet, yes, and faded, but in no distress. Matilda was confused.

"It's okay. Just lie down and close your eyes. Mama and Papa'll wake you up tomorrow."

"Molly, I don't feel sick anymore."

"You're all better now, that's why."

"Why is 'Lacey mad at me?"

I moved my hand down to pet her and Lelacey's tabby back arched and her fur flared out like a mane. With three strokes she settled down again but she kept growling at Matilda from behind my legs with her ears flat against her head and her eyelids peeled back. I said I didn't know why, but I wanted to say other things. That Lelacey didn't like the dead, that Lelacey could smell the sulphur on her; that Lelacey wished she had gone straight on to Zurichia instead of lingering in our safehouse. But I had always been told to be kind to Matilda in whatever form she take: my sickly little sister, my parents' princess, my little follower, my dead shadow.

Matilda lifted her finger and Lelacey crouched down deeper into the mattress. Thank God Matilda didn't try to touch her, at least not then. Instead she went back to bed and she didn't make the floorboards creak, although the sulphur stayed by my bed, and it burned my throat.

***

Micah was born during a Bleeder Storm, so Father made sure the
doors and windows were sealed up and Mother had him in their
bedroom, all over the cream-colored sheets. I was just barely old
enough to help, but Matilda had not aged so she sat in the hallway
outside with her pallid hands tucked between her legs. When I ran
outside to put the kettle on she was staring at the slab of metal we
covered the window with, listening to the Bleeders' howling, their
scratching on our house. I have always hated that sound but Matilda was dead. Maybe she understood what they were saying. I wear
earplugs during Bleeder Storms, and I don't try to pick out words.

When Micah first saw Matilda at the side of Mother's bed he
cried and struggled in his swaddling cloths. He was repulsed and
Matilda knew.

We found her standing over his cradle with her hair drooping
over his face. She was watching him breathe, she said. She was
watching the tears flow down his cheeks—odd wet things that she
only remembered now, and only vaguely. Micah was screaming
bloody hell and Father took Matilda away—she dripped all over
his shoulders, her bulbous eyes lolling out of those sunken sockets
to watch Micah twist up in fear. "But I wanna see him." Her voice
had sunk with her eyes. "Papa, I wanna see him."

"Mother."

She cooed to Micah, offering him her soft glowing face as a paci-
fier.

"What if Matilda's a Bleeder?"

She looked up and stared at me in deep offense. "How can you
say that about your own sister," she said.

"Just because she's my sister doesn't mean she might not turn
into a Bleeder."

I wonder now if I wanted her to be one, despite the danger. Because then they would have to ship her body to Zurichia, and the doppelganger that made our house perpetually funereal, sitting in corners like a cobweb, would have to leave too. I had made friends by then, and I no longer invited them over. Our house was a sideshow—it still had windows, and too many doors. And it had Matilda.

"Well," said Mother, tucking in her lips, "she's not, and I know because I check her everyday, and she's got no lesions. She's absolutely fine. A beautiful little girl." Those were things she said with tangible pride, with her eyes closed in blind faith. Like her mental stability rested upon their truth.

I had already said once, in a fit of childish rage, that she was ugly. I knew it, Micah knew it. Mother and Father looked at her amphibious, clammy skin that pinched her bones and saw her chubby baby pictures. But there was such an uproar when I said it the first time that I wasn't going to say it again. I hate uproar.

Matilda didn't. Her body stayed small and skinny, but her tantrums grew volcanic. Sometimes she'd claw at Father when he tried to put her to bed, and then he'd lean over the bathroom sink putting aloe on the welts so no one asked questions at work. It got bad enough that we couldn't leave her alone in the house else she'd scream so continuously that the neighbors would think we really were harboring a Bleeder, and call the police.

"I hate you all!" she would spit, kicking and contorting into positions worthy of carnivals, because she felt no more pain. Her gums would peel back with her eyelids and she would thrash at us, she would flail. "I wanna leave! Let me leave! Open the door! Open the door!" I sat on the couch comforting Mother, while Father lunged at Matilda to grab her and straitjacket her, but one such winter evening she developed the wherewithal to melt out of his lumberjack arms and manifest herself in the opposite corner of the room, near the umbrella stand.

We were all shocked. When Grandpa waited for Grandma to die, he never flew anywhere, just sat in his rocking chair, creaking back and forth. It's what made him a Benign, so far from a Bleeder—he was passive in death. But Matilda started to teleport.

She tried to use this new power to make her demands clear: dishes thrown at the bolted doors, the cabinets opened and slammed, rattling the china inside. Sometimes she even threw herself against the exits of our house, but her body was not a body, as she had learned. It was a remainder. The leftovers of a life that was permanently gone. Like the gray dust that makes the clouds, she was just fall-out. She had a malleable form and now she would never be controlled again. After she threw dinnertime fits she'd fly up the stairs—Father would tuck the blankets around her only to find that she'd slipped through the mattress and box spring and was crawling out from under the bed. The only rule she couldn't break was the one about leaving the house. That was the only wall she couldn't walk through.

Sometimes at night I would wake up and she would be hanging from the ceiling looking down at me and Lelacey wrapped up like snails in wool and cotton. She never even pretended to sleep anymore.

"Molly I'm so lonely." Even when she was sad her voice was like a growl. The voice of a bear coming out of a little girl. I could not see her eyes through her hair that dripped like seaweed. "You don't love me anymore."

I didn't but I never told her that. It would have been cruel.

***

That was the season Lelacey died. Of course I knew: I knew

when she wasn't on my bed in the morning and her litter box was still clean. For about an hour I fit myself into the smallest crawl-spaces in our decrepit house hoping that she was just hiding. We were, after all, a house of hiders. Even Micah would roll under couches if we left him on the floor. So I screamed into the dark holes. It was down in the cellar that I found her limp little body, her fur cold and stiff as if in perpetual alarm. She must have been frightened. I could see the bruises around her neck, bruises that fit tiny, bony fingers. I touched her whiskers, I tapped her nose. We got her when I was very small—we found her wandering, a mewling kitten asking for a home. She had always been mine. She claimed me.

By the time I went back upstairs Lelacey had come back. She had appeared in the kitchen and was pawing at her food dish, making the most wretched and pitiful sounds. I looked at Matilda, who was sitting on the couch quite pleased with herself, and I finally started screaming: exhaustion of the lungs, drying out the voice box as I hollered terrible words: I hate you! (several times) How dare you! You little brat! Why can't you just be dead! Why won't you go away!

I didn't scream for long. Reason was thrown at me. Lelacey was here, wasn't she—it wasn't as though I had lost her for good, she was just *changed.*

Lelacey came out of the kitchen on rickety legs. Her eyes never used to be such a sickly yellow. I crouched down and called her: Lelacey, Lelacey, come here, darling. My cat's disembodied spirit pulled back and hissed at me. And then she hobbled over to Matilda, who opened her arms and smiled, croaking: Lelacey, Lelacey, come here, darling.

***

For a while I tried not to come home. There was a boy at school—his name was David, and he lived on the other side of town, in a large modern house without doors or windows or chimneys, an impenetrable fortress of sleek metal. No Bleeders and no Benigns. His father worked for the Department of Postmortem Security, and I was too ashamed to tell them about Matilda. I hated walking home, no matter where I'd been. It was always that same road, the row of old sick houses with weak foundations, ready to collapse. It was like I could feel Matilda's eyes boring into me through the walls of metal. I felt them everywhere. Even on sleepovers across town I would wake up with the feeling of little fingers pulling down my sleeping bag, getting lost in my hair, whispering: "Molly, Molly, come home and keep me company."

I knew the neighbors whispered about the house at the end of the road with that "dead little girl that's been there seven years now". The mailman asked me if my parents were all right; on Hallow's Eve little boys from the neighborhood threw stones at the windows and shouted at Matilda to "show yourself". Father went after them with a shotgun but they would scatter into the shadows, laughing.

Who knows how David found out, but he found out. His parents had a talk with me about the dangers of keeping a spirit in a residential area and not shipping it to Zurichia on one of those huge reprocessed oil tankers. Didn't I know it could go bad at any moment, they said. Research has shown that the likelihood of a Benign becoming a Bleeder is sixty, no, seventy percent greater if it's confined to a house as opposed to when it's roaming around in the deadzone. That's what David's father called Zurichia. I guess the international committee thought Zurichia sounded nicer than "the deadzone". More welcoming.

But what could I do? We were so much a family of hiders.

Mother hid in the attic with her books, Father hid in the den with his television. Most nights we said very little at the dinner table. We stared at our food and picked at it while Matilda rioted upstairs. And then we lay on our cold and lonely beds, waiting for the morning, while Matilda and Lelacey prowled the corridors. It was like we were the dead ones.

"She's family," I told David's parents flatly. They concluded I was crazy—we weren't to see each other again.

So I stayed home. Mother thought I was coming around— maybe I was. Father wanted me to keep an eye on Micah, because he was no longer scared of Matilda and actually seemed to favor her companionship. She was teaching him strange games—demented versions of hide-and-seek and tag. Once we found him blue-faced, curled up in a tea chest covered with sheets—he said that Matilda told him to hide there and wait for her to find him. We found her skulking around the attic with no intention of ever going back for him, but of course, she spit at us and disappeared.

Micah was the first to see the lesions. He told me—"why does Sissy Matilda have those dark spots"—and then I started taking peeks at her. There was one under her dense tangled hair and one in the crook of her arm: bulging, dark red sores that spread with every tantrum Matilda threw. Every time her temper rose the lesion would gobble up more of her pale porcelain skin. They looked infected, and painful. And even though there was no blood pumping her heart she was bleeding through those sores: out they came, little drops of pungent rage, dribbled on the carpet. I grabbed Micah and ran.

"Matilda's a Bleeder."

Mother and Father were sitting in the living room when I told them, their faces as blank as the wall behind them. I refused to put Micah down. I had let Lelacey out of my hold and now she was dead and disfigured and spent her days howling in the basement where we buried her.

"She's a Bleeder!" I shouted. "She has the lesions! I thought you were checking her!"

Micah put his hands to his ears and wrinkled his nose. Mother and Father turned their heads slowly to look at each other.

"Are you listening to me?"

Mother sighed and bent her head—Father squeezed her hand. "We know, Molly," he said to me. "But please. She's not hurting anyone."

"This isn't legal! She has to go! She *wants* to go!"

"No." Mother was shaking her head. "No, she doesn't. She wants to stay. My baby wants to stay. And I want her to stay, and we all want her to stay, so why can't she stay?" She had started to shriek then, and there was a dampness to her voice— she was about to cry. All her fretting and crying over Matilda had aged her. She had been young once; now her hair was made of straw. Father gathered her up into his arms and shushed her and said that of course Matilda could stay.

Mother looked at me from behind Father's shoulder. Her eyes were hesitant and defensive and quick to close, quick to break apart from mine. "Molly, she'd be all alone… all cold and alone."

I went back into the hallway to the sound of their sobbing, with Micah still clinging to me, resting on my jutting hip. Ours was a cement house—because it was built before the Department of Postmortem Security's safety standards were passed into law—half its lighting was supposed to come from the sun. Our stringy electrical wiring didn't make up for the loss—although with the weather as it is and was, I suppose it wouldn't have made a difference if our windows hadn't been boarded up. But it meant that our hallways shrank and darkened into tunnels lit by sporadic torches, and the permeability of cement meant that sometimes we could feel moisture coming in through the walls, through the floor.

Matilda was in the hallway—sometimes I wonder if it was her lingering presence that cursed us. Sometimes the house's weight followed her, like she was some kind of vortex of energy that the house groaned and shifted in order to obey and draw closer to. Maybe that was why the house was shrinking. Matilda was a black hole with her mouth wide open. I hurried past her, telling Micah not to look at her.

"I won't hurt you, Molly."

She followed us, floating down the hallway on her dirty tip-toes. I wanted, so badly, to leave, if only to sit in the yard and know that she could not haunt us there. Her fingers brushed the back of my shirt, like a twig in a wood. I turned around and screamed: "Get away from me!"

Her huge drowned eyes looked at me in want.

"Do you remember when we played astronauts?"

There was a playground nearby. We'd go at twilight on the clearest of days, when you can almost see the stars, and swing as high as possible for as long as possible, to make believe that we were in space shuttles orbiting distant planets. Repairing the craft required crossing the monkey bars. Re-entry required the slide. When the wind was high we called it turbulence, a word we'd never experienced.

"I wanna do that again." Another sore was blossoming at her hairline—tiny tentacles of rippling magenta stretched across her temple, itching, yearning, hating. I had nothing to say but Matilda sighed and dissolved of her own accord.

***

There was only an hour left of light when I zipped up Micah's jacket and pulled his hat down so it covered his ears. He had never been to the playground. Micah's time on the outside was really only within the straps and buckles of the car seat that Mother and Father still tied him to, even though he had gotten too big for it.

I guess it was Matilda, forever frozen at swing set age, that reminded me.

"Where are we goin'?" asked Micah, dragging on my hand. The sidewalks were covered with scraggly, serpentine weeds, so we walked on the road, beside the gutters clogged with debris. The houses here were bare and empty. There was no traffic likely.

"To the moon," I said.

The playground was smaller than I remembered. It was part of a neighborhood park, built into an enclave of old trees and marked with wood chips. The light was dimming—our timing was perfect. I glanced down at Micah. He looked reluctant.

"Haven't you ever wanted to go to the moon?"

"No."

"Oh, come on. It'll be fun. We'll just take a little trip around the world. You just keep your eyes on the sky."

I got him on the swing and he clenched the little metal chains so hard that his hands would be bleeding if it weren't for his gloves. He was so afraid when I started to push—he didn't like being catapulted forward, although he only went a few feet at first—but when he felt my hands on his back and realized he was always falling back toward me he relaxed. I heard the beginnings of his childish high—the surprised giggle, the lean-forward, the kicking swimmer's legs. I pushed harder, pushed him higher. The air was searing. It was almost clean.

And yes, I wished Matilda was there.

Then the storm sirens began. From there we couldn't see the

radio tower but even Micah was old enough to know that the sirens meant nothing but the worst. He was in the midst of flight
when they began and when he came back for another push I
did push him, because for the first few seconds I didn't believe
the alarm. All it took was a rustling of the oaks that hugged the
playground. I grabbed Micah off the swing and ran with him in
my arms.

"Molly!" he started screaming. We were on the road. My footsteps hit my ribs like punches. I was looking nowhere but ahead.
"Don't look!"

The route took forever. Hedges moved and so did branches—
I stayed dead center on the winding two-lane streets because
hands more twisted and gnarly than Matilda's were reaching
up through the gutters, sloughing aside the mud and leaf-dust.
Then I hated the fading light. Micah was crying. I didn't have
the lung capacity to tell him we were almost there. When I
slammed my fist on our heavy bolted door I looked back for one
brief sweep and saw the Bleeders swarming over roofs. It is their
world, more and more. Not just the rebellious Bleeders but the
legions and legions of Benigns. When Zurichia is full they will
need another vacant continent.

Father was furious. He checked the door bolts twice and said
we could have died. Mother was in the kitchen doorway, cradling the cold wall—dark Matilda was in the middle of the hallway, staring up at the ceiling and stretching her neck back so far
her head should have come loose. The awful scratching howls
hit the door when he was still up against it and he jumped back
as if shocked.

Mother cried out and extended her arms toward us, her babies,
and after we moved toward her and she took us in she began to
pray. We each had our pendants hanging round our necks—me
and Micah and Matilda. It was all that linked us now, while the

house began to shake and Mother's appeals to the saints were buried in the avalanche of sound that was the roaring Bleeder storm. Father watched the ceiling while they trampled it, watching as family photographs hanging from nails jostled under the weight of the stampede. I don't know why we felt unsafe that time, why Mother hugged us as if the end had come. Could we smell it in the air? Did we know?

The first thing we heard was a crash, not of glass but something heavier, coming from the upstairs. Mother screamed so Micah screamed.

"Maybe it's that cat," said Father, but we all knew it wasn't. Lelacey was no Bleeder. Lelacey was mourning herself in the basement.

What followed were the same sounds of a tempest locked in a cage that Matilda made when she was furious, amplified by three. Then we did hear glass shattering and unbreakable things hitting walls, and after one pressurized pop the sound of a geyser let loose.

"The bathroom," I said. "The toilet. It came in through the toilet."

It must have been the bathroom door that blew open, followed by an eruption of thousand-tongued curses, a fury so hollow that it sent shock waves up and down the upstairs corridor. We could hear the posts of the railing shaking and the wall paint peeling under ripping, scratching nails. Matilda's eyes followed its sound as it ricocheted from room to room above us, dislodging all evidence of life it could find.

"It's in the house."

Father went to the hall closet and took up his titanium bat, muttering to himself. He was giving it a few habdash practice swings when Mother dragged us children over the mosaic-tiled kitchen floor and under the table, the white tablecloth brushing our heads, and locked us into her huddle by her bony arms. "Shut your eyes, my babies, shut your eyes. They won't take any of you away from me." Mother did shut her eyes, fiercely, and so did Micah, but Matilda and I were looking at each other. I saw her slip away from Mother's embrace. In another blink her tiny weightless form, wracked with disease even now after death, had seeped out of the kitchen.

"Matilda! Matilda!"

I was shoved out from under the table to bring her back. But the hallway was so broken it was scarcely recognizable—Father was chasing the invasive Bleeder with a titanium bat like a maniac, smashing walls most of the time. I thought I was in an earthquake. I thought I was dying. Cement was flying like hail and the walls were spattered with blood, the Bleeder's and Father's. I fell. I stepped on broken glass. I covered my ears to keep the Bleeder's words out of my head. Most of all I tried not to look at it. It was so grossly deformed. A walking, flying corpse, a lesion in and of itself, with all traces of humanity lost to its hate and rage. I stumbled up the stairs on hands and knees, cross-eyed because something hard and crumbly hit the back of my head. There were repeated booms against the bolted window at the top of the stairs; the corridor leading off to our bedrooms was filled with strips of plaster and cinderblock dust. Like our house had been stripped down to its skeletal remains.

And there, Matilda, in the bathroom. Suddenly gentle and small: a baby sister. Standing next to the toilet whose lid had been blown off when the Bleeder climbed out of it, looking down into the bowl stained blue. The bathroom, lined with shards of glass, was a house of mirrors, and Matilda was already on the other side. Another lesion was growing, this one on her hand. She knew it was there. She knew what would happen.

"I have to go get better," she whispered. I barely heard her—I saw her filmy lips moving. She must have been trying not to howl, afraid her voice would sound like the banshee Father was fighting. "I can't stay any longer."

I leaned my head against the splintered eave of the bathroom door with my legs falling out from underneath me. "I'm sorry, Matilda."

"I'm going now."

I thought I heard gurgling coming from the pipes. The sudden thought of Matilda, dead and crystallized at age seven, in a world where houses turned her away and Bleeders hid in gutters waiting for enough numbers to gather, assaulted me and I did want to hold her down and shut her in her room for safekeeping but I was sitting by then. Couldn't bring myself to stand but just watched her.

"Go to Zurichia," I said, "it's safe there. Grandma and Grandpa are there, they'll..."

She dove in. There was a splash. She could fit because her body wasn't a body.

"Matilda... Matilda..."

By the time Father chased the Bleeder up the stairs and back to where it came from I was lying on the mess of medicine and soap bottles on the bathroom floor with my eyes closed. I heard it—like a high-altitude plane passing over, a mix of a whine and a roar—followed by Father's footsteps and his unintelligible yelling. Once the thing was back in the sewage system he took a sheet of metal and hammered it onto the toilet, without thinking, feverishly saying, "Keep safe, keep safe, protect the safety of the interior..."

"Matilda's gone," I said, and sighed.

I expected tears. I expected Father to go running out into the Bleeder Storm to find her. Instead we sat at the dinner table, the four of us, listening to the quiet hum of our own breathing and the sudden silence between our ears. The walls of our broken house groaning. We didn't make the place stand much longer. I wonder if she made it. But I think she did. I hope.

AND WHEN SHE WAS BAD

The final girl alive sits down on the dark soil and moans. It's her virginal moan, the one that makes her special, but now, three days later, there is no hint of an orgasmic lilt in her voice. It's fatigue that the earthworms in the dirt hear. There is no one else to hear. The others are dead and the strange white-haired couple whose land this has been since the Civil War are dead, and so are all their animals, even the sad-eyed German Shepherd. Even the chickens' eggs have their tops bitten off and their insides sucked dry, so not even the unborn hear how her voice has changed. The monster, does he hear? She looks at him, broken-legged and broken-winged in front of the barn where he killed her slutty best friend. Poor dead Ann, always a little wild. She promised they were on the road to Aspen. She promised no wrong turns.

***

Thirty minutes later, the final girl wipes her own blood on her face and stands and goes to the monster. He knows no words and begs for nothing as she comes close—his torsal wound has

33

clotted all dark and ugly, and his broken leg has swollen, and if he is a product of nature then he must be in pain. She did not think he was, earlier. She thought he really had spawned from Hell, and she had been hating herself as she hid under the bed and he ate the old woman on top for not being able to remember a single Scripture after spending twelve years in the basement of a church embedding them in her heart. The mattress had bowed down on her back like the pressure of God, or if it was her granola self talking, karma. She thought about her sins and Sodom and Gomorrah and celestial wrath raining down on the plain, washing it of all the devils, and like a good little angel she bit her lower lip bloody and felt the pain and sucked it back in. And then she ran over the monster with a hay baler and broke half his body and realized he was mortal after all. Angel's got herself a sickle now. Everybody's bleeding, everybody's dead. Everybody's made of iron and water and bone.

***

The final girl and the monster go to the nearest town. She's going to bring him to justice, that's what she told him. Going to make sure he never hurts anyone again. She ran him over a second time to be certain and then chained him to the baler and drove it up to the little country road, dragging him behind her. His face is in the gravel. They pass the car that Ann's boyfriend tried to escape to—its tires are still slashed out and Josh is still half in the windshield, with his feet chewed off.

The final girl did not even like Josh the drunken frat boy, but she still screams back at the monster, "Look at that! Look at what you did, you sick freak! Look at *it!*" And she regrets not doing the same thing for Ann, down in the barn. But the monster's face is in the gravel and the monster sees nothing. He learns nothing. He is after all the monster. The final girl feels her ribs compress and little by little she starts to cry. They're anguished tears, the kind of tears she expected when she was trapped in a storage room with the monster breaking in, not the kind of tears appropriate for this moment in her narrative. Now she is free, and the terror is crippled at her feet, and the sky is laid bare and swallows, thin birds, are crossing overhead like little flourishes of hope. Yet she cries and cries and the monster does not respond, and she looks back over and over at the car and then down the hill at the grungy farm, left to languish in the putrid smell of death. She wishes she was dragging back the right bodies and cries some more because this brutality is what she has. This is her prize for being good, this is what was behind door number three, this is her gold star sticker. She keeps her foot on the pedal as her chest keeps heaving and the baler groans on like nothing is happening.

***

The baler stops. It put-puts to a halt as the dark comes in over the trees, and at first the final girl just sits on the uncomfortable little stool, scared to look behind her although she's been listening to the monster drag over the asphalt for the past two hours. Now the two of them have lost all civilization, because the farm is gone and the nearest town, that fabled myth, has not come into view. But then she picks up the sickle she's kept under her foot and gathers the strength to turn and look at the monster. She imagines him standing, his jaws fallen open and dripping saliva, ready to consume her headfirst. But he is not—he is still lying on the road, twitching occasionally.

She hears in the black woods by the road a miniature howl and begins to think of other monsters: coyotes, wolves. She wonders

what he is, this savage thing. She hates that he eats parts of his
victims, but this trait of his also reminds her of the Big Bad Wolf
and oddly enough, this consoles her. Maybe he is just an animal,
like the Beast of Bray Road and the Ozark Howler. Maybe he
is just wired to prey on other creatures. Maybe it's not his fault.
This idea makes it easier for her to envision killing him too. It's
what's always been done to rabid animals, to dogs with mange,
to escaped leopards, to pit bulls that bite little babies.

Dumb beasts, she thinks, remembering her uncle putting
down a horse with a broken leg. Dumb beasts can't help it and
we can't help them. She tries to breathe calmly and accept her
role as executioner of this thing she has captured. But her uncle
let that horse go gently into the night, with a tranquilizer and a
syringe, and all she has is a sickle. That's a weapon with no pity.
She decides the townspeople, when she finally reaches them,
will carry out the grisly job themselves. What would her parents
say if she came home with blood on her hands? Still, she keeps
pity in her heart and nurses it like a kitten. She's always felt
pity for the strangest things. For dying insects. For hitchhikers
ambling down the road looking lost. Earlier on this trip—before the wrong turn—she chastised Josh for mocking those lost
souls, and Ann of course mocked her in turn. "Such delicate
sensibilities," her mother used to say, brushing her hair.

Feeling relieved, the final girl gets off the stool and quickly
unhooks the chain from the baler, then starts to drag. He's lighter than she thought he'd be.

***

The final girl hates that the monster does not talk. All afternoon
she thinks, talk, monster, talk. It is possible that he is dead and
has been all this time, and that those little tics and flutters of

his ragged wings are tricks of moonlight or her own wishful thinking. She's not willing to close the gap between them to check. Instead she just hates him from afar. She would not care if he talked about eating people or how he was going to kill her or how it felt when he killed Ann. She hates her own company much more. Why the hell else would she say yes to Aspen with Ann and Josh if they weren't a reprieve from the deafening white solitude of her dorm room, perched ten stories above the ground like the bell tower of Notre Dame? But the monster has never spoken. He is, after all, the monster.

She says, "I could tell you my life story." He says nothing. "I was born in Grand Forks. I had good parents. I go to college now. I'm an English major." She stops because her own life makes her hair stand on end. There is nowhere to go with that story. "I could tell you why I survived." He says nothing. He drags, that's what he says, his scrapes against the ground are his reply. She imagines it's his way of saying yes. "I survived because I am a good girl. I am not a slut. I am not a pig. I am not…" She thinks of the old couple whose house the car broke down in front of, who narrowed their beady little eyes at them, this pack of teenagers in threadbare clothes, but let them in anyway. "I am not old and stupid. And I can run. I always got good grades. And my father taught me how to…" She remembers her father clapping and laughing after she finished singing the national anthem in the living room, how he said, "Good girl! Good girl!" Her voice trickles off as she watches the moon and the moon watches her. "And it doesn't matter," she finishes.

The monster doesn't reply. She keeps dragging. The stress on her joints burns out all those things she just said, the things that don't matter. The memories of blood and screaming and slamming doors and slipping keys and shotgun cocks fade with every step. The great big amorphous past has risen up behind them on the country road and is swallowing those memories whole. When she thinks of them now all she feels is numb release. It is leaving a long hollowness where her sternum should be. A void. She realizes the chorus that she thought was the moon clucking actually belongs to cicadae in the long grass.

"You see? Even animals can talk," she says, looking back at him. Her voice is quivering. Inside she's begging him to say something. Just a grunt would do. When Ann and Josh left her in the farmhouse to go fuck in the barn she was actually happy to hear the monster land on the roof with a screech that sent the animals into hysterics—else she'd have to listen to her own little voice all night. He drags along.

***

It is night and the dog comes soundlessly from behind. The final girl thinks she hears a growl but as she's turning she gets jerked off her feet and falls. She's lucky the sickle in her hand doesn't tear through her thigh. Her wrist is still being tugged while her head is throbbing and instinctively she pulls back on the chain—it takes her a minute to turn over onto her stomach and see that some kind of stray hunting mutt has the monster by the neck and is trying to drag him off the road.

"Hey!"

The dog glances up at her with urine-colored eyes but it only lasts a second. It's the raggedy monster it wants.

No, she thinks. No, he's mine. She's not sure why she thinks this, but she tells herself it's because she wants to own the coming vengeance, she wants to personally ensure the nearest town burns him alive in the name of Ann and Josh and the Mc-Faydens, she wants to feel the heat of the pyre. She tells herself it's because the monster hasn't killed this stupid dog's friends.

With her heart in her throat, she yanks the chain back again and with the other hand lunges for the dog with the sickle. The final girl bites her lip because already the dog is drawing blood—dark and viscous, it leaks from under the monster's rubbery chin— and she's afraid she's too late.

Then the monster lifts up one clawed, previously dormant hand and grabs the dog's neck. The final girl skids to a rough stop and watches as the dog, suddenly whimpering, gets its neck twisted until its head is barely hanging off its body. The monster starts eating, loud and visceral like he's not ashamed. After ten minutes, the monster throws the mangled body at the stricken young woman. It hits her sneakers but she's seen so much carnage recently that it doesn't even make her jump. She just kicks the offering aside and marches up, shaking, to the monster she thought was crippled. By the time she's leaning over him and her hair has fallen down into grabbing range he's laid down on his back again and closed his eyes. Seeing this elicits a staggered shriek.

"What, are you surrendering now?" She gives the chain a hard yank and the monster's head flops in response. He doesn't wake. His arms and knees have tucked into his body like a baby in a womb. She lifts the sickle. "I'm going to kill you, you idiot!"

The monster opens his eyes. One dig of the sickle will end his life and she can't believe he doesn't know this, being a monster. Still he throws up no defense. His bloody lips don't even hiss.

"Why won't you kill me?" This, she says softer. He did try to, earlier—but he never seemed to put as much effort into killing her as he put into killing Ann and Josh and the McFaydens. He always seemed to miss. He always seemed to give her time to run. And this makes her drop her sickle. Her shoulders slump and her knees go wobbly. "Why me, huh? Why do I get to be the last girl? You don't care about how good I am, you don't care about…" She shakes her head, because all he could have seen in her was a trembling piece of teenaged meat. "You're a fucking monster."

The monster is back to feigning death and subservience and will not communicate with her. She starts walking away, pulling the chain taut. "What, are you lonely?" she asks. She says it sarcastically, but as soon as the words are out there she knows they're true. The monster doesn't reply as she begins once again to drag it down the empty road. The shock of suddenly having something in common with a creature so awful silences the girl he let live, and she wipes her eyes on her muddy sleeve. There's been no cars on this road all day. But then again it was a wrong turn.

***

Sometime between nightfall and sunrise she stops walking and sits down, then lies down. There's no more dragging sounds and the silence bites her now. The monster turns over and folds his good wing over his head. The chain between them is not stretched taut and still he shows no interest in eating her. The final girl is thinking that maybe he should have eaten her; but she thinks this cautiously, afraid that he will somehow hear her thoughts and come on over, jaws gaping, ready to obey.

"You ate all my friends. I have no one now," she whispers at the lump she holds hostage. But she knows she was lonely long before the monster first landed on the roof of the farmhouse like an angel of pestilence. She was lonely long before she went to college and became Ann's roommate (the only reason Ann dragged her along on this trip—it was out of pity). Could people be born lonely? She remembers being lonely even back in kindergarten when all children are supposed to be delightful little cherubs, that is why she wonders. Well, time is nothing. How the void inside began doesn't matter. All that matters is that it's there.

The monster just let her scream about it. The monster let her run. He let her pound her heels into the ground and her heart into her ribs, so angry and vicious and alive, this sweating ugly little girl in the mud with dirt under the fingernails and grease in her hair was now finally filled with real bursting pain, the stuff that burned so much cleaner than internal sorrow. The monster let her bleed. The monster let her swing baseball bats and rip clothes and howl like the Beast of Bray Road herself. He let her break bones and he let her like it. He let her swear. She has said fuck more times in the past three days than she has in all her twenty years of life and each time it's felt like a breaking wave. Doing all that sick ugly nasty stuff has been like vomiting the sad lonely years with their pastel colors and blue ribbons and dutiful pats on the head for the good little girl.

The final girl digs her filthy nails into her skin and wonders what she was really trying to run over with that hay baler when she jammed her foot against the pedal and screamed, "Die, you piece of *shit! Die!*"

"Why did you come here?" she asks the monster that is barely a monster anymore. "Did I invite you somehow? Did I dream you into being?"

Only the void inside responds.

She is afraid that the monster is her golem, and that is why he never talks. But if that is true, he has done well. That she can't argue. The skeleton that is left of her bottled life feels unbelievably clean after the three-day orgy of violence, like boiled bones. That night she sleeps not curled up like a scared snail but open wide. Insects crawl in her hair and nest, as if she is their queen mother.

***

All night she dreams of fists. Every time they are her own. She recognizes her bony knuckles, cut up from punching through the glass of a door that wouldn't open back at the McFaydens' farmhouse. In her dream she is punching through wooden doors too. She is coming down out of a crystalline sky and punching red shingles. She punches the leathery skin of a cow. She punches rib cages and faces and stomachs of people she thinks she might know. She watches them crash. She punches the mattress. She punches the monster; his jaw crunches like it's made of styrofoam. She punches herself. And there's a voice in her dream that sounds like her own saying "Arise, arise!"

There's Ann, dying in front of her. There's the bed that she tears the stuffing from. Late in the dream, when the colors are bleeding and the American Gothic portraits are shuddering down the wall, she is in a bathroom. She looks down and sees that her fingernails have gone black and that she is barefoot. She looks in the mirror and it cracks.

***

In the morning the monster is awake. He is watching her with his blank reptilian eyes. She looks back at him as he sits cross-legged on the center stripe of the road. She somewhat hopes he'll speak but is barely disappointed when he doesn't—as usual, she speaks instead. "I'm going to let you go," she says. "How do you feel about that?" The monster has no reaction, of course. "I'm going to let you go, but only if you give me what I want." He has no objection and she moves closer.

She takes off his tattered devil's wings. She puts them on.

Without them he looks like a shriveled fetus, a burned giraffe, something that was not meant to be and that life was finally, mercifully letting go. He curls up as he watches her adjust his wings. A couple rolls of the shoulder and they feel right. She can feel the wind seeping in through the tears, and one of them has been bent up something awful by the hay baler, but she still gives them a go. She flaps and imagines the monster swooping down and catching the old man and eating him, mid-flight, like an eagle with a hare—she wonders if that will be as hard as it looks. She flaps harder and the wind catches her. With difficulty, the final girl rises a few feet off the ground and awkwardly sways in the breeze.

The woeful little thing below her, purposeless now, emits a strange, guttural squawk and lifts up his webbed fingers. His neck is still tied to the chain and he's starting to get pulled upward the higher she goes. He doesn't want to follow her forever. She unravels the chain from around her hand. She drops it and watches the creature meekly crawl away, wondering what to do with himself now that she has no need for him, until a higher wind rises and takes her over the trees. In the distance she sees a farmhouse, and swoops. She is used to flying solo.

ONLY UNITY SAVES THE DAMNED

"**D**ude, are you getting this?"

Rosslyn Taro, 25, and Clark Dunkin, 25, are standing in the woods. It's evening—the bald-cypresses behind them are shadowed and the light between the needles is the somber blue that follows sunsets—and they are wearing sweatshirts and holding stones.

"It's on," says the voice behind the camera. "To the winner go the spoils!"

They whip their arms back and start throwing stones. The camera pans to the right as the stones skip into the heart of Goose Lake. After a dozen rounds the camera pans back to Rosslyn Taro and Clark Dunkin arguing over whose stone made the most skips, and then slowly returns to the right. Its focus settles on a large bur oak looming around the bend of the lake, forty yards away.

"Hey, isn't that the Witching Tree?"

Off-camera, Clark Dunkin says, "What?" and Rosslyn Taro says, "Come on, seriously?"

"You know, Raggedy Annie's Witching Tree."

The girl sounds too shaky to be truly skeptical. "How do you know?"

"Remember the song? 'We hung her over water, from the mighty oak tree.' Well, there aren't any other lakes around here. And First Plymouth is on the other side of the lake." The camera zooms, searches for a white steeple across the still water, but the light is bad. "'We hung her looking over at the cemetery.'"

The camera swings to Rosslyn Taro, because she is suddenly upset. She is walking to the camera, and when she reaches it, shoves the cameraman. "Bay, shut up! I hate that stupid song. Let's just go, I'm getting cold. Come on, please." But Clark Dunkin is still staring at the tree. His hands are shaking. Rosslyn Taro calls his name: "Lark!"

The camera follows Clark Dunkin's gaze to the tree. There is a figure standing in front of it, dressed in a soiled white shift and a black execution hood. The figure reaches two pale, thin hands to the edge of the hood as if to reveal its face. And then the camera enters a topspin, all dirt and branches and violet sky, as the cameraman begins to run. Rosslyn Taro is heard screaming. Someone—the cameraman, or possibly Clark Dunkin—is whimpering, as if from very far away, "oh, shit, oh, shit."

And then the video abruptly cuts to black.

***

They called themselves the LunaTicks. Like everything else, it was Bay's idea: he named them after an old British secret society, supposedly "the smartest men in Birmingham." There were ground rules not only for their operations, but for life as a whole: if one got caught, the rest would confess or expect to be ratted out; where one goes, the others must follow. Only unity saves the damned, Bay said.

Roz's father thought the boys were a terrible influence on her. These slouching undead fools had metastasized at his front door one day when Roz was in sixth grade, with their uncombed hair and unwashed skin and vulgar black T-shirts. He'd made the mistake of letting the vampires in. Under their watch, his daughter's mood swings escalated from mild distemper to a full-blown madness. The charcoal rings around her eyes got deeper; her silver skull necklaces got bigger. She was vandalizing the elementary school; she was shoplifting lipstick. He'd tell her he was locking the doors at midnight and in the morning he would find her sleeping, nearly frozen, on the porch—or worse, he wouldn't find her at all. So he excavated her room, vowing to take the Baileys and the Dunkins to court if he found a single pipe, a single syringe. He gave up when she failed to apply to community college. The screen door swung shut behind her and he thanked God that he also had a son.

He was not alone. Bay's parents hated Roz and Lark as well; their hatred of the two losers who hung like stones around Bay's neck was the only thing the former Mr. and Mrs. Bailey still shared. They tried, separately, to introduce Bay to different crowds: the jocks, the computer geeks, the 4-H club. Bay said he hated them all *(too dumb too weird too Christian)*, but the truth was that they had all rejected him. Eventually Bay's parents gave him an ultimatum: *get rid of your friends, or we get rid of the car.* So the responsibility of driving down bedraggled county roads—and all roads lead to Goose Lake, the old folks said—fell to Roz and Lark.

Lark's parents couldn't have named Roz or Bay if they had tried. "There's that raccoon girl," they'd say, or "it's that damn scarecrow boy again," before drifting back into a dreamless sleep.

None of the LunaTicks would have graduated high school without the other two.

***

The Goose Lake video went viral, and life started to change just like Bay predicted. They sent the video from Bay's phone to the local news and suddenly they weren't the LunaTicks or the "dumb-ass emo kids" anymore—they were crisp and poignant, *three local youths* who had *captured shocking footage* of their *hometown spook.* People on the street gave them second looks of fear and fascination. A couple reporters came out from Lincoln and Omaha, though their arrogance forbade them from understanding what this video meant to Whippoorwill. They were interviewed on a paranormal radio show, *Unheard Of,* based in Minneapolis. For the first time in their lives, they came with the warning label they'd always wanted. "The footage that you are about to see," dramatic pause, "may disturb you."

Bay had to keep from laughing whenever he watched the Goose Lake video, because of the absurdity of his perky little girlfriend pretending to be a dead witch—for Halloween last fall, Jessica had been a sexy strawberry. He was proud of her moxie, even though she'd whined afterwards that she smelled like a dead rat.

"When we make the real movie, I want a better costume," she said.

"We ought to hire a real actress for the real movie, babe," he replied.

The movie was his big plan for getting out of Whippoorwill. It was all that time spent working at the theater, selling tickets to the "sheeple." Said "sheeple" couldn't get enough of those found footage mockumentaries. But really, they had a lot of ways out of Whippoorwill. There was working on a Dream America Cruise, or hitch-hiking, or Greenpeace. There were communes and oil rigs. The LunaTicks would lie on the asphalt watching jets pass overhead and dream up these exit ramps out of car exhaust. *I can't wait to get out of here,* they'd say, smiling wistfully—they'd been saying it for years.

Lark couldn't stop watching the Goose Lake video. He got the file on his own phone and then showed it off like a newborn baby to his retired neighbors, the gas station clerk, the town drunk who sat outside the grocery store with a whiskey bottle in a paper bag. Lark always asked what they saw, as if even he didn't know the answer. No matter what they said, he'd shake his head and mutter, "That's not it." Bay said he was taking the method acting thing too seriously.

Roz couldn't watch the video at all. This played well during interviews because she seemed traumatized, but after the microphones were off she was angry all the time. She wasn't getting enough sleep, she said. The silver maple outside scratched at her window, as if asking to be let in.

The town bent around them like a car wrapping around a tree during a tornado. Suddenly all these Raggedy Annies—*Raggedy Annie in my yard, Raggedy Annie in my attic, Raggedy Annie in the hospital when my husband passed away*—came crawling out into the sunlight. The entire town had grown up with the same story about a witch who aborted babies back when the town was still being sculpted raw out of the rolling prairie, and they all knew the matching nursery rhyme as sure as they knew Happy Birthday—*we hung her over water, from the mighty oak tree/ we hung her looking over at the cemetery.*

A girl from high school, an ex-cheerleader, chatted Lark up in the express lane at the grocery store where he worked. She was buying diapers, but she wasn't wearing a wedding ring. "Aren't you freaked out? God, I think I might have *died* if I had seen her." Lark said that wasn't part of the story. Raggedy Annie didn't kill on sight. The ex-cheerleader made a mock screaming sound and hissed, "Don't say her name!" She also said to meet her at

The Pale Horse on Friday night, but she didn't show.

So Lark sat at the bar with Bay and Roz. The bartender said he'd always known that bitch Raggedy Annie was real. "Shit, man, every time I drive by Goose Lake I get this weird feeling. I thought it was a magnetic field or something, like Mystery Quadrant up in South Dakota. But nah, man. Our fucking parents were right! She's our demon. She's our cross to bear, if you don't mind me saying. And the bitch can't let go of a grudge. There's just this one thing I don't get though… but why did she show herself to you? Of all the people who've been boating and camping out at Goose Lake, why *you* guys?"

What they knew he meant was why, out of all the great little people in this great little town, would Raggedy Annie choose these losers? Or was it like attracts like: yesterday's demon for today's devils?

On Monday Lark showed the video to a pack of shabby children in the candy aisle. Tears were shed; one kid pissed himself. As a furious mother hoisted her away, one girl pointed at Lark and shrieked, "Mommy, the tree!" Lark's co-workers would later say that they had never seen him look so freaked out, so cracked up. He started shouting—in *desperation,* everyone told the manager, not *anger*—"I know, it's the Witching Tree!"

The day after, Lark neither showed up for work nor answered his phone. He probably would have been fired anyway, given the children-in-the-candy-aisle incident, but Roz and Bay had to make certain he hadn't somehow died—a freak electrocution, carbon monoxide, anything seemed possible if Lark wasn't answering his phone—because where one goes, the others must follow. So Roz drove them to the Dunkins' house on the scraggly edge of town. No luck, no Lark. "I have no idea where he is," said Mrs. Dunkin, from the couch. It smelled more foul than usual. "But he isn't here, raccoon girl."

His parents had really let the yard go—the branches of a grotesque hackberry tree were grasping the roof of the little tin house, like the tentacles of a mummified octopus. They always kept the shades drawn, so maybe they hadn't noticed it. "Nice tree, Mrs. Dunkin," Bay said as they left, but she didn't respond.

***

Bay had the big ideas, but Lark was the smartest LunaTick. He slouched in the back of classrooms, mumbling answers only when forced. Most of his teachers dismissed his potential—as the twig's bent, so's the tree inclined, they said. But there was no arguing with test scores. When the time came to shuffle the seventeen-year-olds out of gymnasiums and into the real world, Lark got the Four-Year-Colleges handout instead of Two-Year-Colleges or The U.S. Armed Forces. He stared at it for a week before quietly applying to the University of Nebraska-Lincoln. If he stayed he knew he would end up like Roger Malkin. Bay would eventually get a job at the Toyota dealership and Roz would marry some tool with bad hair, but he'd take up the mantle of *town drunk*. He had the genes for it. Roger would slur, "You's a good kid," and that meant they understood each other, damn it.

He told the other LunaTicks that he'd gotten into UNL while Bay was driving them to Dairy Queen. Bay was so upset that he nearly drove the car off Dead Man's Bridge, and that moment of gut-flattening fear was the most alive any of them had felt in months. "Come with me," Lark begged, but Roz just chewed her hair while Bay ground his teeth. They looked like scared rats, backing into their holes.

After the university paperwork started coming in—Get Involved! See What's New!—Lark realized that his life in Whippoorwill was a mere shadow of real human experience. He saw himself in an inspirational poster: teetering alone on a cliff, muslin wings outstretched, DARE TO DREAM emblazoned across the bottom. In what should have been his final summer in his hometown, Whippoorwill shrank and withered until just driving down Jefferson Street made him itchy, claustrophobic. He'd stand in the shower stall with the centipedes for hours, drowning out the coughs of his narcoleptic parents, willing the water to wash off his mildewed skin. *All this is ending,* he would think. *All this is dead to me.*

When he loaded up his car in August his parents pried themselves off the couch to see him off. "You won't get far," his mother whispered in his ear as she hugged him, bones digging into his back, and from the doorway his father said, "He'll come crawling back. They always do."

And he was right. After Lark came home for winter break, he never made the drive back east. Classes were hard. Dorm rooms were small. People were brusque, shallow, vulgar. Everyone had more money than he did. The jocks who'd made high school miserable were now living in frat houses behind the quad. He hadn't made any real friends—not friends like Roz and Bay, anyway. They were waiting for him at Dead Man's Bridge after the big December snow, smiling with outstretched wool gloves. "We know you couldn't stay away," Roz said. For a moment Lark considered grabbing both their hands and jumping into the river of ice below.

***

Raggedy Annie stood at the end of the bed. *It's Jessica,* Roz thought. *Jessica broke into my room and she's trying to scare me and she and Bay are going to laugh about this tomorrow.* She tried to open her mouth and couldn't. She tried to pry her jaw open with her hand and couldn't lift her arm.

The thing at the end of the bed—*Jessica, Jessica, Jessica*—stretched two bone-white arms to the black hood. Roz tried to close her eyes but before she could, the hood was gone and the face of the ghoul was revealed. She didn't know what to expect, since Raggedy Annie never had a face in the story—but it was her mother. She was glowing blue-green, like foxfire in the woods, and if not for that glow her face was so flat and her movements so jerky that she could have been an old film reel. Her mother—who should have been a mile away and six feet deep in First Plymouth—opened and closed her mouth as if trying to speak, though only a hoarse, coffin-cramped gasp escaped.

She was a mess the next day. She forgot about make-up and coffee and straightening her hair. She forgot to call the landscaping company about getting the silver maple tree, the one that knocked on her window every night, under control. It was almost as tall as the chimney now; it was overwhelming the house. *The one thing I tell you to do,* as her father would later say. *You're just like your mother. Apple doesn't fall far from the tree, I guess.* She also forgot about the performance review that would have determined whether she'd be made Accessories Sales Supervisor at Clipmann's, and ended up spending most of the review trying to save her job. "Are you on drugs?" her manager asked, disappointed. He'd made it clear how important it was for women to look put-together on the sales floor. "You look terrible."

Old Lady Marigold, who had nothing to do now that her husband was dead except rifle through clearance racks, found her listlessly hanging hats upon the hat tree. They looked like a headhunter's tower. "You shouldn't have messed with Raggedy Annie, Rosslyn Taro."

Roz squeezed the cloche in her hand and took a deep breath

that was meant to be calming. "We didn't do anything to her, we just..." The calming breath hitched in her throat—memories of smearing the white shift in damp dirt, saying *hell no* she wouldn't wear it, watching Jessica slip it on instead—"We were just hanging out at Goose Lake and happened to..."

"You *must have* done *something!*" Old Lady Marigold squinted as if to see through a curtain. "You must have been trying something, you must have invited..."

"You care so much about her now, but the town elders *killed* Raggedy Annie, didn't they? Isn't that the whole point of the stupid story? This town will literally kill you if you step out of line?"

Old Lady Marigold pursed her wrinkled, wine-stained lips but held her tongue for fifteen seconds longer than normal, so Roz knew that she was right. Not that anyone needed Raggedy Annie to teach them that lesson—just live in Whippoorwill long enough for the walls to build up, either behind or beyond you. "It is *not* a stupid story. Good Lord, what did your mother teach you?"

She shoved the cloche into place. "My mother's dead."

"And you don't want to let her down, do you? Now Raggedy Annie was an evil woman, but her story is part of our story, Rosslyn Taro, and for that alone you ought to have some respect. You shouldn't have showed that tape to anyone. You shouldn't have paraded her around like a damn pageant queen."

Roz willed herself to say nothing. Bay had warned them about keeping quiet regarding Goose Lake, to make sure their stories matched. He was getting calls from famous television shows, *Paranormal Detectives* type stuff. He kept saying *this is it,* but Roz couldn't help thinking that more publicity—more pageantry— would only make the haunting worse. Bay wasn't getting visits from anything pretending to be Raggedy Annie, so he probably didn't care. She'd asked him how they would explain Lark's absence and he said, "Say he went insane, it'll sound creepier." She had never so much wanted to hit him.

"That friend of yours has been hanging out in Roger Malkin's trailer. What's his name, *Lark?*" Before he gave up the ghost several weeks ago, Mr. Malkin used to sit outside the grocery store next to the mechanical horses, drinking whiskey from a paper bag. Lark would be sent to shoo him away, but never had the heart to do it. "My hairdresser lives out in Gaslight Village and she says you gotta get him out of there. The debt collectors are coming to get the trailer any day now."

She called Bay on her lunch break, to tell him that Lark had not in fact run off to Mexico, and ask him if Jessica still had the costume—her tongue no longer wanted to voice the hallowed, damned name of *Raggedy Annie*. "Because I think we should burn it."

Bay was in an awful mood, supposedly due to a severe toothache. "Don't flake out on me like Lark."

"I'm not flaking, I just think we fucked up! I think we shouldn't have done this!" She pulled back her hair, sunk into herself, felt the rapid beating of her heart. She thought she saw Raggedy Annie—*Mom?*—at the other end of the parking lot but then a car passed and it was just a stop sign. Talk about this and she'd sound crazy. Forget sounding crazy, she'd *be* crazy. Another loony. Just like Lark. She had to use language Bay understood. "We should get rid of the evidence before anybody ever finds it."

"Well, I have no idea where it is. I haven't talked to Jessica since Tuesday. She's being a bitch."

If Lark was here, he'd say *"no!"* all sarcastic and wry, and she'd let out her horse-laugh and Bay would get pissed because he was the only one allowed to diss Jessica, and she'd say, "What do you expect with some nineteen-year-old Hot Topic wannabe?"

"She's never got the time anymore. She's always working on her damn terrariums." She heard him scoff through the phone. "Here I thought she hated science."

The next day Roz called KLNW news and said she wanted to come clean about the Goose Lake video. "Our first mistake was making the film at all," she said on the six o'clock news. "Our second mistake was showing it to other people. I just want to say to the entire community that I'm so sorry for lying, and I'm so sorry for any disrespect we may have caused." To the nameless, unseen power behind the visitations, she added a silent prayer: *Please forgive me. Please let me go.*

***

The Bailey family tree lived in Aunt Vivian's upstairs closet. Once upon a time when Bay was young and bored and his parents were having it out at home, Aunt Vivian had unrolled it and presented it to him on her kitchen table. It was his inheritance, she said. Just like his father's Smith & Wesson and his mother's bad teeth. Aunt Vivian's lacquered fingernails ran from name to name, jumping back and forth in time. "That's your great-great grandpa Johnny, he enlisted after getting married and then went and died in the War," she said. "And that's Laura Jean, she's your cousin-twice-removed. She wanted to be a movie star, but she only sang back-up in commercials."

"Why is it called a tree," little Bay asked.

"Because we all grew from the same roots. Lots of people draw their family trees starting from their great-grandpas at the top, as if all your ancestors lived and died just so you could be born, you special little cupcake. But that doesn't make a damn bit of sense. You start with the roots—that's Herman and Sarah Bailey, when they moved here from Ohio. The rest of us are their twigs.

We grew out of them."

The chart indeed looked like everyone since Herman and Sarah had grown out of their subterranean bones, children sprouting from their parents like spores.

"Does that mean we're stuck here."

Aunt Vivian cocked her head. "And just what is wrong with 'here'?"

His parents had met in elementary school; they grew into a big-haired, Stairway to Heaven couple with matching letterman jackets. *Whippoorwill born and bred,* they cooed, as if that was anything to be proud of. They'd disproved their own manifesto by the time Bay was old enough to dial Child Services. For a while he was the only one who heard the plastic plates ricocheting off the dining room wall, the *"fuck you"*s and the *"just get out"*s, the stationwagon scurrying out of the driveway and jumping the curb. He wondered how to put that shit in the family tree. Attention, the tree is currently on fire. After the divorce severed his parents' bond, he imagined his own name gliding away as if it had never been rooted to this gnarled monstrosity that began with Herman and Sarah. Yet nothing changed. He stayed tethered to the crown of the Bailey tree: a struggling, captive bird.

His father never liked it when he talked about New York, Vegas, Mexico. He would point a beer can at him and say, "You think you're better than this town? We're not good enough for you anymore?"

It seemed easier to say he was sick of "you fucking hillbillies" than to tell the truth. He knew that would get a response, probably a box in the ear for pissing on his surroundings. But what he really wanted to say was *You were never good enough for me. You were never good enough for anyone.*

***

Rumor had it that the weirdo living in Roger "Alkie" Malkin's trailer in Gaslight Village was an escaped convict. Tweaked-out gremlins in neon-shirts sometimes snuck peeks through the windows, standing on their tiptoes in the muddy swamp-grass that had swallowed most of the trailer's tires. The weirdo was usually sitting in the dark with a flashlight, watching something terrifying on his phone. The glow on his face was lunar. When he noticed them he'd growl and scurry to the window and pull the curtains. The rumor adjusted—now he was a scientist from Area 51, on the run from the Feds.

But he was just a man—a boy, really—who had the misfortune of stumbling upon some hidden fold in the world that he couldn't explain, and knew of no other recourse than retreat. He was just Lark. When Roz knocked on the door of the trailer, distressed because she'd seen feet descend from the silver maple tree in her backyard, he opened the door. And when Bay banged upon the door an hour later, yelling that he knew they were in there, Lark again relented.

"The gang's back together," Lark whispered, trembling and huddling on the piss-stained carpet. He looked like death by then—he'd lost so much weight, so much color. But Roz and Bay were red-eyed too. They hadn't spoken to each other since her confession to KLNW news. He had tried to contact her at first—called twenty-three times and sent seven text messages, including *"Fuck you you fucking bitch"*—but within forty-eight hours he was the one on KLNW, and Roz was the unstable nutjob with the ax to grind. He swore to the town of Whippoorwill that the video was one hundred percent authentic. "Only unity saves the damned."

"I just got fired," Bay said in the trailer. "My manager says she lost *trust* in me since my friend *Rosslyn* went on TV and said we faked the entire Goose Lake video." Roz was clenching her stomach, refusing to look at him. "So thank you, Rosslyn. Thank you so much."

"I was desperate!" she shouted. "You don't know what it's like! You turn every corner and you wonder—is she gonna be there? Is she watching me? Will anybody else see her? And even after I said sorry, she still didn't stop!" She knelt down beside Lark and cautiously tugged on the hems of the blanket he wore like a shawl around his head. "Lark, I know you've been seeing her too."

Lark stared blankly at her, and Bay clapped his hands over his head. "You're unbelievable. It's not Raggedy Annie, fuckwit, Raggedy Annie isn't real! Remember? We made her! She's Jessica!"

"Yeah? And where is your little girlfriend anyway? She's a part of this mess, she ought to be here too."

Bay nervously chewed on his fingernail as he stalked around Alkie's trailer. It was empty save for plastic bags and cigarette butts and half-eaten meals: evidence of a life undone. "Jessica's gone."

The other LunaTicks were silent, but Bay slammed his fist into a plastic cabinet and snapped an answer to a question he'd heard only in his head, "I don't know where! She's just gone, she hasn't been to work, her parents haven't seen her... they think she got mad at me and ran off. When they looked in her room all they found were those... damn terrariums." Suddenly exhausted, Bay slid to the carpet and pulled off his black beanie. "They're all the same too. Just one tiny tree in every one. Looks like a little oak tree." The tiniest sliver of a bittersweet smile cracked Bay's face. "Like a tiny Witching Tree."

"Bay's right," Lark mumbled. "It's not Raggedy Annie. It's the trees. Here, look at the video again." He held up his phone and their no-budget home movie began to play. Roz and Bay were so hollowed out by then that they didn't have the strength to object to watching their little experimental film another, final time. They watched themselves skip stones across Goose Lake, watched the camera find the Witching Tree. They watched themselves act out the script they'd written at Jessica's house the night before—*"Let's just go, I'm getting cold"*—and watched Jessica stand ominous and hooded in front of the Witching Tree. And finally, they watched the branches of the Witching Tree curl, like the fingers of some enormous dryad, toward Jessica.

"Do you see the tree?" Lark whispered, like he was coaching a baby to speak. The leaves of the tree stood on end, fluttering as if swept by a celestial wind, trembling as if awakening. "See it move?"

"I don't understand," Roz whined. "It's the breeze…"

"No, no, no! Listen, I've looked this up, and these beings exist across the world, in dozens of civilizations across time… there's Yggdrasil, there's Ashvattha, there's Világfa, there's Kalpavrishka, and now there's… there's the Witching Tree." Bay was about to punch Lark in the face, and they all knew it, so he spoke faster. "These trees, they connect… all the planes of existence, the world of the living with the world of the dead. The Witching Tree is our Cosmic Tree."

Those words—*Cosmic Tree*—hung like smoke circles in Alkie's musty trailer. Jessica's terrariums. The trees that grew manic and hungry over their houses. The Witching Tree itself, eternal long-limbed sentinel of Goose Lake. And all roads led to Goose Lake…

Bay was the first to break the trance and grapple to his feet. He claimed not to understand what Lark was trying to say. He said he couldn't waste his time on this bullshit about trees, because what could a tree do to him? All he knew was that Lark and Roz had gone completely bat-shit, and now none of them were ever getting out of Whippoorwill, and was that what they wanted all along? Did they want to be stuck in this inbred town forever, maybe open a tree nursery if they were so obsessed with greenery?

"…dude, what are you doing to your teeth?"

Bay was picking at one of his bottom canine teeth, digging into the gum, trying to rip it out. "It's the root!" he shouted through his bloody fingers. "It's fucking killing me!"

Bay waited until he'd returned home to extract the tooth. He was so distracted by the electric pain that he failed to see that the dead cottonwood outside his mother's house, the one that had broken his arm as a child, was growing green again. He used a pair of pliers and the bathroom mirror—the pain was nothing compared to the horror of enduring another moment with the tooth's ruined root in his skull. Yet even as he stared at the ugly disembodied thing lying at the bottom of the sink, he could feel the roots of his other teeth rotting. He didn't know what had happened to them—his bad teeth, his mother's teeth—but he could feel their decay spreading into his jaws, his sinuses. The thought of those sick roots growing into his bones—he saw them jutting out of his chin like saber-teeth, drilling down in search of soil—made him want to die…

They all had to go. By the time his mother came in, he was lying delirious on the tiles, his teeth lay scattered around him like bloody seeds.

The day after Bay was committed to Teller Psychiatric, Roz drove alone to Jessica Grauner's house in the half-light. She went because only unity saves the damned, though she'd hated Jessica when she'd tagged along on the LunaTicks' vandalism operations and petty larceny sprees. Where one goes, the others must follow, and she neither wanted to follow Bay to Teller Psychiatric nor knew how to follow Lark into his rabbit hole. And she had the squirmy feeling that Jessica was still hanging around— *like Raggedy Annie hung from the Witching Tree?*—somewhere on the property.

Roz had been to this house twice—once for a grotesque house party while Jessica's parents were out of town, and once to prepare for the Goose Lake stunt. On neither occasion had there been a linden tree in the front yard, but now a full-grown specimen had broken through the earth to stand in proud, terrifying splendor before Jessica's window. Its roots bubbled across the lawn, disrupting her parents' carefully-manicured ornamental ferns. A large, discolored knot peeked out from the linden's trunk—a malformed branch, right, a sleeping bud? But when Roz got close enough to touch it, she saw that it was a face: Jessica's face, her eyes clenched shut and her mouth stretched open in an anguished forever-scream. Roz ran her finger down one wooden eye, heard Jessica's nasal whine—*I smell like a dead rat!*—and quickly stuffed her hand back in her pocket, running back to her car.

***

Roz's mother died during the Great Storm. She died at home, of cancer, while the world raged around them. Electric lines sparked, cars slid off roads, walls fell in, and smaller trees were torn out of the earth, but their older, larger counterparts miraculously survived. It seemed like a condolence card from God: *the world is filled with death, but Life endures.*

There were strange things said at the funeral. "She's waiting for you, in heaven." "We will all meet again, by-and-by." Roz hated to admit it—because who wouldn't want to see their mother again?—but when these words floated up on desolate roads at midnight, she was frightened. She wanted to hear that her mother was at peace, in a better place, had *moved on*—not that she was *waiting, lingering, hovering,* skeletal hands outstretched to receive her daughter as soon as death delivered her—no. That was ugly.

Her mother loved trees. They were her favorite thing about Whippoorwill. *Don't you love how tall they are, how old they are? These trees are older than all of us.* She was a native, so she had grown up with them—climbed them, slept in their nooks, taken their shelter, carved her initials into their skin with the neighbor boy. Roz's father had agreed to move to Whippoorwill before they got married because it was supposedly a good place to raise a family—what with the safe streets and heritage fairs and seasonal festivals—but when he wanted to move to Lincoln for the sake of a higher salary, her mother had refused on account of the trees. *But there are trees everywhere,* he said. *It's not the same,* she said. *These trees are my inheritance. They're the kids' inheritance.*

She had a special bedtime story about the Witching Tree. It had nothing at all to do with Raggedy Annie. It was about the men and women who first built Whippoorwill, back when America was young. They built the jail and they built the church, they built the courthouse and they built the school. And then they planted the Witching Tree, so after their human bodies died they would stay close to their children, and live forever.

Her father listened in once, and got so upset that her mother never told it again, and Roz never heard it again from anyone else. At middle school sleepovers—before the other girls decided she was just too weird—they only ever whispered about Raggedy Annie, the abortionist-witch. When she asked about *"that Witching Tree story"* they would indignantly snap, "That *is* the Witching Tree story, dummy!"

But one time in high school when they were all smoking pot in Bay's basement, Roz tried to re-tell her mother's version of the Witching Tree story, what little she could remember of it. It turned out Bay and Lark had heard similar shit from their parents, once or twice. Bay and Lark were, first and last and always, the only people she could count on not to lie to her. Lark said, "It's a creation myth. And an apocalypse myth, too. The end and the beginning, the beginning and the end."

Dawn came, and they never spoke of it again. The Witching Tree story—the real one, the one submerged beneath the arsenic-and-old-lace of Raggedy Annie—was only whispered in the ears of Whippoorwill babies, so the truth would soften like sugar cubes right into their unfinished brains. These babies grew up and forgot except when they were sleeping, usually, but sometimes when they looked at the massive, infallible trees of Whippoorwill for too long, that primordial story writhed like a worm and they would shiver, listening to the leaves rustling like ocean waves, wondering who was waiting for them.

***

Raggedy Annie stood, again, at the end of Roz's bed. Roz could almost hear her breathing.

"No," Roz mumbled to herself. "She's not real. Raggedy Annie is not real." And maybe she wasn't, but something stood there. Something had turned Bay into a pile of dirt in Teller Psychiatric. Oh, that wasn't in the official hospital report—the hospital said he somehow *escaped,* from the restraints and the room and the asylum, and the forest-fresh soil that had replaced him in the cot was—what—a practical joke? The LunaTicks knew all about those, but this was something else, something beyond. Roz closed her eyes, telling herself that once she opened them, it would be morning and Raggedy Annie would be gone.

When she opened her eyes the figure was leaning over her, twitching. This time it wasn't her mother beneath the hood. This was the face that looked back at her in the mirror every morning, bleary-eyed and bloodless, sapped of life. It was her. Her doppelganger cocked its head to the side like a bird and stared at her with her own big black eyes—black, then blacker, in the face of the ghost. It was death looking down; she could feel that in her veins, because that wasn't blood roiling inside her anymore. It was sap. *Slow like honey.* Death leaned in and Roz screamed herself awake.

It was midnight. Roz drove to Gaslight Village in a fugue, but Lark wasn't there. Alkie's trailer looked like it had been spat out by a tornado—it had been smashed nearly in half by a fallen tree. Branches had broken through the windows and now grew inside the trailer, as if they'd been searching for him. Her first thought was that the trailer had become his coffin, but after she scrambled to reach a broken window, cutting her hands on glass shards, she didn't see a body in the dark. No soil, either. There was only one place, unhappily, that he would have gone.

She could see the woods around Goose Lake stirring before she even got out of the car. For a second she sat behind the wheel, trying to delay the inevitable, hypnotized by the razor-sharp static that had overcome the radio, until she saw again the figure that she'd been running from since they made the video. Raggedy Annie was standing where the trees parted to make way for a little human path. The hooded ghost turned and disappeared down the trail, and Roz knew this would not end if she did not pursue. Where one goes the others must follow, and Raggedy Annie was one of them. The truth was she always had been. Raggedy Annie and her mother and father and brother and Lark's parents and Bay's parents and Jessica and Old Lady

Marigold and Roger Malkin and everybody, everybody in this town: they were all in this together.

She willed her legs to move into the rippling chaos. As soon as she stepped foot on the dirt path the air pressure dropped, and her bones felt calcified in pain. She'd been hoping not to return to Goose Lake. She'd been hoping to leave Whippoorwill. She'd been hoping… *well.* Hope was just delusion that hadn't ripened yet. The forest didn't smell like pine or cedar or Christmas or anything else they could pack into an air freshener—it smelled like rot. A fleet of dead were howling overhead, and there was nowhere left to go but forward. Just like all roads led to Goose Lake, all of Goose Lake's dirt paths led to the Witching Tree, the oak to seed and end the world.

The Tree had grown since she last saw it. She felt the urge to kneel under its swaying, groaning shadow. Even as worms crawled out of cavities in its trunk, new twigs and leaves sprouted on its boughs. Lark was a dwarf beneath it, wildly swinging a rusty ax. Every strike was true, but he wasn't getting anywhere— not only was the oak enormous, but its bone-like bark yielded nothing except for a few brittle chips of wood. She could see this, even though she could not see stars through the foliage. What stars? The Witching Tree was everything in this world.

Lark looked up and tried to smile when he saw her through his sweat. He looked so weak and mortal, a mere weed next to the Witching Tree. "We can make it, Roz! You and me. Just you and me. You just gotta help me. Help me end this thing."

She shook her head. She could feel the Tree's roots moving like great pythons beneath the fertile earth. "I don't think we can, Lark… I don't think we're getting away."

Lark frowned and paused his work, catching the blade with his hand. "But if we cut it down, it ends," he said, and then cried out and dropped the ax. He was squeezing his left palm—he'd nicked it. Or it had nicked him, it was hard to tell. So the blade was sharp after all—just not sharp enough to slay the tower of space-time that was the Tree. He moaned and pressed his right hand into the wound. "Something's wrong," his voice warbled, holding out his hand. By the Tree's light Roz could barely see it: dark amber where red should have been. It was sap. He was bleeding sap.

"Roz," Lark whimpered. He sounded like the eleven-year-old Clark Dunkin that she had happened to sit next to in sixth grade: sniveling and sullen but still, full of a future. The years of dishevelment sloughed off in seconds, revealing the baby-face below. Was this how the Tree could promise endless life, like her mother said? "Help me."

She blinked, and became faintly aware that she was crying. "Don't fight it."

Now roots were bursting out of his storm-worn sneakers, running wildly toward moist earth—they were trying to find some place to settle, to never let go. Lark was trying to shamble forward but he could only heave his chest, retching until he couldn't breathe. Tree bark tore through his jeans and his arms finally straightened and seized and were destroyed—no, transformed. Only the human skin died. Lark arched his back and would have broken his vertebrae had they not turned to pliable wood; his mouth tore open and a dozen branches leapt from his wooden throat, sprouting blood blossoms. It was almost beautiful.

Roz was kneeling by then, in deference and fear. When Lark's screams finally stopped, she knew that it was her turn. Where others go, one must follow. She lifted her head and saw the great and gnarled Tree, glowing blue-green with something far stronger and far more alien than foxfire, achingly reach its branches toward her and then shrivel back. It was so jealous, so unsure of her loyalty. *"Roz-zz-lyn,"* her mother said, from somewhere in the rush of leaves, *"why d' you want to lee-eave us?"*

Roz picked up the ax. A wail swept through the branches, but Roz only threw the weapon into the murky green waters of Goose Lake. "I'll never leave," she said, and began trudging homeward. "I promise."

It was not a warm embrace. The Tree's branches bit deep into her back as it entwined her, and she soon lost the ability to see anything but heartwood. Still, she melted into the Tree as easily and completely as if she had never been parted from it. Little by little, the walls came down: the walls of Whippoorwill, the walls of her skin. *I'm scared,* she thought as the flesh of her tongue dissolved into sap, and though the only response she heard was a deep and ancient drumbeat pulsing from far within the Witching Tree, she finally understood.

PUGELBONE

I was born in the Warren, and the Warren was all I knew. Both my mother and father were Meers. We go back to the founders. My father was very proud of our ancestry, but he was also very ill. He talked about forging tunnels and building walls and digging rooms for more families, more, when of course the Warren was already finished, and there was no more concrete to dig a new space out of. The rooms had been split as small as they could go without forcing adults to stoop, without making stretching out to sleep completely impossible. Babies were being suffocated, usually under older children, sometimes under their parents. The tunnels had become so narrow that we could only pass through one by one, and even then we had to dodge laundry from the overhead apartments, and falling garbage bags, and other things that people decided they just didn't have room for. I guess before Warrens get finished—get carved up into this Swiss cheese honeycomb as far and as dense as they can go—people have high expectations of how it will turn out. I've seen my father's sketches. There is an order there that is inhuman, it is so exacting. My mother used to say that in a Warren, you eventually lose control. I don't just mean the

jealous lovers that beat each other's heads against the floor, or
the men we kids used to call trenchcoat nasties. I mean you lose
control of the Warren.

And I don't mean to say that everything is shit in a Warren,
because there are reasons people join Warrens, and they are good
reasons. You save resources, save money, you don't drive so you
don't clog the air. You know your neighbors. You're always close
to help, close to home. You share. You keep each other warm.
Warrens have saved lives. I'm not just saying this because my
parents taught me to; I really did see it, every now and then.
Every now and then I'd get a hint of what was so great about
living in a Warren.

But mostly I was miserable. Mostly there were Pugelbones.

***

"You mean the *Helix Warrencola*."

"God, no, I *don't* mean that. I mean..." Dr. Roman's blue
ballpoint pen and razor-thin eyebrow lifted in warning. "I mean
yeah, okay, whatever."

"Unless we're talking about something else. I just want us to
be careful about our terms."

"Well, that's what I mean, the *Helix Warrencola,* but that isn't
what we called them, and you know we saw them first. You
know because we told you, over and over, that there were these
things in the Warren, and we didn't know what they were, and
nobody ever came to check..."

Dr. Roman twirled her pen toward the cavity in her neck.
"Me? I didn't come to this office until last year, Lizbet, and besides, we have nothing to do with Civil Security."

"I don't mean *you* you, I mean..." The ceiling light in her office was very smooth, very large, very creamy and eggy white.

Like a giant flattened pearl. Like Dr. Roman. "Never mind. It's nothing."

"Because remember, I'm here to *help* people like you."

"Yeah, right. I know." There was no way out. "I'm sorry." There was no other way.

Dr. Roman blinked with slow, heavily lacquered eyelashes. She was a woman who had time and space to spare. "Then go ahead."

***

Everyone in the Warren called them Pugelbones. But I learned it from my sister—Katrin, two years older. She was a fiddler until our old man neighbor asked our father to smash the fiddle up. Our walls were thin, some no thicker than a hand, and Katrin wasn't a very good fiddler. But she was very good at telling stories, and after our parents sent us to bed so they could hiss at each other in private, Katrin would lean down from her hammock, her eyes all big and jaundiced, and say, "I want to tell a story. Listen to my story." And we had to, my brother and I. He'd reach up from his hammock and grab my hand, sometimes my hair. We were stuck beneath her; her words had nowhere to go but down.

She said that sometimes bones don't make it to the grave with the rest of the body—in the Warren, cemetery space closed up fast, and people had to be buried on top of other, older corpses. Hopefully blood relatives. People die the way they live, I guess. So sometimes a bone would get washed up to the surface in a rainstorm, or get left behind in a moldy apartment where some poor hermit died without anybody noticing. Anyway, loose bones were always turning up in the Warren. My uncle said he'd found a skull once, although he never showed us. I found a bone myself, once, a back bone, a—vertebra. It was lying all by its lonesome in the hall outside our apartment. I picked it up and buried it, because this is what my sister told me: bones that don't know they're dead, that don't feel that blanket of soil and realize "my time has come, the worms inherit me," they will act like they're still alive. And they go searching for clothes and trash to cover themselves with, because bones aren't accustomed to being naked in the world. The very first time this happened, the bone was a femur of a garbage man named Johan Pugel. So we called them Pugelbones.

Nobody really knew what it was that Pugelbones did, because many of us had never actually seen one. On first glance they look like any old heap of clutter and waste. There were a lot of sightings, but the Warren is filled with shadows, see—nothing is flat. Even the walls bulge like they're filled egg sacs, so you see these shapes everywhere. Our old man neighbor complained to you people about an invasive species but a lot of grown-ups only mentioned it when we were being bad, like, shut your mouth or I'll sit you outside with the Pugelbones. No more whining now, I bet. And then you spend the whole night with your hands over your mouth, listening for the sound of something shuffling in the hallway. It's not footsteps. It's too soft and slow and continuous, like the sound of pillows falling. Walls no thicker than your hand, remember.

***

"Did you fight with your parents often?" Dr. Roman tilted her head to the left as if on an axis, as if she could swivel it all the way around if she wanted to. "Did they hurt you when they punished you?"

"What does that matter?" But it mattered. Because Marget

was still in the holding center with a wrist band and a change of clothes, it mattered. "I mean, not really, no. We didn't fight. Fight's not the right word."

"Because it sounds like a toxic relationship." Dr. Roman let the "x" in toxic linger on in all its crisp and nasty consonants; maybe it was her favorite word. "It doesn't sound like you had any positive role models in the Warren. It's not unusual…"

"I don't need one to raise Marget." And then, because the stench of the old apartment and its phlegm and germs were defiling this lovely egg-white office, "My father was very ill. He didn't even know what he was saying at the end."

"Why, what did he say then?" Goddamn, she could catch a scent.

"Something about population control. He talked about rabbits and foxes…" Dr. Roman had gone very stiff and bloodless. "Like I said, he was very ill."

"The *Helix Warrencola* were a newly discovered species. The idea that they were in any way created as a weapon of some pogrom against the Meer people is not only offensive, it's inaccurate." So that was offense showing in her face. "Grossly inaccurate."

They were fond of "grossly" too. Grossly unfit to care for a child. Grossly deluded. Gross conditions and gross behavior. Maybe that was why it took them so long to respond to the Warren's distress calls—hard to keep clean in the muck of a massacre. When Civil Security finally arrived the officers in their camouflage armor could not stop complaining about the Warren's smell and its soggy streets. It was true that the Warren hid nothing, that there was no space in the Warren to provide the illusion of disinfection.

"You asked me what my father said. So I told you."

"You need to let go of this anger you hold toward us. Really we've done a lot to try to help the Meer people."

Anger beats at the heart like a call, like a drum, like a march. It is quick and to the point—it is easy. It Gets Shit Done. It Makes Shit Happen. Guilt, on the other hand, is a worm that burrows. "I wish I was angry." Hooks into the heart, hooks of all kind: metal hooks, hooks of green glass, hooks like anchors and hooks like hands. Some worms just cannot be un-dug.

Dr. Roman opened the case file and flipped through sheets of multi-colored paper. "You had a lot of anger as a child. You threw... bricks off rooftops? You punched one boy's teeth out of his head?" She wanted a response, but what would be correct? An apology? An excuse? More confessions? Tears? Would tears bring Marget home? "Why do you think you did that?"

***

Because I liked to break things down. My father built, I broke. My sister crafted, I destroyed. When our old man neighbor asked my father to smash up Katrin's fiddle, you know, he didn't have the heart to. So I did it. Ripped out its strings and pulled its neck off. It isn't that I wanted to hurt Katrin. We may have lost touch since moving to the city but she is still my sister. I just liked to see things come apart. I liked to see things in their rawest form, re-duced so far they can't be reduced any more. Fiddles, bread loaves, radios, socks. Didn't matter. I had loved peeling layers ever since my mother handed me an orange when I was a baby—but I didn't start breaking things that weren't meant to be broken until I got older.

I was breaking pieces off the ledge of the rooftop playground. You know if the smog's not too bad, you can see the city from up there. It always looked so open and flat and sparse, like God the Creator just scattered a bunch of boxes over the plain and strung them together with long gray roads. Sprawling herds, my father said. Overfed cows in their golden barns.

Anyway I took a break to watch geese flying south—I never got to see the sky from our apartment—when I saw the Pugelbone in the far corner of the roof, near the storage shed. It looked like a pile of abandoned shit: some kid's torn-up corduroy jacket, a garbage bag, doll skin, drain hair, curdled milk, dead rats. Stuff that would have ended up incinerated or washed down the sewer into the River Becquerel. Except this pile was alive. I could tell. It was *breathing*. Like all these dead things had been wound together and reanimated. It was beautiful, and I wanted to strip it to the bone.

It didn't scare me like I thought it would. Didn't scare me like it should have. It was staring right at me, even though it didn't have eyes, and there was this innocence about it, like it knew it was rude to stare. When my father stared it felt like rubber bullets. With my mother and Katrin, more like needles. And with my brother... well, my point is: when this thing stared at me, all I felt was a flutter of eyelashes.

I should probably say that I didn't have much in the way of friends. The other kids thought I was a waste of space and carbon and oxygen—it's why I went after that kid Benjin, punched his teeth out. But Benjin was right about what he said. I *was* a leech, I *was* citizen failure. I was only ever good at breaking things, and in a Warren you have to be useful or you'll get ground up into fodder, living in some lonely crawl-space, eating other people's garbage because you're a good-for-nothing, can't-contribute-nothing, burden on the community. And I couldn't wire electricity. I couldn't fix drains or people or food. I had dreams where I'd find this tiny crack in the wall that I could fit my finger into, and then my hand, and then my arm, until I'd mash my whole body inside the concrete like a wad of gum and hope the renovators wouldn't come in yelling, "We need this space! Move out!"

So when the Pugelbone looked at me in fondness, well, I guess I paid it back.

***

"You wanted it to be your friend."

"I thought if I was nice to it, then it would be nice to me."

Dr. Roman's eyes appeared to be closed, but she was only looking down. She was writing something secret on her little scented pad of paper.

"Is this a common theme in your relationships with other people?"

Other people were bodies in traffic, plump and heart-shaped faces like the ones on billboards and commercials. Polished and empty as the great big boulevards with their seasonal garlands and deserted buses. Foreign people, foreign lives. It's all about keypads and time sheets now, little Meerkat. "I don't know."

"What about with Marget's father?"

"I don't want to talk about that."

"You need to be forthcoming with me during these sessions." She tapped her pad of paper with the ink end of her mighty pen. "It's very important that I make an accurate assessment of your capacity as a caretaker."

"I don't know who he was." Blue shirt, iron-on logo of a red-crown. He'd heard Meer bitches were little tigers in the sack. He came and left without warning, while something on the stovetop burned down to an unrecognizable lump of char. Give and Ye Shall Receive. "So I guess I can't say."

Dr. Roman raised her eyebrows again but this time, for once, the room was quiet.

***

The Pugelbone followed me home that day. I used to ask myself this but now I know: I invited it. Not with words, because I didn't think it would understand those—but when I opened the door to go down below, I looked over my shoulder. You know, to see if it was coming. When I went down the metal staircase I could hear it shuffling after me, dropping its mass step to step. I thought I heard a muffled sort of panting but for all I know it could have been me. That stairwell was very close quarters.

I had never been followed before. Not even my little brother followed me. Not even the tiny brown mice that the crawl-space people hunted followed me, and I had even left them bread crumbs. I said to the Pugelbone, "I'm glad you're here," and its smile was like the curve of a rusty spoon. I could see the two of us running out of the Warren, over the plain and away. Not to the city. Just away.

I thought I would lose it in the street—someone kicked it, thinking it couldn't feel pain, and I picked out a rock I had in my pocket and threw it at the bastard—but when I got to our building and opened the door, the Pugelbone was right behind me, brushing up against my legs.

My brother was the only one home. He was drawing spiders on the floor where our mother usually stood to serve us dinner. He always liked spiders—he used to let whole packs of them crawl on his face when he was a baby, I don't know why. He said, "Hi Lizzie," and then kept on drawing. I don't know if he saw the Pugelbone behind me, but Timot was always such a space cadet. When he was three he sat himself down in the middle of a street to pick up a marble and was nearly trampled by the passers-by. We found him wedged in the dirt, bruised and smiling. "Too stupid to live," people said.

In the Warren, people will walk right into a space and take what's inside. There is the assumption, if your door opens, that you are either generous or dead. So I stepped aside to lock the door. It was only for a second. Three seconds, at most. What none of us realized is that there are mouths everywhere, and they find their way around doors. You have no idea how many mouths there are in this world, and all of them are open. All of us are food.

I screamed, but Timot didn't. I tell myself now that it happened too quickly for him to feel pain, but then I remember that his arms and legs were shaking—no, convulsing, slapping the floor so hard that I could feel the vibrations under my feet all the way on the other side of the apartment. I hope that he was already gone by then, and those were just the... twitches of a dying body. I heard a sound like someone sucking milk through a straw and I realized that the Pugelbone was drinking my baby brother dry.

The Pugelbone went up into the air duct and I lay down. I held his hand—I thought he'd want me to—but it was so limp, like an empty glove. There was blood tracked all over the floor and the wall, and as I lay there I thought to myself that the pattern read like some kind of message. But I don't know what. I never figured out what.

***

"Lizbet."

The room shifted. Dr. Roman was calling.

"Was this really an accident?"

"Yes, it was a fucking accident! Don't even ask me that!"

"But you said that you liked to break things."

"No. No, no, no! That is not fair! I would never fucking hurt him! Look at the case file, it's in the case file!"

"The case file only says that your brother was killed by an unknown entity. Later determined to be a *Helix Warrencola*. It doesn't say anything about whether or not you manipulated the situation. And I don't hold you responsible for that, Lizbet. You were a child. You were living in terrible conditions…"

Mother and Father had believed in the Warren, and cried when it was fumigated. Afterwards they'd wandered in and out of bungalows and parking lots, too old to build another life. "I didn't know. I swear I didn't know."

"I'm going to recommend that the Department of Child Welfare wait a little longer before returning custody of your daughter to you."

A "little longer" is not a schedule. A "little longer" is a young snake. This particular "little longer" was already five months long. When the Warren told the city that there were monsters in their walls, the "little longer" had stretched into a full, bloody year. "Tell me. Is there anything in that damn file that says I've ever hurt Marget?"

"But that's the reason you're here, Lizbet. You took Marget out of pre-school. Forcibly. You pushed her teacher's head into a white board. That is not acceptable behavior for any parent." Dr. Roman prodded the air with her chin. "Even a Meer."

"There was a Pugelbone in that classroom. It was in a cubby hole, and it was looking straight at Marget. It was like the time I took her to the city zoo, to the cages where they keep the predators. Most of the animals are stoned off tranquilizers, but there was this long, skinny, yellow-black tiger that stared at Marget with a living hunger, you know? A mother knows."

Dr. Roman sighed and glanced at the large clock on the wall. "We've already talked about this. You were hallucinating. You were stressed and you were tired and you'd been drinking the night before. Lizbet, sometimes I wonder if we've made any progress at all."

Were there Pugelbones in the holding center? Government

closets ran deep. "Okay, okay. Forget I said anything."

"The *Helix Warrencola* is extinct. Do you understand? That's already been confirmed. And even if there were a few surviving individuals, they'd be stuck in the landfill where the Warren used to be." She leaned forward and whispered, because she was only trying to help, "I really don't want to add paranoid personality disorder to this case file."

Let Marget not be running, let Marget not be screaming. Let Marget be sitting quiet, playing cat's cradle with herself. "Just tell me what I need to do. Please, if you just give me…"

"You aren't ready, Lizbet." The case file fluttered shut. "I'll see you next month, same time."

***

In dreams she had been consumed many times. On occasion it was an act of sacrifice, and she would see Timot and later Marget tottering away on little mushroom-stem legs. More often it was just an attack, sudden and meaningless. In grocery stores, in the factory break room. No safe place. She'd wake up slapping her stomach, trying to put herself back together.

From City Plaza, southbound traffic was non-existent. A raccoon-eyed woman in a coat of chinchilla got off the bus at St. Greta's Hospital, and a pale man in a long tan raincoat got on. A wool scarf was wrapped under his chin so thoroughly that his neck looked like a swollen goitre. The bus was lurching forward when he sat down in the middle of the back row and placed his briefcase on his lap. Then he closed his eyes and sighed.

The small mass under his scarf began to tremble. His fingers pulled the scarf down and revealed a faceless knot of matter cradled in the wool, like a baby in a sling. It was latched onto the man's neck, but it disengaged with a pop and turned its large red sucker toward Lizbet. Blood ran from the withered wound.

"What do you want," drawled the man, scratching at his skin. "Goddamn Meer."

Lizbet drew her knees up as fortresses and gnawed on her nails. The broad boulevard stretched through the half-empty city, blind and merciless, and on into the night.

RED GOAT, BLACK GOAT

I t had been raining for five days. The Gunawan estate, riddled with wool and dung, was rank. Its position on a hill had saved the mountain villa from the floods wracking West Java, but the moon orchids were drowning, and the Mercedes was sinking in the mud. Twenty-some feral goats watched the driveway roll down the slope. Then they started to bleat, because a little human figure was slogging up the hill.

Ina Krisniati was covered in mud by the time she conquered the hill, but by then she was no longer feeling her aches. She had walked two miles, in rising waters and darkness. The small and the weak—frogs, stones, flowering weeds—had succumbed. And Kris had nearly given up too, halfway up the hill. She'd nearly decided to go home to Cililin and marry some fisherman on Saguling Lake. But her grandfather had fought in the war, partaken in the 1946 Sea of Fire—Kris came from strong stock. The goats followed her as she fought her way to the house. They watched with sad, beady eyes as she rinsed her hands in rain and wiped her flip-flops on the mat. When she rang the doorbell, they resumed bleating.

A woman came to the door. She was, to Kris's surprise, not

a maid. She had bags under her eyes but she was dressed like a soap star. Behind her, the house was glowing with spun glass and gold. The warung-keeper in Bandung who told her about the job did say that the Gunawans were born lucky. The woman cleared her throat.

Kris mustered a smile and bent her head. "Asalaam 'Alaykum," she said.

It took the woman half a minute to answer in kind. "Wa 'Alaykum as-Salaam," she muttered. "Are you the new babysitter?"

Kris nodded.

"Ya Allah." Mrs. Gunawan rolled her eyes and stepped back from the door. "What a mess. Don't move." She threw towels at her until she stopped dripping. "You know you're late. And you'll have to wash those, of course."

"I'm sorry, ma'am. The bus I was on broke down. Then I took a wrong turn, back on Tunjukmanis…"

Mrs. Gunawan rolled her eyes. "Right. Well, you're here to watch the children, and they're already in bed. I expect you to watch them *constantly*. My husband took off, my son fell off a horse last week, and… " She took a deep breath and flexed her jeweled fingers. "You have experience with childcare, yes?"

"Four little brothers and sisters. It's been tough for my parents, my father was ill… "

Mrs. Gunawan gave her a long look. "Don't even think about sneaking a little extra. I'll make you regret it."

"Yes, ma'am."

"You didn't touch the goats, did you? The ones roaming around?"

They had seemed to want her to. They'd been nudging her, blocking her path, making needful little grunts. "No, ma'am."

"Good. Don't. Only the children and I can touch them. Oh!" She cocked her chin up and pointed. Whispers trickled from the second floor. Soon little footsteps came down the staircase, and little heads popped out of the shadows. "There they are. Number one and number two."

The children looked like a pair of big-eyed malu-malu. Two of those shy little primates had once climbed into a power switch center on Saguling Lake and fried themselves as well as the hydro-electric plant. Kris smiled at the children. They did not smile back.

Mrs. Gunawan made no introductions. "Take them to bed," she said, with a flip of her wrist.

The bedroom was so cold that Kris thought there had to be some kind of draft. She checked the windows in vain while the children sat side by side on the bed, eating chocolate goo out of plastic tubes. On the wall, over their heads, hung a protective charm made of wild goat hair.

"I guess it's just cold in here." Kris plastered on a smile and walked back to the children. The little girl was the older of the two. She looked like her mother, especially when she had her chin up so she could look down her nose. The little boy was cradling his arm, which was wrapped in a cast and a sling. "I'm Kris. I'm going to watch you from now on, okay?"

"I'm Putri," said the little girl. "This is Agus. And you're not going to be watching us, because we already have someone who does that." She poked her little brother in the shoulder. "Don't we."

He nodded vigorously, but only after a pause, and when he looked at his petrified arm he frowned.

"Really? And who's that?"

"The Goat-Nurse. She's taken care of us since we were born." She sniffed. "We've never had a babysitter."

"Well, that's fine if the Goat-Nurse wants to watch you too. But your mother wanted someone to come and make sure that you don't hurt yourself falling off horses anymore." She smiled at Agus, who made a quivering attempt to smile back.

"We can't trust people from outside the family," Putri said. "The Goat-Nurse says so."

Kris had wondered why such a rich family had no servants. "Well, you don't need to worry about me." She wiped the chocolate off their mouths, the little malu-malu. "I'm not going to hurt you."

***

In the daytime the children showed off the family's goat herd. These were not the feral goats that roamed the estate and the wild woods beyond—these were fat, gentle livestock, happy to spend their lives in a backyard enclosure before being sold off to butcheries. They passively chewed their grass while the children sat on their backs and braided their white wool. The goat keeper Tono spent most of his time lounging under trees and staring off at Mount Tangkuban Perahu.

"Don't they want more space?" Kris asked him.

Tono shook his head, cracking his knuckles. He'd been digging out the sunken Mercedes. "They're scared of the wild goats. The ones that eat up all the grass."

One such wild goat—thin but fearless, with a pair of odd gangly legs—was roaming in the bushes outside the idyll of the enclosure. It looked at Kris and there was something not-quite-right about its face.

"Those goats will charge you," said Tono. "But mine are a lot nicer. They know they have it good. You don't even need a stick to corral them."

He had given his herding stick to Putri to play with, and she lorded it over the animals like a kingpin. Now and then she'd bop them on the head for eating flowers or urinating, though it had no effect on their behavior. "I'm the Goat-Princess!" she declared, and her brother saluted her like soldiers saluted the General during parades, like the General saluted the flag.

Tono smiled at Kris, then bit down gently on his cigarette.

Putri refused to surrender the stick when it was time for afternoon prayer, so Tono let her keep it. Only when the Gunawans sat down to dinner did Mrs. Gunawan tell her the stick could not rest at the table. It fell on Kris to put it away.

The upstairs hall light had burned out. There was a window fifty feet away, but a rainstorm had rendered the moon useless. Kris crept down the hall, trying to remember how many doors away Putri's bedroom was. All the door knobs were cold. Oily. The walls felt coated with a wax that smelled of soil, and sweat, and corpses. When Kris tossed the herding stick onto the floor of Putri's room, it rolled back toward her in affection. The Goat-Nurse, she thought.

It had to be a ghost. Maybe she'd been a babysitter like Kris, some hundred years ago. Maybe she'd been Dutch. A prison nurse. Someone cruel. And maybe something horrible had happened to her, something that earned her such a nasty name. Maybe she lost her legs in an accident. Maybe they had to sew on a pair of goat legs as rudimentary prosthetics...

From the end of the hallway came a *clop clop*. Kris looked to her right into the dark. *Clop clop* again, but closer. Back at home she'd been able to pick a human shape out of a moonless night if she gave her eyes enough time. So far the hallway was a mess of undefined clumps, but they'd straighten out. They'd clear up.

"I'm not afraid of you," she said, but the days when she didn't fear the dark were gone.

Her eyes adjusted, and she saw something standing at the wall. It had a face, of a sort. A long neck. Below that was something like a body in a smock, and then—livestock legs. Bristled. Filthy. Complete with cloven goat hoofs. Then the entire shape shuddered and the façades of skin melted back like a drawn veil. Beneath it darkness came a-crawling.

Kris fell all over the tiles, unable to feel her legs. Some distant part of her reptilian brain realized that she had been shaking for the past five minutes. She tried to stand—no, her legs were leaden. No more *clop clop* now, just a rush of overboiled air. She glanced up once and saw a curled blackness filling the hallway, floor to ceiling, like smoke but thicker, heavier, almost woolen. Kris slapped her hands over her eyes.

Maybe you should lose your legs

Maybe I should have them

"Kris!" It was like being pulled from drowning. "What are you doing up there?"

Was there a safer world? The monstrous breathing had pulled back from her neck. She looked up through her fingers and the hallway was bare. Just curios lined with velvet. She shoved her numb feet beneath her body and staggered downstairs.

"I hope you weren't in my jewelry…"

The expression on Kris's face must have cut Mrs. Gunawan off.

"The hall light's burned out," Kris said, but she could not hear her own voice. Light bulbs were part of a surface world that was no longer relevant. Light bulbs and dinner plates and chandeliers. From some distant plateau, Mrs. Gunawan told her to tell Tono in the morning—but Mrs. Gunawan was a blur. So was the room. Only the children were in focus, with their bullet eyes and their heart-shaped mouths.

***

Dark things swirled on the periphery of the flashlight's ray. These things made a pretense of hiding, but it was purely symbolic, part of a great game they were all playing. Kris saw them and so did the children. Agus even traced their movements with his finger, as if they were watching a wayang performance.

"I don't think she likes you," Putri said, pulling her sheets up to her chin. "You should be careful."

"I thought all *she* did was take care of you."

"Yes, of *us*, and our goats. But she gets mad easy. Do you know where my daddy is?"

Kris shrugged. She assumed he was off cavorting in Bangkok or Bali. Possibly skulking in a Jakarta lounge popping shabu, but she doubted it.

"He had a fight with Mama about the Goat-Nurse. Then he walked into the forest. The Goat-Nurse says he's dead. She says he got eaten by a tiger."

Kris swallowed. She thought she heard a *clop clop.*

"She has *power*, Kris." With a sigh, Putri closed her eyes. "You *have* to be respectful."

Kris went next door. She didn't knock and would never knock on a door in this house again, not when the Goat-Nurse lurked in the walls. The little shape under the sheets jolted awake.

"I'm sorry," Kris whispered, quickly closing the door and kneeling by the bed. "I need to ask you something, okay? It's very important."

Agus chewed his cotton top-sheet.

"Did the Goat-Nurse break your arm?" Silence. "Gus… you need to tell me."

"I really did fall off the horse. He got all scared and went up on his back legs. I fell into the ditch. But the Goat-Nurse didn't catch me. Mama says she's supposed to make sure I never get hurt." After another pause: "Are horses scared of goats?"

The children's mother was smashing peanuts on the sofa when Kris rushed this information to her. Mrs. Gunawan raised her eyebrow. "Why do you think I brought you here?" she said flatly. "The damn Goat stopped looking after them. I don't know why, but… it is what it is."

Kris carefully perched on the edge of another chair. She didn't want to encroach, but Mrs. Gunawan was slouched over, looking breakable.

"The night he left, my husband told me the Goat took one of his brothers. Little brother, long time ago. And I told him—I thought this thing worked *for* your family—and he started…" she flailed her hands, "throwing plates."

"Ma'am… have you considered asking an imam to come?"

Mrs. Gunawan wiped her eyes and laughed. "She's not a jinn. God knows that would have made it easier. Imam get rid of toyol all the time, don't they?"

Yes, they did—Kris had seen it done, at a sideshow. A morose man brought the imam a glass jar, large enough to hold a baby, and said the toyol inside had gotten so out of hand—attacking small animals, biting people—that he couldn't use it to run errands anymore. The imam proceeded to pray over the jar, slap its lid, and scold the baby-jinn for bad behavior. Then he gave the jar back to the morose man and told him to bury it in the woods and let the spirit be at peace, for God's sake.

"You thought it was a toyol?"

"She made the crops grow! She gave us those fat goats in the shed! It was a *drought* the year they found her. Or she found them, I don't know." Mrs. Gunawan crushed a peanut shell. "My husband said the goats just came to the door one day. The wild ones, you know, the ones you shouldn't touch. They just came to the door, April 1962. Like God had sent them."

***

A few days later, Tono was caught taking money out of Mrs. Gunawan's purse. She drove him to the front stoop. First he made excuses—she owed him last month's payment, the money fell out and he was putting it back—and then he tried to return the five hundred thousand rupiah with a gap-toothed smile.

Mrs. Gunawan grabbed Tono by the wrist. He looked startled. "Keep it," she said. "And here. Something else to remember us by." She thrust a thick tuft of goat wool into his hand.

The wool was far too coarse to have been shorn from the sweet, docile goats in the enclosure. Tono made a horrified croak. He tried to drop the feral wool but it clung to him; he tried to rub it off like pollen but it spread. "Please!" he cried. "I'm *sorry!*"

She pointed, but it didn't matter anyway. Even if he huddled on the doorstep he'd still be marked for death. So Tono went off down the hill, sobbing. His threadbare shirt glowed white under the moon.

"You'll kill him," Kris said. "And you'll destroy Bandung."

Mrs. Gunawan slammed the door and bolted it. "But maybe she'll get a taste for other people." The blood-strained whites of her eyes were nearly unbearable to look at. She had been beautiful, once. "You don't want to die, right?"

Kris shook her head. The windows went dark and the electricity blinked as something large slipped over the roof, momentarily drowning the house in a deep digestive rumble. Mrs. Gunawan clenched her jaw so hard her chin shook. Kris cowered.

Then it passed. The walls settled as if exhaling. The water heater and refrigerator hummed, but all else was calm.

"Maybe you should leave," said Kris. "Before it comes back."

Mrs. Gunawan shook her head violently. "*She* is out *there*. We are safer *here.*"

People had started screaming down below. Kris put her head in her hands. Trees broke and roofs collapsed, but they were only punctuations against the steady roar of the Goat in bloom.

"It's just like the Tasikmalaya earthquake," Mrs. Gunawan said melodically. "That's all. Just another earthquake, just another mudslide... just another volcano, ripping open..."

A gurgling cry arose from the staircase, where Agus stood with his hands clapped over his ears. His mother was catatonic, so Kris hurried to shush him.

"She's out killing," he whined. "I hate the noise she makes." As if the Goat heard him, a gut-wrenching aerial moan burst out from the city. It must have carried all the way to the crater of Tangkuban Perahu. The docile goats, crowded near the walls of the house for protection, were bleating plaintively.

***

They didn't see the Goat-Nurse for another two months. Those were not a happy two months, although they were bloodless. Bandung authorities had passed off the Goat's attack as a violent mid-season tropical storm. Twenty-one had died, but they'd been impaled on branches, crushed under roof beams. The only casualty who'd been consumed was Tono, whose head fell out of the sky and onto the front porch the day after.

The children were quiet; nervous. Kris counted the days and held her breath, waiting for a hoofstep or a grunt. And in her dreams she would lie in the goat shed, watching an endless herd of feral goats come trampling out of the stalls. Their wool would blanket her. They would nuzzle her and bare their teeth and smile.

"She isn't far," Putri said at breakfast. Kris couldn't tell if she was pleased.

That evening Mrs. Gunawan had a visitor: her father-in-law, accompanied by a mute, kowtowed son. He was wearing an old black button-down suit and centimeter-thick glasses. He took a deep sniff of the air and knew.

"Where is she? Where did she go?"

"Why don't you ask your son."

"If you chased her away, you ungrateful bitch… "

"Look, that monster—*she*—doesn't belong with us. She hurt my son, look what she did to his arm!"

The elder Mr. Gunawan leaned down and inspected Agus's cast with a jut of his jaw. He smelled heavily of menthol. He was missing several teeth, and Agus stared unabashed at the black spots eating away at his gums. The old man hissed at the evidence. "That's it? That's all? Do you have any idea what she *is?*"

"You promised me my kids wouldn't get hurt!"

"I promised that you'd have grandchildren." He knotted his lips in disdain. "Same promise that was made to me."

Yet the old man need not have worried. The Goat came back—on the eve of jum'at kliwon, no less, spirits' night. She descended onto the house and draped her many woolly arms over the windows, blocking out the moon. Then she seeped through the roof and drenched the walls with wool-grease and the dirt of twenty cities, the blood of six hundred. The house had always been hers.

Agus and Putri cuddled into the Goat's familiar warmth. Mrs. Gunawan woke up throwing the sheets back, gasping for air. Kris lay on her stomach like a snake, hoping the Goat would pass her by.

Mrs. Gunawan didn't get out of bed the next morning. They heard her coughing from the kitchen.

"Where's Mama?" Agus asked, while Kris tossed the fried rice.

"She's sick," said Kris. "We should go down to the market and buy her some jahe."

"I don't think we should go anywhere," said Putri, and that was that.

The house felt unbearably quiet—no Tono, no Mrs. Gunawan. Just a hovering stillness that left the children sleepy and Kris scrubbing oil off a coffee table. The spot wouldn't clean; the streaks kept morphing back into the shape of a goat head. She threw down her sponge. "Let's go outside."

"Why are you trying to separate us from her?" Putri asked, yawning.

"Because she is a danger to you!" She hissed this, because she was afraid.

"She would never hurt us, or leave us. Not like Mama and Daddy."

Kris groaned and helped Agus off the couch. "*We* are going to go for a walk. *You* may stay here with your Goat-Nurse, since you like her so much."

Putri looked disgruntled, almost hurt. In the backyard—they walked and walked, but could never step out from under a great gray cloud—Agus asked if his sister would be okay.

Kris snorted. "She'll be fine."

"Agus! Look at me!"

They looked over their shoulders. Putri had gone up to the second floor balcony and climbed the terracotta shingles until she was standing like a weather vane on the top beam of the roof.

"Ya Allah, Putri! Come down from there!"

"You watch! She'll save me!"

"No she *won't!*"

Putri grinned. Then she bent her knees and jumped, flapping her arms, giving over complete faith. As she dropped past the second floor windows, smog emerged from the house and

swarmed her little body. The enormous black cloud slowly drifted her down to a nest of grass. For a second the cloud seemed to
have consumed her; then it dissipated, and left the unhurt child
behind.

Putri was still smiling. "You see? She loves *me.*"

Agus hung back, looking at his own broken arm. Despite
weeks of cast-life, the fracture just wouldn't heal. He began to
gnaw at his shirt collar—and Kris was about to tell Putri to be
nicer to her brother—when Putri reached her hand out toward
him and said, "Never mind. Let's go see the goats."

Agus took Putri's hand after only a second of hesitation, and
the two children walked solemnly through the grass to their inheritance.

***

Kris woke up sluggish. She had overslept, she could tell. How
could it still be dark? She looked at her bedside clock, but it had
jammed, apparently, at 5 a.m. The goats must have jammed too,
because for once she didn't hear them mewling through the wall.

She had a flashlight, thank God. She fumbled her way into
the main rooms of the house. All the clocks were stopped, and
all the skies were dark. There was something too velvety about
the night, like immense cosmic curtains had closed around the
house.

Something was struggling upstairs. A muffled fight, but in a
house so silent, Kris heard all. She found Mrs. Gunawan choking in her bed.

Kris rushed over out of occupational instinct—*what can I do
for you, ma'am?*—but once she was leaning over the cursed bed
she froze. Between the rows of perfect teeth, behind the bluish
tongue, gobs of black wool were filling Mrs. Gunawan's throat.

Kris clapped her hands to her own mouth as Mrs. Gunawan thrashed.

"I'll call the doctor," Kris muttered, but Mrs. Gunawan grabbed her wrist and made a wretched croaking sound, like she was trying to scream through the wool. Her eyes were peeled back so far that even the blood vessels writhed. Kris jerked back. In another second the seizures stopped and Mrs. Gunawan's eyes rolled backward. Wool poked through her lips. Kris said a little prayer, but there was no peace to be had.

There was a little sound behind her. It was the children, standing shock-still in the doorway. God only knew how long they'd been watching their mother die. They made eye contact with Kris, then bolted.

She chased the little white figures down the hallway. She called them—"Gus! Putri!"—but they had their backs to her. She'd had nightmares like this: running, chasing, and then the children would turn around with hissing kuntilanak faces. Kris caught up to them downstairs, and said a little prayer before grabbing their bony shoulders and spinning them around.

But no—they were children. Bitter and breaking, but still apple-cheeked. Kris threw her arms around them, spewing any and all bullshit that would calm them down, but Putri shoved her away.

"We don't need you! We don't need Mama!"

"I know you're sad." Hoofsteps were running rampant upstairs; doors were slamming. She heard a thump that had to be Mrs. Gunawan's body being dragged off the bed. "But you need to stay with me, okay, we need to go get help."

Agus started crying, and Putri's snarl escalated into a scream: "The Goat is our real mother! She is *everyone's* real mother!"

Kris bit her bottom lip so hard it drew blood. Then she grabbed hold of Putri's arm and dragged her out the back door.

Agus came running after them, practically howling. They were still trapped behind the night-curtain. The yard was torn up, like someone tried to plow it, and Putri kept jamming her feet into little ruts in the soil. Kris kept yanking her forward.

"Come on! You think that thing is your mother, I want you to see what it does to its children!"

More screams. Kicking. Biting. But when they reached the goat enclosure, all resistance stopped. It was too quiet, and it smelled absolutely foul. Wet things squelched under their rubber flip-flops and oozed between their toes.

"Look at what it does!"

Kris turned the flashlight on, and immediately choked back vomit. There was a lot of red, a lot of bones. Stubby little horns and milky eyes lay scattered in a sea of lush wool.

Agus shrieked and buried his eyes in his hands. Putri said nothing, but as Kris leaned down to shake sense into her—she had loved these creatures, hadn't she? given them names?—tremors began to wrack the child. Putri was crying.

Kris teared up too, in relief. They were going to run. They were going to run down the hill toward Bandung and it would be all right. They'd go to a mosque or the mayor and the Goat-Nurse would fade into oblivion. She even had a fleeting thought of taking them home to Cililin. They'd be happier there. They could dive for snappers in Saguling Lake, wake up clear and unburdened for the first time in their lives. "Don't worry," she said, stroking their hair. Yes, they were going to survive. "Don't worry."

"Look! One of them's still alive!"

Near the shed, a little slip of flesh and bones rose on a pair of shaky stick-legs. It moved inch by inch, in trembling jerks. Under the flashlight's gaze, it looked fur-covered—it was certainly dripping blood. But those legs were the rods of a puppeteer; that was the shape of Arjuna pressed against the screen, not the god himself.

Kris told her no. She *screamed* it. She ran after Putri to strain and sideache, but the little girl was damn-near flying toward the shed. Kris pushed her leg muscles harder and they gave, as if they'd been sliced out. She skidded on the grass and landed chin-first in entrails.

The little slip had become elephantine. It was fundamentally shapeless, a lumbering mess of smoke and wool and a hideous desire to consume—and yet it wore a human face, strapped on like a dancer's mask. It was the grotesque, plasticized face of the feral goats, of the thing in the upstairs hall. Long and misshapen and *false*.

Kris scrambled to her feet. The Goat was at treetop-level now. She was swelling, breathing blood and matter. The human mask bent down toward Putri with its eternal tight-lipped smile, black wool pouring forth behind it. The child was whispering something—some plea with God? The Goat whip-snapped her into the air.

I love you I love you I love you most of all

"Kris, help me!"

"Reach for me, reach for me, reach for me!"

The faith had been ripped from her eyes. The Goat inhaled, exhaled, and swallowed her whole. Putri did not scream; her mind had already emptied out onto her babysitter, who pulled her own hair and clawed her own skin and unremittingly howled.

The Goat departed. She hovered briefly over Agus like a cloud—he peered up into her frothing underbelly as if hoping to see his parents and sister peeking out—but she had long deemed him unworthy of her love. She moved west.

Then came the feral goats, field-destroyers, farmers' bane, servants of an older god. They ate the blood-red remains of the docile herd with long tough teeth and slurping lips. They licked the goat shed clean. They gnawed off Kris's legs as she lay face-up in the grass with barely blinking eyes—and then they wandered into the forest, following the scent of the great and ever-wanting Goat.

Agus was left squatting in the grass with his broken arm, begging to be loved.

SEVEN MINUTES IN HEAVEN

A ghost town lived down the road from us. Its bones peeked out from over the tree line when we rattled down Highway 51 in our cherry red pick-up. I could see a steeple, a water tower, a dome for a town hall. It was our shadow. It was a ghost town because there was an accident, a long time ago, that turned it into a graveyard.

I used to wonder: what kind of accident kills a whole town? Was it washed away in a storm? Did God decide, "away with you sinners," with a wave of His hand—did He shake our sleeping Mt. Halberk into life? My parents said I was "morbid" when I asked these questions, and told me to play outside. So I would go outside, and play Seven Minutes in Heaven—freeze tag with a hold time of seven minutes, the length of time it takes for a soul to fly to God—with Allie Moore and Jennifer Trudeau. When the sky turned dark orange we would run back to our houses and slam our screen doors, and after my parents tucked me in I would sketch a map of the ghost town by the glow of my Little Buzz flashlight: church on the bottom of Church Street instead of the top, school on the east of the railroad tracks instead of the west. Then I would draw Mt. Halberk, and take a black sharpie, and rain down black curlicues on those little Monopoly houses until every single one was blanketed by the dark. When I got older, and madder, I would draw stick-people too— little stick-families walking little stick-dogs, little stick-farmers herding little stick-cows. And last, the darkness.

When I was in junior high school they told us the truth: the accident was industrial. The principal stood up in the auditorium and said there used to be a factory over there, in *that town,* and one day there was a leak of toxic gas, and people died over there, in *that town.* A long time ago, he said, nothing to worry about now. Some parents were angry; they said kids were getting upset. But gas leak sounds a lot less scary than a volcano, ask any kid.

Nobody would talk about it, except when we needed to dwell on something bad. Some families said a little prayer for the ghost town during Thanksgiving, so they could be grateful for something. My uncle Ben, the asshole, told my cousins that he would leave them there if they misbehaved. Politicians in mustard suits pointed across the stage of the town hall and said, "My opponent supports the kind of policies that lead to the kind of accidents that empty out towns like Manfield." That was the ghost's name: Manfield. I lived in Hartbury.

***

Allie Moore was afraid of bats; she didn't like the way they crawl. Jennifer Trudeau was afraid of ice cream trucks, and nobody knew why. We only knew that when she heard the ring-a-ling song coming around the corner she'd rub her scarab amulet, to remember the power of God.

Me, I was afraid of skeletons. It was mostly the skull, the empty hugeness of the eye sockets and the missing nose and the grin of a mouth that could bite but couldn't kiss. But I also hated the rib cage and the pelvic butterfly and the knife-like fingers splayed apart in perpetual pain. It made me sick to think about what waited for me on the other side: the ugliness, the suffering. My parents took me to church and Pastor Joel promised that there would be none of that in Heaven, when I finally exhausted the cherished life that Almighty God had given me, when I finally decided my seven minutes were up and I was ready to go. "But that won't be for a long, long time from now," he said, patting my head. "So run along."

That was all well and good, but Pastor Joel didn't stop the nightmares. He didn't stop that Hell-sent skeleton from crawling out from under my box spring, clacking its teeth, tearing my sheets and then my skin. I would try to run but could never move, and those rotten bones would clamp like pliers around my neck, squeezing and squeezing until I woke up. I stopped telling my parents; their solution to everything was sleeping pills. The only thing that calmed me down was drawing and destroying Manfield, to remember that I wasn't dead like them.

It was Miss Lucy who stopped the nightmares. Miss Lucy loved Halloween, and come October she decked the classroom in pumpkins and sheet-ghosts and purple-caped vampires. She also hung a three-foot skeleton decal from the American flag above the white board. I could not stop staring at it, because it would not stop staring at me. "I know ol' Mr. Bones is kind of creepy," Miss Lucy whispered after I refused to go to the board to answer a math problem. "But you shouldn't be scared of skeletons, Amanda. You've already got one inside you." Then she reached out her finger and poked me in the chest, in what I suddenly realized was bone. I'm proud to say that I only wanted to dig myself apart for a few gory seconds before I realized that Miss Lucy was right, that a skeleton couldn't hurt me if it was already part of me.

"Memento mori," Miss Lucy said. My parents thought she was witchy, and corrected things she told us about the Pacific Wars—*we never promised that we would help Japan, we never threatened Korea.* She was gone by next September, and a woman with puppy-patterned vests had taken over her class. Mrs. Joan didn't like Halloween. Parents liked her, though.

***

I was seventeen the first time I went to Manfield. Allie Moore's boyfriend, Jake Felici, decided it would be a hard-core thing to do for Halloween. Jake was a moody, gangly boy who played bass guitar, and Allie's hair had turned a permanent slime-green from years on the swim team. They were the captains of hard-core. Allie invited me and Jennifer Trudeau. Jake invited Brandon Beck, who I loved so frantically that I thought it might kill me. So while other kids in Hartbury were drinking screwdrivers in somebody's basement or summoning demons with somebody's Ouija board, we piled into Jake's beat-up Honda Accord and drove down Highway 51, Brandon and his perfect chestnut hair smashed between me and Jennifer Trudeau.

We were expecting something like those old Western gold-miner towns—wood shacks, rusted roadsters, a landscape still dominated by barrels and wheelbarrows. We were expecting something that had been cut down a hundred years ago, when companies were still playing around with chemicals like babies with guns, before regulations would have kept them in line. But that was not Manfield. Manfield had ticky-tacky houses and plastic lawn gnomes and busted minivans. There was a Java Hut coffee house, a Quick Loan, a Little Thai restaurant. That is, Manfield looked just like Hartbury—only dead. Only dark.

We were standing in what had once been the town's beating heart. Jake's flashlight found a now-blinded set of traffic lights. Allie's flashlight found something called Ram's Head Tavern. Taped to the inside of the tavern's windows were newspaper clippings from twelve years back: the local high school had won a track meet; an old man had celebrated sixty years at the chemical plant that would kill them all; and they had held a harvest fair not so different from the one we celebrated in early October. Kids in flannel struggled to hoist blue-ribbon pumpkins, white-haired grandparents held out homemade pies, a blonde girl with a sash that read *Queen of Mount Halberk* waved, smirking, to the camera. Hartbury was the only town on Mt. Halberk now.

"Are you sure this is safe?" asked Jennifer. "What if there's still poison in the air?"

"It's not like it was radiation," said Jake, trying to muster up the certainty to be our Captain Courage. "Gas dissipates, so it's all gone now."

Allie echoed him enthusiastically, but she also pulled her plaid scarf higher up her neck. I looked at Brandon, but he wasn't looking at me. No, Brandon was hanging back with meek, slight, big-eyed Jennifer—telling her that it would be all right, kicking pebbles in her direction. None of it seemed real. I saw the five of us standing like five scarecrows, five finger-puppets, five propped-up people-like things that were, nevertheless, not people. My heart was pounding like a wild animal inside my chest. I wanted to get out—out of Manfield, out of my body. I don't know what I thought was coming after me. I could only feel its rumbling, unstoppable and insurmountable, like the black volcanic clouds I had once drawn descending upon this town.

No one else seemed worried about the fact that everyone had lied about how recently the accident destroyed Manfield, and in the years to come we would never ask our parents why. I suppose we assumed that they had been so traumatized, so saddened by the loss of their sister-town, that they decided to push Manfield backward into the soft underbelly of history. "They never said when it was exactly," Jake said, in their defense, "just that it was a while ago."

A while. All our understanding of time is made up of slipshod words that you can rearrange to cover up the fact that somewhere, somebody was wrong. In a while, Brandon Beck started dating Jennifer Trudeau. In a while, I decided to leave the state for college. For a while, I dreamt of my parents driving five-year-old me to a harvest festival, buying me a pumpkin, crowning me Queen of Manfield, and then leaving me to vanish into a gently-swirling fog.

***

I gave myself an education at Rosewood College. I learned that Seven Minutes in Heaven was not, in fact, a kind of freeze tag, because it was not, in fact, the length of time it took for a dead soul to reach God. I learned that boys would lie to you about hitchhiking across the Pampas to get you to sleep with them, and I learned they probably wouldn't call. I learned that I had no memory of several headliner incidents that took place the year I turned six—not the three-hundred-person Chinese passenger aircraft that was mistakenly shot down over Lake Dover a hundred miles from where I grew up, not the earthquake that killed sixty in Canada, not the Great Northeastern Chemical Disaster that saw a pesticide gas cloud submerge Manfield and then float westward toward Hartbury—and that I actually had no memory of kindergarten at all.

My parents couldn't help me. I would call and they would

grunt and hum and rummage through the kitchen drawers; when they got anxious, they needed to fix things. My mother remembered so many of my little childhood calamities—how I once tied our puppy Violet to my Radio Flyer and made her pull me "like a hearse"—but she didn't remember much from the year that Manfield gave up the ghost. So I tried to forget that I'd ever forgotten anything by drinking, making sure I met enough new people at each party that I'd be invited to another. I'd eventually cycle through everything and everyone, throw up in every floor's bathroom, memorize every vintage poster for every French and Italian liqueur on every dorm room wall.

I had hoped to get along with my freshman year roommate, a poker-faced redhead named Georgina Hanssen who was also from a small town, but Georgina was not the bonding type. She lived and breathed only anthropology. She had pictures of herself holding spears in Africa and monkeys in Asia, and eventually the truth came out that her parents had been missionaries, and she had been raised Mennonite. Sometimes she ate dinner with me in the white-walled cafeteria, and we would take turns insulting the slop that passed for food, but she didn't give me any ways in, and at night she would turn down hall parties to hunch over her weird yellow books and munch her mother's homemade granola bars. One morning I woke up drunk, half-in half-off my bed, and found her staring at me like a feral animal, like she was seeing me for the first time. "What are you reading," I asked, the only question that could start a conversation with her.

"A History of Forgotten Christianity," she said. Her finger scratched an itch on the open page. "For Professor Kettle's class. I'm on the chapter about cults of universal resurrection." She paused, then started reading. "Cults of universal resurrection have experienced cyclical fortunes throughout American history, typically reaching peak popularity during periods of economic

depression. An estimated three hundred and fifty such commu-
nities have been documented across the Northeastern region.
They are commonly found in small towns with high mortality
rates due to exposure to natural disasters, poor medicine, and
unsafe industrial conditions."

Something slithered around my shoulders. "So?"

Georgina took a deep breath. "Cult-followers believed that
God had bestowed upon them the power to return the dead
to life. When an untimely death occurred in the community,
church pastors and town elders would quickly perform a ritual
to prevent the soul from leaving the dead person's body, holding it in a state of 'limbo' until the more elaborate resurrection ritual—often involving a simulated burial and rebirth—
could be performed. Although resurrection rituals varied, all
cults of universal resurrection held the dung beetle—famously
worshipped by ancient Egyptians for similar reasons—in high
symbolic standing, as the insect's eggs emerge from a ball of its
waste. Rather than Christ the divine worm, cultists worshipped
Christ..."

"Christ the divine scarab," I finished. Yes, I had learned that
line in Sunday school, along with *God bestows the gift of life unto
those who have faith*, and yes, we hung scarabs on our Christmas
tree, but only as a reminder that God was all-giving and we were
His life-possessing children, and I had no idea what *that* had to
do with bringing people back from the fucking dead.

"So? What happened to them?"

"During the Great Evangelical Revival, they were mostly
pressured to convert to mainstream Christianity." A fingernail
scraped a page. Something tore inside me. *"Mostly."*

***

I left school after my freshman year. There didn't seem to be much point in staying. I went into the city, because I couldn't go home—not to that town full of the walking dead. Not to Pastor Joel and whatever he had done to us on the night of the gas leak. Not to my parents. Before I burned their pictures I would search their frozen smiles for some sign, some hollowness, some fakery, some *deadness* in their eyes. Depending on how much time I'd spent with Brother Whiskey and Sister Vodka, I sometimes found it, sometimes didn't. Regardless, I took their money—I had to, what with the economy and the price of liquor. They sent me Christmas cards with green-and-gold scarabs on them, and on the off-chance that they had the right address I burned those cards along with a lock of my poisoned bleached hair, because Lily Twining said she was a witch and that was how you severed family ties. "Doesn't purify your blood, though," Lily warned me, cigarette jammed between her teeth. "Believe me, I've tried."

When I was twenty-three my Aunt Rose, wife to Uncle Ben the asshole, died of a stroke. My parents picked me up at the bus station with glassy eyes and the old red pick-up, and oh how I longed to slide back into a gentler, dumber time when I could simply be their daughter, Amanda Stone, twenty-three years old. It did not work. *Memento mori.* I remembered.

Things had changed in Hartbury. My favorite Italian restaurant on Church Street had gone out of business, replaced by a plasma donation center. Everyone looked like ghouls, the skeletons that we all should have turned to grinning through their sagging skin. And a new dog—a black and white spaniel—came bounding off the porch. "Where's Violet?" I asked.

"Violet died last year," said my mother, without a hint of sadness in her voice.

"Life is cheap," I replied, rubbing New Dog behind its ears.

My parents didn't know what was happening to me. They were frightened by my tattoos: a black outline of my sternum where Miss Lucy poked me, followed by three black ribs on each side. They were worried about Brother Whiskey and Sister Vodka, not realizing that those two had seen me through a lot of darkness. They were embarrassed by how I behaved at Aunt Rose's funeral. They didn't understand why Pastor Joel's numb routine of *o death where is thy sting* and *o grave where is thy victory* made me hysterical with terror and laughter. I went to Manfield on my final night in town, and took New Dog with me—like Violet, this mutt had immediately adopted me, apparently willing to overlook the question of whether or not I was undead. I said I was going to see a friend, as in *hello darkness my old friend,* and my mother asked if I was going to see Allie Felici and her new baby. "Sure," I said, and slammed the screen door.

Manfield looked beaten-up. Windows had been broken into, storefronts had been tagged with unimaginative graffiti—a reversed pentagram here, a FOREVER LOVE there. Another car with an unfamiliar set of self-indulgent high school stickers was already parked at the mouth of the main street, and it didn't take me and New Dog long to find the occupants trudging along in the half-light, posing for pictures while making stretched-out corpse-faces. We crept behind at a safe distance, New Dog and I, just close enough to hear the sharp edges of words.

"You hear about that other town that got hit with the same stuff, except nobody died?"

"Why? They closed their windows?"

"No, joker. Look, my mom was a 911 operator. They got so many calls from Hartbury that she thought the whole town was toast, just like Manfield. But when the rescue workers got there, freaking Hartbury just closed up and told them to go home, said everything was fine."

At Aunt Ruth's funeral, my father told me that I had no respect for the life this town gave me. I said that he had no respect for death. I said that if he respected life so much then why didn't he just dig up Aunt Ruth and bring her back? His face collapsed like a withered orange. "Aunt Ruth was ready to go," he said. I flailed out of his grasp like a wildcat. I ran to the parking lot over the graves of strangers who had decided to stay dead, under the watchful eye of the great green stained-glass scarab in the window of the church. *But I am a scarab, and no man.*

***

It sounds romantic when you first hear it: seven minutes in heaven, seven minutes for your soul to board its tiny interstellar ship and set the coordinates for God. Seven minutes for you to change your mind. But that time is spent in nothing but the dark. The empty. Just like underneath Manfield's carefully preserved skin, behind the Ram's Head Tavern sign forever creaking in the wind, there's nothing but gas masks and body bags.

The world was changing, very fast. I had stolen food out of children's mouths, helped a man I loved pilfer from plague corpses, thanked God I wasn't pregnant because I didn't want a calcified stone baby at the bottom of my stomach. I'd seen a lot of skeletons, but only on a cross-country bus in the dead of summer did my own return to me—howling, ushered in by smoke. Its bones were just as coarse as I remembered, but its agony was so much deeper, that much richer. My skeleton had grown up. That time, I let it win. I unclenched my fists and let go. I let God.

I woke up when we stopped to let new passengers barter their way on in exchange for gas. Outside my window, one man was beating another to death for whatever the dead man had in his bag—soldiers who couldn't have been older than fifteen ran off the survivor, the killer. I might have tried to see what I could salvage from the dead one, as ghouls go after corpses, but was interrupted by an old man on the other side of the aisle with rotting teeth and a black fedora. He called me young lady, though I felt like I'd lived forever, and asked where I was from.

It was a question I hated answering. Sometimes I named the state. Sometimes I lied. Sometimes I said something crazy—"outer space" or "hell" or "beyond." That time I told the truth. *Memento mori*—the skeleton made me. I told him about Hartbury, about the harvest festival. I told him about Seven Minutes in Heaven. I told him about playing dead—laying frozen in time in a bed of fallen leaves, waiting for someone to pluck you back to life.

"Can I tell you a secret? I died there." The shadows of nearly all my bones were tattooed across my body—I wanted to command the world to pay witness to my death. "I've died."

The old man grinned and wiggled deeper into his suit, as if he and I and every other loser on that bus were buckled into a fantastic Stairway to Heaven. "Join the club, living dead girl."

***

The third time I went to Manfield, I was thirty-four. I walked, because my sponsor was big on cold night walks with a backpack filled with stones, to symbolize the burdens we all carry in our Pilgrim's Progress. I was alone, save for the county dogs that smiled at me with bloody gums as they trotted up and down the cracked remains of the interstate. New Dog, whose name turned out to be Buttons, had been hit by a car on Highway 51. I invited my parents, but they frowned sadly and wondered why on Earth I'd want to go. "That's a dead town," they said.

How strange I must have always seemed to them. They must have spent my life blaming themselves for my choices, wondering why I wasn't more like sweet little Jennifer Trudeau, who had her head wrenched off in a freak accident with an ice cream truck. Seven minutes in heaven can't undo that kind of fatality. "It's peaceful there," I said.

So it was. There was a stillness in Manfield that you couldn't find in Hartbury, because when the blanket of death came for us we kicked it off and were left naked and shivering in the world. But in Manfield there was grass carpeting what had once been the sidewalk, vines crawling up Ram's Head Tavern, rabbits nesting in the seats of long-gone drivers. Rehab always stressed peace in our time—there are some dragons you must appease, my sponsor said, because there's no fighting them. And truth's one such dragon.

A new flock of teenagers had landed in Manfield. Two girls, three boys, all on crippled bicycles whose parts had been cannibalized for the war effort. I hid behind a termite-eaten column as they wobbled past.

"You know this place is haunted. My older brother knew a guy who went up here on a dare and saw a ghost... a girl with a dog. One of them red-eyed demon hellhounds." In hiding, I smiled. Buttons was going to live forever. "I think that guy got deployed." As had Brandon Beck, his perfect hair shorn down to the scalp before he left for the front. The town used to hold candlelight vigils for his never-recovered body, before his parents passed and so many others followed in his footsteps. "I think he's dead."

Everyone was dead; everyone was alive. A fighter jet roared overhead, right on time for its appointment with the grim reaper. The teenagers stopped their pedaling to watch the angel pass and I took the occasion to run silent and deep, head down, fire in the belly.

GIRL, I LOVE YOU

My best friend, my blood-sister, decided to make the Ultimate Sacrifice to destroy Asami Ogino. We were drinking chuhai on an overpass, and as the world roared beneath us, Yurie showed me the letter she planned to send to the Ministry of Education. It was a four-page, four-year chronicle of the sins Asami had visited upon her. She had, of course, used a PO Box and Anonymity Seal. She wrote: *Don't try to find me. Just make it stop.* I almost let the letter fly over the barbed wire toward the smoke-covered sun, because I already knew the Ministry wouldn't care, just like our teachers didn't care. That was the difference between me and Yurie: I had accepted that life was shit, not just in school but beyond; Yurie still had this perverse expectation of joy. All that tightly-wound, brightly-colored hope was her downfall.

"If I don't hear back in a week," she said, "I'm doing it."

This is something people often misunderstand: Yurie didn't want to do the Ultimate Sacrifice. But she already tried everything else. Two dozen Vengeance Charms bought from skeletal bloodhounds in the grimy alleys behind malls, cooked up from the bloody floor planks of haunted houses. A zip file of a black-market video-bomb, *Grudge of a Predator:* a so-called documentary on our so-called war crimes (she refused to tell me how much she paid for that one). We also took a two-hour bus ride up to Rika Yamazaki's shrine so Yurie could wish for Asami's death. Miss Yamazaki had an 80% satisfaction rate, on account of the enormous rage cloud that spawns when you're shoved off a balcony by a jealous ex-boyfriend—but even then, Asami was fine.

Asami was so fine that she had some of her friends burn Yurie's arms with cigarettes before school. I hadn't been there—I was slumped at the foot of my bed, staring at the clock—but I saw Yurie showing off the bleeding black wounds to curious first-years. The math teacher scolded her for upsetting everyone; I wondered if Yurie had lost her mind. Maybe this is where Love of Life takes you, in the end.

"That Yamazaki bitch just sits on people's wishes," Yurie complained, but Miss Yamazaki did have a lot of wishes to answer. It wasn't just junior high students anymore, but sad middle-aged couples and bespectacled professionals and families with little kids in bear hats. I thought it was fucked up to take your kids to the grave of an angry murdered stranger, but who am I to judge. "That's why we need regulations on shrines. Not that this government can get anything passed."

Yurie didn't like the Prime Minister—thought he was a fatalist unable to grab the wheel and stop this car crash we were all in. On my worst days, I worried she secretly thought the same about me. After all, my father had been a bureaucrat, servant to the impotent government—very particular about following state recommendations on psychic energy, even though he hadn't written them. He was in the labor ministry. Research. No research in the world can save you from your destiny, I guess.

"It's always a gamble, using dead people."

Yurie's phone beeped—we didn't need to look to know the message was some variant of DIE DIE DIE with UGLY and SLUT tossed in for extra color. I said, "None of them are worth anything."

"Michi, I lost everything. Choir, the girls I used to know, how teachers look at me… my stupid bicycle. You don't know what it's like."

"I know what loss is like."

Her face crumpled with apology. She had been with me three years ago when, halfway through a crosswalk, I looked up at a giant screen and saw something about Riot and Government Worker and a somber photo of my father on top of the tortured remains of a black sedan. My brain had floated out through my eyes, trying to escape this new post-father existence, while my body stayed rooted in the street. It was Yurie's screaming that brought me back to this shit-covered world.

"But we've got weapons now. And I'm going to use them, even if you're too scared."

Yurie called psychic energy an arsenal. She was always stocking up. But at a certain point you run out of money, out of options. I'd heard of precisely one dead banker with a 100% satisfaction rate, but his shrine was perched on an island in Matsushima, and who had the money for that? Eventually all you've got to spend is your soul. Traditional fortune-tellers call psychic energy "dismal energy," probably because they're afraid of losing their customers now that anyone can pluck that power out of the ether, but maybe they were right: maybe nothing but suffering can come out of psychic energy.

"And what are you paying for that weapon? It's called *Ultimate Sacrifice* for a reason."

She snorted. "Life's not much of a sacrifice. You know that."

Yeah, I knew. I was the one that pointed out black companies and the cyber-homeless. I was the one that buried my father after his car hit a cyclist and a mob stomped him to death. It wasn't fair to ask me to argue for a beautiful future, and bam: I was angry. Yurie grabbed my sleeve.

"Don't hate me," she hissed. I thought, *if I promise never to forgive you, will that keep you breathing?* But I couldn't keep my face stern, not to her tears. "I could never hate you," I said.

Of course Yurie never heard back from the Ministry of Education. Of course Asami never got pulled out of school. So Yurie bought the script for the Ultimate Sacrifice from a glass case in one of the city's first psychic shops, a converted pharmacy with a red door. The old woman who unlocked the case asked her if she understood the sanctity of life, had her look at pictures of babies and ducklings.

"What if I don't want you to go," I said. We were standing at the intersection where we'd have to part ways. I had used up everything in my own arsenal to dissuade her, and now I was down to the raw, wriggling emotional stuff that I hated handling. "Will that make you stay? Will you stay for me?"

She didn't answer right away. Instead she hugged me and said, "Girl, I love you," before tugging the straps of her backpack and walking resolutely up the hill, like a Himalayan mountain climber. Her answer came that night, when Yurie's mother called to say Yurie had jumped off a building, to her death.

***

I was calm, all things considered. Ever since my mother put her arms around me and said she had some terrible news, a numbing chill settled on my shoulders like a shawl. During Yurie's funeral I could only think of how cold I was, how strange everyone was acting. People with faces out of half-remembered dreams kept asking how I was doing since Yurie's "accident." I'd never heard "I know you girls were close" so many times. I'd say, "Yurie's coming back," and that always made them look away.

I spent a month waiting for Asami to die. I wanted front-row seats for Yurie's Revenge—I was scared I'd miss it if I looked away for a second. But Asami kept on giggling, pointing, whispering—at me, at the fat sad kid, at the quiet soprano that had become her new whipping girl since Yurie died. Asami picked at the weak like the obsessive-compulsive pick at scabs: she just couldn't seem to stop. When I nearly set everyone on fire in chemistry, Asami mouthed at me, "Kill yourself, worm."

"You're not taking your future seriously, Michi," Miss Tomoe said after class. She was unmarried, childless, tending to her parents, forever trapped in high school. I couldn't imagine anything worse. "It's so important that you don't slip up now."

I wondered if Yurie had messed up the curse—written the words wrong, done something out of order. Bold, reckless Yurie—it wouldn't have been the first time.

"I'm sorry about your friend's accident. You don't blame yourself for what happened, do you?"

Obviously, I blamed myself—for failing to keep her alive, for being too weak to suffer with her at school. After she walked away on that final evening of her life, I yelled at her to call me, and she waved back without turning her head. In some of my dreams she did turn, but had no face to speak with—just an endless curtain of brittle ombre hair. In other dreams she whispered something different when she hugged me: "Girl, come with me." But as always, I was too scared.

"I don't know," I said. "Why do you pop anti-depressants between classes?"

Miss Tomoe's plate-like façade shattered and she burst into tears right there at the desk, surrounded by all her little beakers.

Not long after that, she was fired for forcing a failing student to drink hydrochloric acid. She'd poured herself a beaker too, saying "Here's to failure!" The student spat his out; Miss Tomoe finished hers.

The sun was setting. I was trudging down the hill under stringy electrical wires when I heard a voice call my name: a deep, deliberate "Michi," like a summons from a northern volcano. Each syllable kissed my bones, rippled my blood. State recommendations tell you to never seek the mouth that releases a voice like that—it's going to be an ugly one, or a hungry one. But I knew the human marrow gurgling inside that voice. It had asked to borrow my pencil, laughed at my morbid jokes. "Michi!"

I turned. Yurie was hovering behind me, the untied laces of her shoes barely scraping the sidewalk. She looked different; terrible. She was covered in blood, like a newborn or a crime scene, but her skin was marble-white. Her joints hung crooked as a carelessly-flung ragdoll. Her neck was so twisted that she could barely keep eye contact with me; her jaw smashed so deep it was hard to believe she could speak. My blood-sister. "Asami," she hissed. For a second I thought that in the trauma of death she had forgotten who I was, and the thought of being ripped apart by Yurie's hands nearly stopped my heart. "I-I-I can't." She kept stopping and starting like a scratched recording. "Reach Asami."

I forgot that you aren't supposed to engage ghosts and stammered to ask why not.

"Ah-ah-asami!" she yelled, although I didn't actually see her mouth widen. Suddenly her hands were reaching toward me as if to give me another hug—I stumbled backward. "Veiled."

The Ultimate Sacrifice was supposed to be so strong—it was always linked with either a murder or a miracle, like the Brave Boys of Shizuoka who committed suicide to save their school from yet another earthquake—that we never even considered the possibility that it wouldn't work. "Yurie, I'm sorry." Yurie wasn't blinking anymore and her eyes were red spider webs. She used to carry eyedrops—she had to be in pain. "I miss you. I'm sorry."

"Michi, help me!" I'd heard this so many times from her: after-school cleaning duty, the robotech competition in junior high, every doomed day with Asami's foot upon her neck. Yurie's were the hands that dragged me out from under my bed. She'd been dragging me into her battles for years.

This time, I didn't answer. Yurie's plea hung between us, suspended across her grave like a very, very long game of telephone. Somewhere a screen door opened and a man shouted, "Yeah, yeah, I'll call you later!" I became aware of birds chirping on the electrical wires, the sound of traffic, the ache in my shoulder... I exhaled, letting out the sweet and sour stench of a broken-down body and breathing in garbage, detergent, fish. Yurie vanished, and my relief criss-crossed almost immediately with sadness.

***

Yurie didn't give up. Really, I should have known she wouldn't; she'd been friends with me for six years. A normal person would have dumped my ass on the curb after my first crying spell, but Yurie was a sucker for lost souls. I used to say she had a Good Nurse complex, but Yurie insisted the love came first, and the care-taking after. And I won't lie: after my father died, I clung to Yurie.

And now she clung to me. We stared at ourselves in my bathroom mirror. We walked together to school. We sat together in homeroom, Yurie behind me with her bloody arms childishly locked around my waist, hissing "help me help me." Back before Asami destroyed Yurie's bicycle, we used to ride around the suburbs like that, except she'd be pedaling in front, veering to scare me, and I'd be sitting rigid and tense in the back, shrieking at her to be careful. I felt suffocated. I could almost taste her blood in the back of my throat. On some subterranean level I was terrified of her—terrified that she was drowned in blood because she'd been out killing strangers, because she couldn't touch Asami.

At lunchtime I wound up on the roof, gulping what passed for fresh air and trying not to vomit.

"Did you come to kill yourself like Yurie?" I whipped my neck back. Asami was sitting under one of the roaring air vents, smoking a clandestine cigarette. She blew a little nicotine cloud toward me. "Well? I know you were her other half."

It sounds absurd given the tears we'd shed over this bitch, but I was relieved to hear someone admit that Yurie's death was no accident—unless her whole life was an accident, and if so then why not mine, why not Asami's or my father's or the Prime Minister's? Asami shifted and something around her neck caught the light—a tiny sun beneath her chin. She budged again and I saw what it was: a glassy choker, nearly invisible beyond the glare, tight as a lattice tattoo across her throat. She saw me staring and slapped her hand over it. I could almost see something human breathing beneath her bone-fine face. "What are you looking at, freak?"

Asami shed friends so fast, I bet she'd never had a blood-sister—someone her heart had twinned to, for better or for worse. Maybe she envied me and Yurie. "Why did you hate Yurie so much?"

"She was the one that hated us," said Asami, voice dripping steel. "She rejected us. You know how she was. Always had to be different. Always a loudmouth. How do you think that made us feel?"

I couldn't tell if she was being sarcastic. "She's dead because of you."

Asami lifted the pink-banded Pianissimo to her lips and shrugged. "So she was weak, like all the rest." I wondered if anyone else had ever turned into a mess on a sidewalk because of Asami. "The strong survive, that's the rule."

And that's when I knew I had to do it—because Asami was wrong about that. The real rule, the one my father taught me, was this: anyone can bite you, so be good to other people. "Everyone has to pay their due," he'd say while we watched news segments on terrorists and corrupt politicians and faraway blindfolded hostages. He believed so much in cosmic justice that when he died I wondered if he'd once done something heinous. But maybe it wasn't that simple. Maybe justice had more arms, a longer reach, than we ants could comprehend.

"Everyone has to pay their due," I said. Asami's plastic laughter followed me into the stairwell and I thought, *she doesn't have a soul to lose anyway.*

Asami and her devotees were waiting for me after school. I was on bathroom cleaning duty, so they nearly drowned me in the toilet. Here's something else people need to understand: kids buy curses like arcade tokens—some of them counterfeit, sure, but others real. Asami did the sort of stuff you wouldn't do to anyone unless you knew they couldn't stick you with a visit from Hanako-san. But I held it together in the toilet bowl; Yurie would have been proud of me. I told myself this was nothing, nothing in comparison to what she'd been put through. My feet slipped on the tiles as Asami rifled through my purse, looking for "spending money" that she didn't need, and I didn't have.

"You're paying your due right now, freak," Asami said. "For talking back to me."

At Rika Yamazaki's grave, I had wished for my father to find eternal rest in that great vinyl office chair in the sky. I didn't want him returned, even though I heard my mother cry at night. With the earth being shaken and stabbed and poisoned at every turn—mad cow, mad bird, mad people—he was better off making his peace with the other side. His suffering had ended. Good.

***

The beauty of psychic energy—the reason my father worshipped the state recommendations—is that protection is nearly impossible. A psychic attack, the public service announcements explained, is like a natural disaster. There's no kicking it back. That's why the cheerful cartoon ghost on the PSAs chirps that "The best way to protect yourself is to be a good person!" And some preliminary studies have hinted that the rate of infidelity is decreasing, because cheating hearts are afraid of waking up fused to their lovers. We're not turning into better people, but our retribution is getting closer.

Of course real life isn't that simple, because some people will always be able to pay for the impossible, and if there's one thing talent's drawn to, it's artillery and armory. We're doing well. We're killing ourselves off at record speed. And a very few of us—a lucky, golden few—have the means to hurt without repercussion, to escape the judgment of peers, to skate above this shitty, brutal world. Internet chatter says the Prime Minister has a talisman, *or else he never could have dissolved Parliament twice,* and common sense says the Emperor surely has one too. And so did Asami Ogino, third-year high school girl in western Tokyo. I wondered how her parents decided to buy her one—had she bitten other babies? Or did they just want give their little princess every advantage?

This is what I thought about while I sat in the auditorium waiting for the choral concert to start. This is what I thought about so I wouldn't think about the fact that I was going to kill the star soloist.

I had already promised Yurie. I'd been sitting in the library, searching yearbooks for pictures of Asami and checking for the necklace—the tiny sun cloaked in clouds—when Yurie's pale bloody hand snaked over my shoulder. I remembered painting those nails sky-blue, when blood still ran under the skin instead of on top of it. And now I couldn't even look her in the eye, because I knew she'd seen hell.

"I told you I'd never let you down," I said, although this was the first time I was sure about that. "But once I do this, you'll be gone forever." She would never hurtle us down another hill on a bicycle death-ride. She would never curse me out again, just like she would never forgive me any more of my weaknesses. She would never ask me to do anything else to win a war, or live my life.

Yurie squeezed—not hard, but all softness was gone from her—and whispered, static from a pirate radio, "Come with me to the beautiful land."

The weight of the world, of Yurie and my crying mother and my years upon years of unhappiness, tumbled onto my shoulders and for a second my spine caved, heaving, toward my dead blood-sister. I was so furious at her for doing this terrible thing, for forcing me to help, for abandoning me to struggle on alone in a world that no one would admit was a post-apocalypse. "Not yet," I said. I couldn't say I was afraid of hell. Knowing Yurie, she'd just try to convince me.

It turns out that it's true what they say about being on stage: the audience disappears into a void. You feel them watching, but really it's just you and your demons, doing battle. Asami was a

million-dollar angel up there, with the stage-light halo and the
talismanic necklace blazing like an open wound, but I like to
think that when she saw me step out of the dark and into the
hot bath of incandescent light she realized that retribution was
on its way.

I knocked her down—her head hit the floor with an ugly
clunk—and dug my fingers under the necklace, scraping the
mortal flesh of her soft perfumed neck. Asami was spitting in
my eyes, yanking my hair, but I won. I wasn't stronger. I wasn't
tougher. But I took bigger risks, because I had nothing else to
lose. Yurie—Yurie had been the last thing. The necklace un-
clasped in my hands and instantly, the fire left Asami's face—her
eyes softened, her teeth vanished. The little deer had seen death.
I rolled away just before the roof of the world opened up and
hell rained down upon her.

I looked for Yurie in the torrent of red and black liquid lightning gushing in and out of Asami's ribs, but there were no faces
in the storm. No faces at the end of the world. Not even Asami,
by the end, had much of a face. But if I strained, if I blocked out
the yelps and sobs, I could pick Yurie's mezzo-soprano voice out
of the demon chorus. She was the only one singing in the blood.

"Girl, I love you, too," I whispered.

***

I'm holding Asami's choker over a trashcan fire. I've been wearing it for the past two months; it might be the only thing keeping me alive. Asami's family has connections—that's how they
got the talisman. So a demon-horde might be hanging over my
head right now, waiting for my shield to lift.

Now I can see why Asami was so impassive, so callous: the
necklace submerges you in a viscous superfluid, and everything

else becomes virtual, dreamy, distant. The world's your doll house; nothing matters and nothing moves you. Once I tossed a cigarette over my shoulder at a park and an old man on litter duty cursed me with an enchanted megaphone—but nothing happened, so I lit another. Maybe burning other people's raw nerves was Asami's only access to the live wire of emotion. I know I've caught myself forgetting that this fishbowl is not reality, and the true world is spinning on without me.

I drop the necklace in the fire and soon amber flames are skating across black metal. Each flame is its own nuclear devil—an undead spirit, an undying wheel—racing alone down a freshly-tarred highway. I've been dreaming about hell and *the beautiful land*, even without Yurie's guidance—I still miss her, but I know she's waiting for me on the burning plain. Sometimes I hope I'll see Asami beside her, finally holding her hand—blood-sisters of a different kind. Other times, I hope it'll be years before I see either of them. The necklace starts to smoke, and I start to count. I've vowed to stand in the open for three minutes before going back to my mother's dinner table. With Asami, it had only taken ten seconds. I pass that mark. I pass it three times. Four times.

Then I hear a noise, like a flock of gulls diving into a sea. I turn.

ENDLESS LIFE

The most famous person to die at the Hotel Armitage was a tall, sturdy man named Jon Henry Fest, son of Herbert and Gloria, fisher-folk from the southern rim of the Bronze Sea. Jon Henry chose the Armitage, it was later said, so he could look upon the sea of his boyhood as he died, the place where he had stalked crabs and bottle caps and later, girls in pink ruffled skirts. They called him Jonny then, and when he traded his parents' blue wooden fishing boats for a train ticket inland, they said he could be anything—a doctor, a senator, an actor on a daytime soap. For reasons unknown to them, Jon Henry decided to take a very different path to renown.

By the time of his death, Jon Henry was known as General Fest, or the Jackal, or—by foreign armies tasked with bringing him down—Black Ribbon, for the award he gave himself after he executed one hundred and five dissidents in a rebellious border province. He died in Room 305, at the age of fifty-nine—half-empty glass on the bedside table, all-empty tinfoil sedative packet in his palm, international police on his heels.

He was the first to die in 305 but not the last. Seven years later a maid named Melanie slipped on a puddle of water in the bathroom and bled to death under the sink. Jon Henry moved on; Melanie didn't.

***

Ed and Lauren had been everywhere: the Devine Air Field where twenty-four guards, porters, bureaucratic underlings, and Foreign Minister Bello, a critic of the Jackal, had met their ends; Victory Prison, site of various atrocities that the tour guide had presumptuously compared to Red Cliff and Project Beauty; the mass graves at the St. Simon churchyard, the highlight of the trip—definitely the most authentic, with barbed wire and black birds and that gloom that meant the locals considered the place supernatural. You can't fake that quiet, Lauren said. They tried to visit South Cross Valley—executions there, by a river, with the dandelions? But the Valley was on the wrong side of the eastern border now and some very angry soldiers had turned them back. So Ed suggested the Hotel Armitage.

"Nothing happened there," said Lauren.

"What do you mean nothing happened? The Jackal killed himself there."

Lauren sat with her nails between her teeth, thinking about her father. He had lived in this country when he was young, in a white villa on a hill; son of a starch-suited lieutenant governor. "Of course this was a long time before the Jackal," was how he always started his stories, "way before those people fucked themselves over. That's independence for you." He was what polite company called old-fashioned, an Empire Man. He disapproved of this vacation. "What do you want there that you can't get in the Keys? The bloody history? The death?"

It was useless to explain, even though he kept death in his den—the bear skin rug, the pictures of his brother's platoon in a landscape as cratered as the moon, the heirloom rifle.

She jolted when Ed touched her. "We have nowhere else to go," he said. So they went.

They requested Room 305 even though they considered paranormal tourism a low-brow cousin of dark tourism—Brad and Ashley, college friends, went to rickety tourist traps and sat expectantly in the dark, waiting for an orb or a white lady or a gentleman soldier or *anyone dead* to come through the walls and be *undead.* But Ed and Lauren had to get as close as they could to the scene of the death. They had to sink themselves in the rot-saturated air.

On the beach they talked about the Jackal's last days and watched shrimp trawlers chug back and forth on blurry waters. It was not high season for the hotel—if high season even existed; the Armitage was such a lonely building. Lauren was trying to align herself with the hotel, high upon the rocks and spiny ferns. "I think he died looking right here," she shouted, over the growing roar of the waves. "Right where I am." She had her arms out. She was trying to catch the gaze of mortality, the swiftness of life's passing—getting there and stepping back from the brink was a high like no other, the same one she'd had as a child with her father's shark tooth collection, pressing a mako tooth into her tongue until she tasted blood and cartilage—but after a few minutes she threw her arms down and said, "It's just a beach. I don't feel anything."

In bed they whispered sweet nothings to each other: *maybe this was the mattress he died on, maybe he lay just like this, what do you think he was thinking?* They made love defiantly under the imagined shadow of the Jackal's angry face. Then Ed went to sleep and Lauren stayed awake thinking about the pictures of the dead at the museum shop of Victory Prison: faces burned away or chopped away or eaten by animals, hair a dank mess, teeth leaking blood. The flesh already dying. She wondered what the Jackal looked like in his own moment of mortality. Had he deflated from that stoic, cruel ideal of a man's man—an Empire Man, if only he'd been from the Empire? Did he look like someone's father?

Lauren woke from this dream to a strange sound, a wood-rattling beat that she took to be an earthquake before she saw the glimmer on the wall. The mirror was shaking as if suffering a seizure. *Death,* it said. *Death is just a way station, a point of transformation. Look what comes after. Not scavenger birds, not a solemn plot on a quiet planet, but a mirror in rapture.*

"Ed," she said, but her voice was strangled.

Stop, said the mirror. *Stop and look at me.*

Tears filled Lauren's eyes. She thought the Jackal was staring down at her from that wall, and she only wanted to be near that wretched man as long as he could not talk back.

***

No one knew that it was Melanie the maid in that mirror. She did not show herself despite her visual medium, and no one alive remembered that she had worked at the Armitage, let alone died there. Melanie was from the dense forest country carved up with highways and quarries that the government dubbed "The Interior": a moody, stressed region that had been turned from a cautious pessimist to a vicious misanthrope by General Fest's reign of terror. Like many girls from The Interior, Melanie had run away from home. The guard who found her body had died himself, penniless in a bar. Most of those who worked with her had gone on to similar fates, and Melanie had left so little impression on the survivors that their memories of her death were vague, formless: "Some girl died in one of the rooms, but I don't remember." It was a testimony to the strength of her haunting that when they tried to recall the incident, Melanie's face would pop up out of the white fog, a black-haired Medusa. She wanted to be remembered.

Melanie hadn't been outspoken in life but she made up for it afterward. Guests in 303 and 307 reported "crashing" sounds in 305, and maids sometimes unlocked the room to find the light bulbs shattered, the windows opened, the faucet dribbling. The Armitage rarely had a full load of guests and the management tried to reserve 305 "out of respect," they said, "for the history," so Melanie didn't get much opportunity to pull others into the warp she was locked in. Ed and Lauren were the first in a long while, and certainly the first to call the press.

The couple had looked to Melanie like pale globules, grossly fleshy, with limbs like tumors that flailed and smashed against objects instead of seeping through them: clumsy, heavy sacks filled with coarse bones and blood-bags. Her time on the bathroom floor stuck in that horrible corpse, begging someone to *take this body off me*, had soured her soul on the human form. Sometimes she feared that she had never really gotten loose, because she would find herself lost in a sea of brittle hair, pounding against a wall of yellow teeth exposed by long-decayed gums— eventually a dull halogen light would rescue her, return her to the rose-colored prison of 305. *I love it I hate it.* At least here she could float in the ether.

It was *lonely, alone, a loner's world,* and yet when she got close enough to smell a flesh-globule all she could do to it was rage. *TREMBLE BURN DIE.* She once saw herself enter 305 in a clean gray smock, pushing a cart, magically alive again—but joy turned to misery when she got close enough to the face to see that it wasn't hers. She'd screamed her hollowness at that stranger until the stranger flinched and retreated and closed the door.

She'd leave marks. They'd remember. A stain upon their break-able bodies, touchable bodies, bodies in the street, bodies limp as burlap sacks, stacked like cargo waiting for a ship.

***

Ghostcrew came in with the tide. It was early evening, and the hotel looked water-logged in the copper half-light. The mermaid sconces appeared to wear barnacles. Most of the crew was too busy untangling the equipment to notice, but one cameraman named Ricardo did fondle his crucifix. He said nothing about the disorienting plug in his ears. Second-rate psychic babble, the others would have said. High electromagnetic fields.

Their shouting in the night—"General Fest, are you here with us?"—roused Melanie's ghost. This was her first memory of General Fest: she is nestled on her father's lap in a fish restaurant, eating rice grains off his plate. A man named General Fest appears on television and everyone goes silent, as if he has stretched out an enormous hand and lowered it over the whole room. His voice is ocean-clear, submarine-deep, totally unstressed. Her father is frightened, and would be fearful unto death. General Fest is the Bogeyman, the Night Hag, the Vampire.

"Come out and show yourself," the crew shouted. "Give us a sign of your presence."

Melanie crawled down the walls even though they had not asked for her.

There were three of them, wrapped in black cables and staring into space as if they were ghosts themselves: Ricardo, a woman named Phoebe, and a man named Tobias, whose face was as de-ceptively placid as a crocodile pond. Tobias had found the three-second video of the Tall Man at Deerview Penitentiary that se-cured Ghostcrew's second season, as well as the infamous "I hate you Alice" EVP of Guinness Sanatorium. People like Tobias were flesh-globules too, but had eyes like rocks instead of clouds. They at least could *see* the withered shapes on the walls of rooms like 305, and know why they felt funny. People like Phoebe and Ricardo, like Lauren and Ed and most of the maids and maintenance men, wandered the haunted world blind.

"There's definitely something here," said Tobias. He stared at Melanie, who was lying belly-down on the floor like bullet-ridden bodies in village ditches—on bad days she felt their fingers reaching through the soil toward her—but his gaze passed through her as her hand would pass through him. He did not see. "Try talking about the war."

"Are you sorry for what you did, General Fest?" said Phoebe, holding out a small recorder. Her eyes were everywhere but here. "All those people that you killed?"

Melanie was surprised that General Fest didn't answer. She would have guessed that he of all souls would have outlasted death. Certainly his shadow had, like a billboard long gone dark and blank that could not be knocked down. She was surprised he did not creep into 305 from whatever hell he'd gone to like he had crept into every crevasse of the countryside in life. He'd held them close and said they'd always be his, "because I will always be your General."

"Maybe you want forgiveness, that's why you're still here. For what you did in the war."

The war. What a curious thing to call it. It sounded better that way, like a noble sepia dream, but there were no winners here. General Fest had taken all the spoils with him.

"A jackal's a dirty animal. It eats corpses in war. Is that what you do, General Fest?"

Their taunting summons were ignored. General Fest had dropped the baton. Melanie imagined it lying on the carpet, a golden scepter inscribed with the query, *Is that what you do, General Fest?* The urge rose in her to take the scepter and all the black banners of power that went with it. Everyone knew *his* name. Everyone feared *him*. But he was such a wicked man...

"The mirror's shaking," said Phoebe.

"General Fest?" Tobias said. "Is that you?"

Melanie hesitated, retreated slightly into the wall. The mirror settled. The woman Phoebe placed a flashlight on the vanity at the foot of the mirror, her hand quivering like flan, and immediately returned to her submissive crouch, never turning her back on the mirror. Would she be this frightened if she thought this was the ghost of a little voiceless maid, the kind of wispy ghost that hides behind corners and weeps? Would she be acquiescing, saying *I give, you are the stronger one?* "If you're the spirit of General Fest, please turn the flashlight on."

Hard to say if Black Ribbon would play along—he was rumored to have enjoyed cricket and polo and other colonial games, and smiled frequently. Some said he always *seemed* like a good man (others said the Devil rides in with a grin). Yet he made it clear in broadcasts that he would not "play" with enemies of the state, that he did not "joke" about the drumming march of economic progress, that the nation's safety was not a "game." Melanie turned the flashlight on.

Claiming that name was so exhilarating—*I am the podium, I wield the people, everything is available, I will do as I will do as I will*—that Melanie turned the flashlight off just to turn it on again—*I am the missile and the shield! Even in death I shadow you!*

"Jesus, look at it."

Yes! Look at me! Tremble! Burn! Die!

"I feel strange," said Phoebe. "Like being in a jail cell with a killer."

But he was more than a killer. Killers were cheap, easy to come by: every other man on the block during the worst purges. It was Melanie's father, with a shaky hand, and her cousin Rudy with his *Strength and Honor* badge. "Better to join in the work than let others do it for you," General Fest said. Killing was just work. General Fest was a carver of peoples. He was doing something more. Something greater? Something with a bigger impact crater. Something remembered, even if the people on the rim slid immaterial into the drainage pit of history.

The flashlight shook so hard that it rolled off the vanity and onto the carpet, still flashing on and off like an airfield runway light. Ghostcrew gasped. "General Fest, are you angry that we're here?" Phoebe asked; her voice was trembling now. "Are you still upset about the war?"

Must be yes. To shred the people like a wheat reaper, to leave the graves uncovered, he—I—must have been angry. His soldiers always bore his face like their uniforms bore his Black Ribbon, and they did hack and yell and empty their cartridges like men possessed. The most merciless purges did come after General Fest's angriest speeches. In his stained clothes, Melanie felt she understood. *I am so angry too. Do we get scared? Is that why we took up the hammer?*

The flashlight flew into the wall, smashing in a brief spatter of yellow-white glow. Ricardo suggested they leave the room.

"Are you kidding me?" hissed Tobias. "This is the ghost of the fucking *Jackal*, man, when are we ever gonna get a chance like this again? I'm talking one of the most notorious war criminals—most *brutal* military leaders—of all time, and we've *got his ghost.*"

Ricardo whispered, "If he was a bastard in life then what d'you think he's like now?"

I was a bastard, yes. Shudder, shudder. Jealous, jealous.

Tobias ignored him, and stood up despite Phoebe's pulling

on his leg. "Don't you regret *anything,* General Fest? Killing all those innocent people, doesn't it ever eat at you?"

Nothing eats at General Fest. Even the worms leave General Fest alone, the divine specimen, body of kings. What is there to regret? What did General Fest lose? The freedom of this imagined life overcame Melanie for a moment, before she remembered: *We regretted.* Her father shot out his chin to repay the blood-debt; Rudy took opiates to get away from the ghosts. The first wave of victims were long-dead, but this was a wound that would not stop bleeding.

Tobias strode toward the mirror. Ricardo said, "Don't do that," and Phoebe said, "We should get the others," but Tobias forged on. He pointed his finger and barked at the mirror the way General Fest would have barked at the camera:

"You know what, you old shit? You got off easy. What kind of sick bastard butchers his own people? Didn't Mommy love you enough? You and all your pathetic followers. And you couldn't even man up and own it." He snorted derisively as if he was a battle-tested, mud-covered enemy soldier, rifle over his shoulder, fighting the good fight against General Fest—not a paranormal investigator on Ghostcrew. "You ran away here! Like a dog!"

Melanie watched this flesh-globule express his indignant rage and thought, *You don't get to talk to General Fest that way. Not when he can't say your name and kill you, take your children.* She saw him swelling, stiff with a stake of pride, but the fields were barren now. He had missed the carnival. Even the killers had been culled. *Where was this bravery when General Fest was holding us close? Where was your courage then?*

The tormented mirror tipped, and Tobias's reflection tipped with it as if his body was being swung on a pendulum. He caught the gaze of his own stone-eyes and was transfixed by the softness and smallness of his face.

Melanie beat at that mirror until Tobias saw what he would have really been, had he lived in her neighborhood—*wish you were here!*—and then a rope snapped. *Mortality!*

***

After Tobias's accident, 305 was put on permanent ice. For the Hotel Armitage it was a walking liability, like the cracked steps leading down to the beach and the lack of fire exits in the Violet Room. "There's something wrong with the lighting there," the front desk told the curious. They might have flaunted their paranormality if the ghost was an anonymous dead maid, but General Fest? The Jackal? Management was afraid the old girl would be burned down.

And it had so much potential, the owners lamented—most of the stately five-star hotels were still owned by colonists-turned-foreigners; the Hotel Armitage had been a valiant attempt at *locally-owned luxury,* a symbol of sovereignty—and then it got itself this weeping sore, this aching reminder of the biggest calamity to hit the post-independent nation. *If he would just go away!* Even those stubborn few on the staff who thought General Fest had been given a bad rap by history did not want to be near him in spirit; they hurried past 305 faster than anyone else.

In time tourists stopped asking about the room, and then stopped coming altogether. Fancier hotels shaped like obelisks sprouted up like warts along the coastline—the Armitage staff heard laughter and jet skis in other bays where palm trees had been planted, and thought to themselves that they were sliding into history with General Fest, the old bastard, as their anchor.

Nearby townspeople tried to help by pointing tourists to the Armitage and ominously whispering, "They say General Fest's ghost lives there," but the tourists just said, "Sorry, who?"

For the elderly it was like watching the earth fall away, and then they recalled that even their children had forgotten what it was like—they were caught up in new jobs, new lovers, new vehicles circling new roundabouts—and their grandchildren didn't know his name at all.

***

But some remembered. Pilgrims journeyed to the Hotel Armitage, went to Room 305 with or without asking, and called upon General Fest just as the dead crawl to the doorsteps of those that wronged them. Given the choice between confronting bones in the sun-baked national cemetery and the General's own soul, they chose the soul.

They stained the walls with anything they could cough up, tore apart the beds, and cursed General Fest. There was a time when statues would have been built in his name, anthems written, hospitals dedicated. Now it was all final reckoning and bloody hands. "They said you would bring this country into the future and you did that, didn't you? Brought it grinding to its knees, with shit in its mouth?" Most of the pilgrims spoke of Hell, their only course of vengeance: burning and cutting and devouring by demons. "On Judgment Day the human pile before you will wear skin to show you their faces." This they promised General Fest.

But Melanie was the only one lingering in the plaster, crumbs of construction where her teeth should have been. General Fest wasn't there to answer them. General Fest had gone. Her mother had told her back when her body was new and soft that only the tormented dead stayed behind, while the peaceful moved on. Thus the ditches are thick with haunting, as are the soccer fields and the barb-wired city walls and all those flat overgrown buildings with faded military signs and rusted locks. And also the washroom in the back of her childhood home, where her father shot himself—she could admit now that she had felt a texture like smoke by the sink. That was the touch of his agony. But General Fest was gone. He was floating over mountains, swimming through cotton-swab clouds. He had left them, in the end, to suffer in his place.

But the pilgrims could not know this, so Melanie absorbed their venom like a sponge. It slowed her; weighed her down. She did not play games with them, not even a little side-sweep of the curtains—as General Fest it would have been an assertion of authority, and she wanted him to be silent. Present, but silent. The pilgrims' agitation turned to sadness as Melanie laid her spirit down: *Abide with me,* she was saying, *abide with me.*

The pilgrims left little cysts of hurt buried in the carpet of 305, and never returned. Maybe it was their departing sighs or all the talk of souls in the land of forever, or simply the culmination of a thousand stories of pain and loss blended into a cloud of endless suffering and endless life—but 305 was no longer much of a room to Melanie. The roof had opened and the walls turned to milk, and Melanie herself was stretching and thinning as her borders collapsed.

The final pilgrim she tended to was a very old, very shriveled woman named Lorena Onde, who was helped into 305 by a maintenance man. Lorena was calmer, wearier perhaps, than the average pilgrim. She only wanted to tell General Fest about her son. "He was just another troublemaker to you," she said, "But he was a happy baby. A fast learner. I had to run to keep up with him, almost broke my ankles. His father said he would get himself killed if he wasn't careful, but not like this. I thought that silly motorcycle would do him in."

Melanie imagined General Fest as a child; her father as a child;

herself, in tight braids, sitting under a bright red sun. *Abide with me,* again, but her grasp on 305 was fading.

"You should know, when you see his bones at your feet, he was loved."

Lorena exhaled with a soft cry and the maintenance man peeked in, afraid she was hurt. And of course she *was.* When she carried those bones in her womb, they'd been soft, malleable, capable of building any sort of human being—in the end, all his possible futures had been bound by bloodshed. True forgetting was not an option for the pilgrims, nor indeed the Armitage staff and anyone else born to this nation. Even those that claimed they couldn't remember and didn't know the touch of endless life had the grit of bone dust in their teeth. Their children would be born with ash in their stomachs, unaware that the bittersweetness on their lips was memory.

The walls melted. Melanie could not see the room. There were no more curtains to hide her. She did not stay long enough to see gray-haired Lorena Onde leave.

***

Melanie had not wanted to enter 305. They said you could still smell General Fest's stench in there, and Melanie preferred to believe he had never existed—and the 500,000 that died, even her father, had perished in a divine intervention. She held her breath as she unlocked the door but the room was empty, thank God. She only smelled the sea. The barely-there curtains of the window were fluttering like a mother's skirt. She checked the bathroom—a steady drip from the showerhead beat against the tub, and the floor was spattered with water. *Everything is okay,* she thought. *Everything is normal.* And then she heard the scream.

Her body did not know reason. Her eyes widened, her neck jerked back, and her feet shot backwards; she thought the bathtub was shrieking. Her right heel came down too fast and too uncertain on a shallow puddle, and once the fall began there was no stopping it. Her right foot slid toward the tub, tipping her body like a lever—face turning upward to the cold ceiling light—and though her left arm grappled desperately for the sink, the porcelain slipped out of her grasp.

The bedroom entered her peripheral vision and as she dropped backward she saw the screamer: a bird. A green parrot with red swarming its face. It was perched on the window sill and it stared at Melanie with eyes that were not quite vacant—then shrieked again, that human scream. As the back of Melanie's head hit the tiles, the cry brought the darkness with it.

VIOLET IS THE COLOR OF YOUR ENERGY

Abigail Gardner née Cuzak was sitting on the bathroom floor, thinking about the relationship that mice in mazes have with death, when a many-splendored light shot down from the stars like a touch of divine Providence. Abigail hurried to the bathroom window above the toilet, but just as she put her fingers on the smudge-stained glass, a loud noise—not an explosion, more like a diver's plunge—burst from the field and pushed her back onto her heels. The impact tripped the perimeter lights; she could see shockwaves rippling the corn. But there was no smoke, no fire, only the faintest tint of red-blue-purple now rapidly melting into night.

She heard Nate throw off the covers, muttering, "What the fuck?" And then, sharper, "Abby!"

The two of them rushed downstairs, a shadow of the team they had once been when they were first trying to forge a life together out of the money they'd saved in college, him at the chem lab, her at the campus store. "I bet it's our buddy Pierce," Nate muttered, barreling through the kitchen, running into a chair in the dark. If it hurt, he didn't show it. "He probably cooked up some radio-controlled boondoggle to mess with the crop. Probably aiming for the sprinklers. Or just trying to nuclear-waste the whole damn thing."

Abigail did not think that sounded much like him. Ambrose might have enjoyed eating up the little farms around him, counting up his tripling acres with a glass of whiskey, but he hated parlor tricks; didn't think he needed to lower himself to sabotage. She said nothing to Nate. It was better to let him cling to that bone if it kept him occupied.

Nate had his gun. Abigail had a fireplace poker. Her farm cats were skulking by the flower pots, making low scratchy howls at something in the corn. Abigail followed him to the front as quietly as possible, her bare feet curling around dry stalks and kernels and poisoned insect corpses, but she had the feeling they would not find what Nate was looking for. They would not find any ruddy farmhand with a twistable neck, nor a small broken remote-controlled drone. Nate would periodically shush her and veer in a new direction, but Abigail knew there was no life out there. The field was so quiet, she could hear the cats' growling. Though the air sure smelled strange—pungent and tart with a hint of curdled sweetness. It prickled her skin.

Between the rows, Nate turned and whispered, "There's no one here."

She could have told him so, but Nate had to know for himself before he'd turn around. Had to go all the way to the state border before he admitted that maybe he had missed the turn for Salt Creek Road. That was just his way. He liked being careful; she liked that about him. "Maybe it was something on the road," she said, so he would let them get back to the house. The thought of the road and the real world beyond the gravel driveway had reminded her that the children were alone. She had dreams about them growing up that way—little feral masters of the house, sunken and sullen and riding the dogs like wolves.

"Maybe somebody blew his tire."

Nate seemed to be chewing the whole interior of his mouth. "That wasn't a tire, Abby."

"You can look again in the daytime," she tried.

"I'm gonna call up that son of a bitch Pierce in the daytime is what I'm gonna do," said Nate. "Teach him if he thinks he can intimidate me."

When they slunk back to the house, the boys were standing on the porch, the dogs at their heels. Zeke was trying to project his authority with his Little League baseball bat; Merrill was wiping his eyes. Teddy asked if a comet had crashed, and Nate gave him a little push to the head and said, "Don't get too excited." Underneath the porch, the cats' diamond eyes were shining.

***

Their harvest was surprisingly healthy that summer—bigger and greener than any others since they moved out of their south Lincoln bungalow three years ago and decided to make a more wholesome life in the country. Nate didn't have the nutrient content analysis back yet, but when he took bites off the blond-haired cob he said he knew. Abigail thought it tasted off—sour, like the air in the field since the crash that wasn't a crash—but Nate said it needed processing, and when was the last time she won any farming awards? Well, he was right about that.

And it was good to see Nate happy. She had never allowed herself to doubt him—before she married him she had asked herself, *do I trust this man to lead this family?* and she had decided the answer was yes, come hell or tarnation—but it was still good to get good news.

"What kind of Frankenstein corn are you growing now, Gardner," said Ambrose Pierce when they ran into him outside Horwell's general store, sipping a Dr. Pepper. "I thought you were all about that hippie organic tofu living and here you are pumping your crop with steroids."

"You're the only one growing Frankenstein GMO corn," Nate said, puffing out his chest. "Some of us haven't forgotten what it means to be a real farmer, growing real food for a real family." Ambrose wasn't married. Nate had suggested he was gay, but he was not. "Guess you Big Ag types wouldn't recognize real corn if it rose up and kicked you in the ass."

Ambrose made a guffawing sound. "Aren't you from Omaha?"

Nate shifted the bags in his hand and went to the truck and didn't answer. But Ambrose caught Abigail by the wrist before she could follow, and said to her, "Abby, something's off about that corn. I don't like it. I don't know what *he's* been doing but you gotta get that shit cleared by the FDA." A good wife would have stiffly told him he was just jealous, just sorry that he couldn't quite yet eat up Nate's land, but she must not have been a good wife. Nate unlocked the doors and shouted, "Abby! Let's go!" The *"go"* had a punchy desperation to it, probably because that was the moment he saw Ambrose touching her hand.

So Nate was already in a bad mood when they started the drive home. Zeke and Teddy had been late meeting them at the truck, and Merrill had knocked down a chocolate display at Horwell's. Abigail understood. They were restless children. Sure, they had all the bicycling down country lanes that they could want, all the smashing of rotten pumpkins, but they needed people. They needed to look at things that weren't stalks or clouds. Teddy especially. She could see the look in his eyes getting pounded in deeper all the time: the look of a cornered animal.

"Did you get that nutrient analysis back?" Abigail asked, and she really shouldn't have.

Nate, chewing on a thumbnail, widened his eyes. "What?"

"For the corn."

"Why would you ask me that?"

A welt of worry in Abigail's stomach became a full-on ulcer as she searched the horizon—just corn and trees and ditch and road—for something that would answer Nate's question to his satisfaction. "I just was wondering." No, that wasn't good enough. The ache didn't stop.

"Did Pierce tell you to say that? Back at Horwell's? Huh?"

Her mouth was opening and closing, but only breath was coming out. She heard something constrict in Nate's ribs and he suddenly ripped the steering wheel to the right, pulling the truck to the shoulder of the road. She knew the boys were holding their breath so she felt the need, then, to make some noise of protest on their behalf.

"Are you sleeping with him?"

"What?" Her voice broke. "Nate, the boys are right…"

His shout punched down like a hammer of God. "Answer me, Abby! Was this some whore's bargain? Said you'd jump into bed if he'd just cut your poor idiot husband a break?"

The radio was playing a mellowed-out beach-pop song by a local band that made it out. They used to get her dreaming about coarse California sand from the anarchic desolation of Sokol Auditorium. This song always made her think of breaking surf, of drinks with plastic umbrellas. Maybe they should go on vacation. Maybe they should never come back. "No," she hissed. "You know I would never do that. You know I would never want to." She nodded toward the backseat. "Can we *please* talk about this later?"

For three minutes, they all breathed together. Then Nate changed the station with a sudden strike of his hand, muttered "Hate that song," and drove back onto the road. So the rest of the way they listened to Dr. Touchdown on KMKO out of

Lincoln. "Wear them down," said Dr. Touchdown, "the key is
to wear down the defense, go for the throat, and don't let up.
Lights out. Bam." From the backseat, Merrill echoed, very softly, "Bam!"

She was ready—no, not ready, never ready, but resigned—for
a fight, but when they got home Nate went into the field and
started running the combine even though there was nothing to
strip anymore. He watched in a state of near motionlessness.
And Abigail watched him from behind the muslin curtain, and
the boys watched her over the stained pages of their homework,
and the dogs watched the boys with sad bovine eyes. Boys and
dogs alike asked for things—food, drink—and eventually, after
the sun began to set, Teddy put down his American History
book and asked for an explanation of Croatoan. When the Roa-
noke Colony disappeared, he said, they left that word behind.
Yes, a sign post. Salvation, five miles south of Cripple Creek.

"Nobody knows," said Zeke. "They probably got eaten by an
Indian tribe."

"Maybe they ran away," Abigail said. "Maybe they wanted to."

***

The cats were gone. She waited for them by their little bowls of
dirt-colored pellets for a week, but they weren't coming back.
She had looked everywhere. She even peeked down into the well.
She didn't know why, exactly. Cats didn't just jump into wells.
Did a tiny piece of her think that perhaps someone—*who?*—
had killed the cats and thrown them in? There was something
down there, ding dong bell, but the flashlight revealed a collar, a
yellow tag, a long nose. It was the dogs. She had last seen them
the day before, pacing near the corn and whimpering. Nate had
gone to tie them up, and she assumed, to untie them.

She was watching the kitchen clock tick toward 3:30 and wondering how to tell the boys when a silver Dodge Ram pulled up to the house. Like a crocodile, or a tyrannosaur, sidling up to its prey. Ambrose Pierce stepped out of the cab and she immediately calculated how long it would take Nate to get back from his meeting with Ticonderoga Mills.

"I haven't seen you and the boys in town much." Ambrose looked aside at the barely-tilting wind chimes. "Haven't heard from you lately neither."

Abigail ground her teeth, head shaking slightly to the internal retinue of all the things she'd really like to say to Ambrose, to Nate. Finally, she conceded that "Nate's been acting a little different lately. Since that light came down…"

"What light? Different how?"

Different like standing in the sea of corn, humming at the sky? Different like telling Zeke he couldn't go out for Junior League baseball this year, because he was "needed" at home? Different like picking up the phone and telling her sister that she wasn't home when she was just around the corner, fixing dinner? No, that was more trouble than it was worth.

"Just different. He's stressed. It's hard, you know, worrying about feeding a family when your neighbor's lying in wait, drooling over your property." She gave him a look. He wasn't fazed. He'd long-ago reconciled himself to the vulture's life. "Maybe the water's gone bad. All the fracking they're doing out by the aquifer."

Ambrose clicked his tongue, muttering something about "hippie bullshit," then leaned in, putting his right hand on the door frame as if he owned the place, as if she wouldn't have slammed the door on his fingers. His voice lowered. "Do you need help, Abby?"

"No, I don't need your *help*. What kind of *help* could you give me?" She grabbed the door. "Nate's coming home soon. I don't want to be a witness in a murder trial."

Actually Nate didn't come home for another hour. She heard his truck pull up but he didn't come in, and when she ventured outside he was standing and staring at the freshly scalped corn field with his keys dangling from his right hand, as if hypnotized by an inaudible sermon. She asked if he was all right, but her fingers wouldn't quite rise to touch his arm. His exhale seeped out like a deflating balloon.

"What did the guy at the mill say?"

"Max Beecham is a motherfucker."

"What?"

"Max Beecham doesn't believe in us."

Abigail hurried back inside. She called her sister's cell but it was off; called her house phone and only got her five-year-old niece. "Will you tell mommy to call Aunt Abby? Aunt Abby, in Cripple Creek." She dropped the phone when she heard the porch squeak, but it was just the boys, who dropped their dusty backpacks and started clapping and calling, "Here boy, here boy!" Of course no dogs answered.

All day she'd been hoping that some vagabond, some wanderer, had snatched up the dogs in the middle of the night and dumped them in the well. Or that perhaps they'd been run over on the highway, or slain by a disease, or just spontaneously died—and that Nate had thrown the bodies in the well in a well-meaning attempt to protect the boys from the reality of death. But when the boys were still mewling out in the field well after she'd called them in for dinner, Nate said, "Boys, I told you, they ran away. Told you we didn't train them well enough. Probably halfway to Colorado by now."

He turned to the little spoons tucked into the little chipped serving dishes, her meek attempts to ward off sadness. "Why aren't we eating our corn? Wasn't that the whole point of moving out here?" She thought they ruled out subsistence years ago. "Growing our own food? Living off our own land? Unless you think there's something wrong with it. You and Pierce."

She waited until after the boys were in bed and she had promised Merrill that they would put up lost and found flyers all over town, to say something to Nate. That was how long it took to sculpt the nauseous worry in her heart into something spear-shaped. She lingered at the top of the staircase, rehearsing her words—*did something happen to the dogs last night* or *I found something in the well*—when Nate rounded the corner at the bottom of the stairs and started laboriously climbing up.

"What happened to the dogs?" came stammering out when he reached the second floor.

He sighed loudly. She willed herself not to apologize. "They ran away. Like I said."

"But I found them in the well."

Nate's red eyes finally focused on her. Her poor husband was so horrified—so honest-to-the-bones horrified—by this revelation that he grabbed her by the arm, saying he needed to explain something to her—*explain*—then pulled the string on the door to the attic to drag her up into that spider-webbed lair of things unwanted, things unexplained. He pushed her down toward the boxes of books that they never bothered to cut open after the move and descended the ladder again, slamming the door shut behind him as she lay shaking in a cloud of dust.

***

At the very beginning she was relieved to be alone. The dark erased everything that taunted her in the light—the carved-up acres of a burned and spent, uniform earth, the harrowing passage of time. She made believe that she was nothing but a set of lungs, expanding and shrinking. She curled up near the door with her palm against the cold wood and slept.

But when sunlight leaked in through the tiny attic window and the attic door was still closed, the muscles around her ribs started to cramp. She tried pounding her fist and then a flashlight against the attic floor. She tried shouting—first at Nate, then at Teddy, then at Zeke. She avoided yelling Merrill's name until she had no choice. The boys' voices seemed so quiet, like they were many islands away across a great sea.

But someone was moving down there below the attic door. She tried everything to talk to it. "Nate?" she called. "Nate, please listen to me. Nate, I love you." When that got no response she started to scream—complicated accusations about his failure as a pharmaceutical sales supervisor and his need to maintain a sense of moral superiority that degenerated into words that degenerated into noise. She chewed off the tips of her nails; she dragged her fingers through her hair so many times that strands began to come off in her fist.

And then, after the sky's white-blue started turning to pewter, the door swung open. She was slow crawling toward it, but it was Teddy. Teddy, her wonder. Her savior. The only boy they'd named after a president. "Come quick," he whispered. "Daddy's in the field."

It did not work. Nate must have been waiting downstairs, because she woke up back in the attic with a welt and a throbbing pain in the back of her head. She resumed screaming because now the attic was drenched in fading amber half-light and that meant she had been locked in that room for almost an entire day. A child's voice screamed back at her from somewhere on the second floor. The *"mom"* dragged like a serrated knife through the wood and the insulation and she realized it was Teddy. He shouted something about *"dad"* and *"crazy"* and *"room,"* and she thought at first that he was talking about her plight but no. Nate had locked him in the spare bedroom, the one they saved for family—family that never visited.

She told Teddy to apologize to Nate. She told him to ask Zeke for help. But in the end all she could do was press herself flat against the floor and sing, "I love you. A bushel and a peck. A bushel and a peck, and a hug around the neck."

That night she stacked up broken furniture underneath the attic window and tried to signal Ambrose with the flashlight. His truck was hurtling by ten miles over the speed limit; he was probably on his way back from Cellar's Bar and Grill and he was probably rushing home for another, but she didn't have a choice. She switched the flashlight on and off, on, off, on, off until his red tail lights disappeared behind the cottonwoods. Had the truck slowed? It hadn't stopped.

When the attic door was pushed open she had to bite her knuckle to keep from calling Ambrose's name.

"You have to let the boys go," she said. She could not see Nate's expression, but his face had been a dark blank to her for months now. That light from the sky had come and eaten all the color off his face—all the variegation, the jokes he'd told her, the promises he'd made her. Every time he had shown her what a good father he was. "I'll stay with you, I'll help you through this, but you need to let someone else take care of them for a while."

"I need you to prove your loyalty to me, Abby. You and Teddy both." He pushed a cob of their corn—tiny shriveled kernels bounded their grotesquely swollen cousins like rings of baby teeth—toward her on a paper plate. The big awful kernels looked like unblinking eyes. "Please eat it. Please show me I'm not wrong."

She picked out a little tooth-kernel and tucked it down between her lip and her gum. It immediately dissolved and filled her mouth with something that melted like pixy stix, something that tasted like bloody soap. "Let them go stay with my sister."

He nudged the plate with the long barrel of his gun. "More."

So she ate more; but Teddy must not have, because his little voice dwindled to nothing but a whisper that Abigail eventually realized was her own ragged breath, tearing in and out.

It took Merrill hours that might have been days to speak to her. He would only push the door open by an inch. She crawled toward him in the dark, chewing another kernel—she was hoping they were poisoning her, and was taking the fact that she couldn't feel her legs anymore as a good sign. "We have to be quiet so Daddy doesn't get mad," he whispered. Pale blue eyes rolled down toward the light. "Teddy won't come out of that room."

"I know," she said. "Listen, baby. You gotta tell your daddy that you're going to the well. Tell him you're going to get water and then go to Mr. Pierce's, okay? Go. I love you."

Pale blue eyes blinked, very slowly. In between she saw her little boy smiling, crying, sleeping, dead. A great many colors passing so quickly they were all bleeding together into one monstrous, endless whole.

***

When Abigail woke it was day. Rainbow sunlight filled the room with glitter, though she wore a cloak of shadow. The attic door was open, and Ambrose was clambering up to see her. "Abby? Abby, are you in here?" He sighed green mint toothpaste. "You're okay now. Nate's downstairs, he's messed up bad. I don't think he can move. I don't know what's happened to him, he... I think he needs a doctor. I can't find... any of the boys."

She started to take off the shadow-cloak. The light started to touch the old useless leather skin she could no longer feel. Her hair wrapped around the sun and started to burn.

"Abby? Honey?"

The shadow-cloak pooled around the stumps that had once held her feet. All her cells looked at Ambrose, waiting to be embraced, but when his eyes and only his eyes looked back at her they wept with horror and hatred and he shot her with his unseeing fingers that cradled the gun like a baby. The pain was not a pain but a liberation. She rose as Ambrose fell, rose all the way to the ceiling and blossomed like a rose, filling the house's every nook. She saw Nate on the couch, dying and then dead and still shuddering, pieces of his mortal coil stubbornly struggling along on the floor. But he was fractured; she was whole.

The walls of the house peeled open like an onion for Abigail. Outside, the well was beating like a brilliant magenta heart, a small nuclear star. The boys were inside with the dogs; they were all waving to her. The many-splendored light was in there too, curling and coiling as it prepared to spring-board off this world and into the next. It wrapped her in electric seaweed tendrils and promised her oceans. It promised her color. But when the boys weren't broken down into simpler matter, they were saying "Mama" and for them she floated down. Crimson and indigo and violet, for violence.

TRUTH IS ORDER AND ORDER IS TRUTH

I didn't go alone into the outer darkness. A huddled legion came with me, men and women and children, all of whom would have been purged for their devotion to my mother. My mother was dead, so she could not summon any army. My father was dead, as well, so he could not protect me. But I was alive, their only child, and I'd promised my mother's followers that I would deliver us to strength and sanctuary in my mother's homeland, Jungkuno. Because all the rivers flow north and Jungkuno is on the southern shore, we had to go overland.

We had no soldiers. Those men were loyal to the Prime Minister, Jaya Megalang. He was their god. They would have followed him anywhere. It was to my parents' credit that the soldiers let us pass through the brick split gate. We had one healer, a very old man who I didn't think understood what he was giving up. There were my mother's friends, disgraced and confused and clinging to their jewelry, more convinced than I that we would rally an army in Jungkuno and re-take the Alunijo throne. There were farmers. I'd expected them all to be farmers, because they were the ones whose crops my mother blessed with irrigation. Then there were my mothers' servants, some of whom would have been gladly buried with her, others who just had no family to vouch for them—these few slogged behind, bemoaning their fate and the insects and the heat.

Except for the reluctant servants, they came of their own accord. No, they didn't choose to trek through the infested rainforest toward a half-forgotten kingdom. But they did choose to bow to my mother Dyah, to call her "Mother of Kingdoms," to see divine providence in her. They saw her Truth, as stark as the silent face of a cold, white moon. Once you have looked into her eyes, once her fingers have grazed your scalp, she is hard to shake. She was my mother. I should know.

When I walked away from Jaya Megalang for the last time, when he laid bare his sordid accusations against my mother, he yelled, "Who knows where you come from? You belong to the outer darkness!" I bit my bottom lip until my mouth filled with blood so he would honor my request to rebury my mother's bones. Then I forced myself to continue walking past the dead kings' banyans, through the brick split gate, and into the wilderness that birthed me.

***

Jaya Megalang called my mother a shaman queen. He dug her up and looked under her shroud and said her skeleton was misshapen, that her eyes were too large and her mouth too wide. He said her fingers and toes had grown too long from "too much magic." He said she consorted with demons while my father secured Maluku and her body paid the price. This was ludicrous because my mother had been agelessly beautiful. The concubines stood no chance against her, which is why they pinned their hopes for power on their sons, my half-brothers.

I wasn't worried, at first. I didn't care that Arda and Murti were men who looked like my father, because I was his only legitimate child. And then he—Jaya Megalang our Prime Minister—said my mother, the "sorceress," had been unfaithful. That I wasn't *really* blood.

As early as my father's funeral procession, I could feel the landscape shifting—temples coming down, houses going up, clouds moving fast as warships. I realized after I screamed at a maid who brought the garden's last jackfruit to Arda instead of me that I had lost my footing. Jaya Megalang had a far stronger voice and reach. Amassing power was not a skill I'd been taught between courtly dance and batik painting. Sycophantic courtesans went slithering after Arda's heels, whispering things about my mother, each more terrible than the last. My ministers would not meet with me. I had been buried, alive, with my parents.

***

A gap-toothed child grabbed my hand and asked, "What will Jungkuno be like?" I didn't have an answer. So, I murmured, "My mother's people will meet us. Do you remember my mother? She was the Queen. We will hear them singing. They will give us crowns of seashells. We will eat fish. We will swim home ...." I don't know what I was saying after that. The air was so heavy, the ground so unsteady. I remember squeezing the child's hand until someone snatched the sprite away. I heard whispers of "Princess" and didn't know who that "Princess" was.

I had never been to Jungkuno. None of us had. All I knew was that my mother ate spiny purple crabs in what she called "harbor-style"—raw and salted—and told only one story about Jungkuno, and only when I was feverish. It began, "My Mother and Father live under the sea." I don't remember the rest, except for bone-fragments about a thousand siblings, whirlpools and swimming "all the way up" to Father's golden eyes. They were an opiate. I asked her for them nightly—even pretending to be sick—until she shook me off.

"You aren't ready," she said.

She'd come inside Alunijo's brick walls to pay tribute and renew ties, on the twentieth anniversary of Jungkuno's acquiescence to the Alunijo Empire. By then, the man who'd subordinated Jungkuno, King Tungga, was dead, and it was my father Sora who was sitting in the pavilion when she emerged from under the banyans, this wide-eyed woman wearing so much gold she was shining. Sea-music, the kind you hear from a conch, flooded his ears. The hermits said it meant she was the Mother of Kingdoms, so my father married her right away. Her few attendants disappeared soon after. She never went back. I asked if she got homesick and she said, "The water is too shallow here," which I took to mean, "Yes."

Maps couldn't decide exactly where Jungkuno was—behind that cove, on that headland? On some days, trees didn't seem to change and bad thoughts would worm in like ants chewing under fingernails: *Jungkuno does not exist. My mother was insane. I have killed us.*

***

Jaya Megalang cast his wives aside like rotting fruit, and hated kneeling to my mother and me. I felt the sourness of his hate and snapped my teeth at him like a cornered dog. Once, I called him an impotent ogre. He called me a demon. I was seventeen.

"You need to humor him," my father said. This was years before he was trampled by the elephant—my father believed he could control everything, and had indeed expanded the empire to Maluku and tamed the Bugis, but his mind weakened after my mother died. "What proud general wants a little girl talking back to him?"

"My brothers don't have to kiss his feet and they're not even princes."

"Arda and Murti also don't argue with him. Consider the battles he's won for us."

Jaya Megalang once subdued a small, restless kingdom in western Java by arranging a marriage between their princess and my father, and then deciding after their ship docked in Alunijo that their princess was to be a concubine instead. They objected, so he killed the entire royal family. My father, only fifteen, sent them riches in atonement.

"Dhani, the best kings, and queens, know when to be diplomatic." So self-satisfied. "You see?"

I did see, but I never bowed my chin deeply enough for Jaya Megalang. Couldn't stay out of matters of kingdom that were none of my concern. I said those *were* my matters because I was the future Queen. He said I never listened, and when I said I saw no reason to listen to a bitter old soldier, he spat, "You'll never be Queen, you spoiled wretch!" That is why he called my mother a shaman queen and I a creature of the outer darkness.

***

Tigers stayed away from us. The jungle is full of them; they carry off scavenging children. But they left our children alone. One night, I saw amber eyes peering at me through foliage, but when I shifted my gaze for a moment, they disappeared. My people cried, "We are blessed!" and "Dyah watches over us!" but I couldn't feel my mother anywhere in that suffocating greenery. I wondered if the tigers knew we were marked for something worse.

About a week in, someone suggested that we should be on the coast by now. These destitute people, half-mad with heat, looked to me for leadership and I froze, as if I were still staring at that tiger. Every forward step brought me closer to my greatest fear: I would make a terrible Queen.

They could have left me. They would have had the right. My title was worthless, I didn't know the way, and I couldn't speak. I still believe it was fear of tigers that stopped them from deserting but no matter—they gathered at my feet, stroked my hem, and muttered good-luck incantations.

A few days passed of this quiet praying. And then the old healer saw me cradling a woman so sick she seemed to melt and asked if I wasn't scared of disease. By then, we had lost four; tigers may have ignored us, but flies and mosquitoes didn't. But plagues never touched me, nor my mother and father, I assumed because we were royalty. I once smiled when I heard a handmaid say Arda and Murti had water poison—she later told Jaya Megalang that I'd rejoiced at my brothers' suffering, but it wasn't that. I'd rejoiced to know I was sole heir to my father's throne.

"No," I said, "because I am my parents' daughter. I have their blood."

This was nothing new, but from then on, "Their Blood!" became a rallying cry. They tested me: Fed me foul water and spoiled fish, had me bury the infected woman when she died, had me sleep in insect nests. Every time I survived, our collective trust in my being, in my essence and power, swelled. They threw themselves to the ground. I could have walked across their backs.

***

My mother's death had undone me. I'd believed she would live forever. With that rule broken, nothing else seemed real. I started swimming maniacally, paddling across dingy palace canals, sleeping in rice paddies. My father sent me to a house on the beach to "recover." If I'd gotten hurt, I might have been shocked back to reality, but even when I crashed into a rock at sea, my body just swallowed the impact and washed ashore.

I realized, as I lay on the sand watching black coconut fronds stir the white sky, that though the sun is blinding, we are ruled by a great dark Truth. The first Truth is this: People Die. The second: There Is A Place Beyond.

My father took me home after I agreed to sleep indoors again and declared me cured. Truly, I was altered. When the elephant tossed him off its neck and crushed him, I did not cry. "He has joined my mother," I said. "I will see them in time."

***

After My Blood and I were hailed as bearers of the kingdom eternal, I made up my mind about four things: We were going south; we would continue until we reached Jungkuno; there, I would receive my inheritance; and we would take back Alunijo. I rolled my conviction up with my people's devotion into a little leaden ball in my head that I called "Truth."

At first, it was strange to carry Truth inside me instead of worshipping its black shadow-shape from a distance. But as soon as I accepted that these four things were True, the fecund jungle began to make sense. I started to smell sea-salt and hear the caw of gulls under the giggles of jungle-birds. I chose easy-going paths. A profound calm that only comes from self-assurance settled upon me. It can lead you into folly, if you are like my father. So, you must wind your focus tight as a closed fist, as my mother did, and listen, not only to the whine of your own hunger but to the roar of Truth. In our final days in the jungle, I thought only of Jungkuno, never of being Queen. In my dreams, clouds roiled like tentacles above wind-whipped flags. "There is a place!" I cried when I was particularly overcome. My people cried with gratitude.

***

A month after our father died, Murti and I met beside the pool where Arda once drowned a palace pup. Murti was just a little boy trying to grow a mustache. He was born when I was five. When he melted into crybaby tears, I'd often had to console him. "You must leave," he said. "Arda will hurt you if you stay."

It was only natural that my brothers betrayed me. Nestling birds peck their siblings to death, to eliminate competition for love or food. The boys' mothers always whispered to them, at sunbaked ceremonies where they sat two rows behind me—but my mother whispered to me, too: "You are the one, my sweet. You were made to be Queen."

I told Murti so. He'd read the law enough times. I was afraid to say it aloud, but if my mother was Mother of Kingdoms, the Kingdom could only reside in me.

"Sister, I know. But the Prime Minister has the soldiers... they don't answer to you." His eye twitched. I think he was suggesting he become my minder and talk to men on my behalf—a terrible idea, since he was just a weak-spined scholar.

"They have no discipline," I said, "and Jaya Megalang is a brute. Decline's already started. Since my mother died, it's been nothing but accidents and terrible weather. We have no luck at sea. Soon, all our rivals will come to our gates and start nibbling."

Murti shook his head. "Don't talk about decline, Dhani. They don't want to hear it."

***

"Declined" is a polite word to describe Jungkuno. More accurate is probably "abandoned." We saw the remains of houses, temples, guard posts—now, all was water-logged and riddled with seaweed. Tiny white snails like maggots crawled across every manmade surface. And there was not a single soul. It felt as if we'd been delivered out of Hell, only to find the world of the dead.

We camped on the beach. There were scattered protests from those who wanted "a roof, after all this time," but I was taught not to go uninvited into the houses of strangers. "The weather is fine," I said, trying to keep my voice calm because I too was close to ruin. "We sleep outdoors."

There was barely any talk, save when a girl shouted that the surf was "full of fish!"—then we quietly reaped that harvest that belonged to whoever had lived in those dark, time-eaten houses on the dunes. I didn't know if we'd survive this disappointment, if I could coax them to accept this dilapidated village as compensation for their lost membership in the Alunijo Empire. I went to sleep curled like a nautilus. What else can you call a dark sea but the end of the world?

Then, in the dead of night, they came: out of the houses, and out of the sea. Those from the houses had long gills like knife slices instead of ears; their gray skin shone in the moonlight. Their mouths opened deep into their cheeks. Long, gangly fingers dangled at the ends of long gangly arms. The ones from the sea looked even less human. They stood slumped and uncomfortable, with water thrashing their legs.

"Princess Dhani," said one from a house who wore an old fishing net like a shawl. Its voice was too pure for its soggy corpse-skin. "Why did you come back?"

No one knew what to say. My people were so startled, still stuck in a restless sleep, that I don't think they understood it as language. I was the only one who could look at them without wanting to scream, because I'd been looking into those black, bulbous eyes my entire life: my eyes in the mirror; my mother's eyes, after midnight; my father's eyes, when he was hungry. "I have never been here before," I said. "I don't know you."

"Truth. We are Wong Jeru and you should be Queen of Alunijo." Little smile. Long teeth. "Where is your mother? Your father?"

"Both are dead," I said and the creatures howled. After a few anxious heartbeats, I realized they were yelling, *Murdered!* "No! My father had an accident. My mother had a sickness...." I lost my voice, remembering her sudden disintegration—one day, we were watching the boats haul in fish, breathing in sea-salt because my mother said it kept us young—the next, she was dying, a blackened and bloody mess on a foul bed. I was ushered out. *Princess might get sick.* But what about Our Blood?

The creatures did not like this explanation, either. They sounded like gulls swarming a school of fish and children began to cry. *"Sickness! Sickness!"* The one wearing the net lunged forward on thick frog-legs and hissed, "She was a daughter of Dagon! What sickness could touch a Wong Jeru? Your mother was murdered, girl!"

It was the first time I heard the name of Father Dagon. This must have been how my birth-father felt upon seeing my mother and hearing music swirl around her like a ribbon coming unwound. It isn't lust, nor fear. It's an awakening. It's the blow of the heavy gong of Truth. I saw the great golden eyes my mother spoke of and felt his two-note name *("Da-aa-ay-gonnn....")* drum against my bones. It gave my people an uncomfortable shudder—they are human through and through, nearly numb to Truth as I now understand—but I was cracked open, my raw soul quivering and metamorphosing before this tremendous power.

By the time I could think again, some in my party had started to argue with our hosts, these "people of the deep." Who did these clammy Wong Jeru think they were? What abominable place did they come from—"Sea is home," the Wong Jeru interrupted, pointing webbed fingers at the dark water, "with Mother and Father forever"—and why they were telling lies about Queen-Mother Dyah?

"Silence!" I screamed. My people closed their mouths and hunched their shoulders. The Wong Jeru curled their lips and the heavy blackness at the center of their eyes fell upon me. "I want to hear what they have to say."

***

They came from water. They are all descendants of Father Dagon and Mother Hydra, whose tentacles touch the surface from time to time. They reached out to the villagers of Jungkuno, and offered them enough fish and gold that they could gobble up three nearby settlements, including a struggling trade town, and prompt Alunijo to come bearing gifts and collecting tributes. The only "tribute" the Wong Jeru collected for all this prosperity was the chance to make hybrids. Strong, undying hybrids who would serve Father Dagon and Mother Hydra on the only terrain that posed a challenge: land. Jungkuno made a pragmatic decision and many hybrids were born.

Some hybrids looked just as amphibious as their Wong Jeru parent; others, like Dyah, were beautiful, with faces like drowned stars. Prince Sora was another beautiful hybrid, though he was raised in Alunijo and had no waking memory of Mother or

Father, or the Wong Jeru female who birthed him after meeting his father, King Tungga, on the beach. As a baby, Sora was brought to Alunijo and presented to his royal father. "Here," the mother gurgled, "your heir." King Tungga's queen was infertile. She had little choice.

So, together, my mother and father made an empire for the Wong Jeru, for Father Dagon and Mother Hydra. Until Jaya Megalang killed my mother. Until my father thought he could tame elephants. My stupid father. No wonder he failed. Fish do not tame elephants.

***

The beach was cold; the night had endured forever. A clammy hand touched mine, and I took a sharp and painful breath. "Take back the throne, Princess. Make Alunijo great again, as your mother and father did. Show them what immortality means."

"You're the only one that can, Princess Dhani." That time, it was one of mine, a human. My long-suffering people looked terrified, their eyes swollen nearly as badly as the Wong Jeru's, but they let the Wong Jeru squeeze close and drool on their shoulders. Only one Wong Jeru gnawed a human. They were all my people now. "Your brothers don't have The Blood."

But I only said yes after I asked the Wong Jeru what they wanted with an empire. They answered simply, "Mother and Father want to grow and be glorious," and we suddenly understood each other perfectly.

I told my people to return to Alunijo and stay quiet, to tell the court I'd drowned. I promised to return on the first Kliwon of the next month. We would need time for the swim and for me to grow my gills. "I'll remember every one of you," I said. "You will not be unrewarded." They kissed my hands—my alien hands, but they did not care; they loved me so—and said they would meet me at the beach. I might have cried if Truth weren't armor-plating my heart.

Then I turned, shed what remained of my soiled clothes, and went into the water. The sea was no longer dark but glowing, not from moonshine but from something deep and hidden. Something within. The lumbering Wong Jeru are full of grace beneath the waves, silken and smiling and cosmic blue, not gray. The music down below is overwhelming.

***

My half-brother Arda was getting married. I didn't know the girl. I assumed she was some princess of another subordinate people. She seemed excruciatingly unhappy, even before I made it clear that I had not come back from the outer darkness to wish them well. I like to think that when I removed her head, I was saving her from a lifetime of pain.

Arda ran as soon as the Wong Jeru climbed onto the stage, leaving behind his bride. This did not surprise me. He had shown me no loyalty, either. Some warriors think family must "take care" of family—I respect such honor codes, but Arda surrendered the right to be killed by me. I sent the Wong Jeru after him, after giving them license to consume. Best not to waste fuel, I say.

But I did kill Jaya Megalang—not to do him any honors, but to be sure he was dead. This was the man who had killed my mother and dug up her bones. After his bodyguards had been knifed or bitten or bludgeoned, after the wedding stage was slick with blood, I approached him. "I always knew you were a monster," he hissed. "You and that damned witch you called a mother. I should have slit your throat when you were a baby."

"Yes, we are monsters," I said, "but so was my father. You live in a monster's empire. You're only upset because you're not the biggest monster, anymore."

"You're mad. You're *mad* if you think you can run a kingdom with salamanders. Do they even have brains?" His breathing was heavy. He was, finally, the fearful one. "Or just teeth?"

I smiled. "They are Truth and you only have lies. Truth is Order, Prime Minister, and Order is Truth."

I did not kill Murti—I saw him standing dumb like a manservant and told my army, both human and Wong Jeru, not to touch him. Instead, I let him stand in the center of his unraveling world, and when it was all over, when I took my seat on the throne of Alunijo and lifted my bloody keris above my head, he knelt with the others. By then, it was dawn. Someone shouted, "Hail Queen Dhani the Undying!" and a great roar of triumph burst out from the sea, sending waves all the way to the coconut palms tied with batik, swaying high upon the sand.

***

Ask about Queen Dhani the Undying, Priestess of the Faith, Shaman Queen. Ask the traders and longshoremen at any of Asia's busy harbors. Ask at any of the courts of Song, Chola, Khmer. Ask them if they have ever seen a dead Wong Jeru. The answer will probably be no. If a sailor tells you he's killed one personally, you've met a liar. Ask to see something from an Alunijo tradeship and they may show you, for a price. Alunijo gold is probably their greatest treasure. You will not find it on the market because no one ever parts with it. It is handed down on deathbeds, mother to daughter and father to son, often as little dancing idols fashioned in memory of me. If you ever see one, in the Asian Peoples wing of some European history museum, note the arms—an Alunijo idol will have arms like a sea-snake. Or you could simply ask the curator if the museum is "haunted." That will probably show you the Truth.

Ask and you will hear fear. We weren't unfriendly, but we were ruthless. Our boats never sank. Even if they had, our people never drowned. When I was nearly fifty, Father Dagon gifted me control over sea-winds and currents. In the Indo-Pacific, that is all that matters. I only unleashed a monsoon once, against over-confident Nippon; fear did the rest.

If you're unlucky, you'll meet a "true "believer in this or that Abrahamic religion. To them, I am the Demon Queen. They'll say I was in league with Satan, even though I only ever served Truth. And Truth is brutal, yes. Truth does not care for human dreams. But I had no interest in converting anyone, least of all the weak and foolish, the ones unchosen by Father and Mother. Truth is Order and Order is Truth. Their place is down below, with Jaya Megalang and other detritus. Fear's the primal god of humans, anyway.

If you are extraordinarily lucky—and ready—you will find a man or woman who knows R'lyeh. It happened to me when I was 412 and I met a shipwrecked chieftain from the Bird of Paradise, Papua Island. "Queen Dhani," he said, grinning to show his chattering teeth, "I have been to the most amazing city."

Insane people are the reason I never got bored. I usually let the Wong Jeru eat anything they pulled from the sea, but this time, I stayed them. My guard, the latest I had named 'Little Murti,' licked his grouper lips impatiently. "What city, little man?" I asked. "Is it better than Xanadu?"

"Oh, yes, Queen Dhani. In his house at R'lyeh, dead Cthulhu waits dreaming."

Then he tumbled over laughing and promptly died. Little Murti asked for permission to eat him, which I gave with an absent nod. I had already begun once more to alter. I felt My Blood boiling over, felt the rest of my sensory life go numb. I saw the lead ball of Truth opening before my eyes, cleaving once, then again.

***

When I turned 500, I left. I dove off my ship at sundown and swam away. By then, I took no joy in empire—the alliances and processions, the shallow exotica. I thought of nothing but R'lyeh, of waking this High Priest Cthulhu. I no longer cared for names, or faces, or food. I did not sleep. I saw my great empire for what it Truly was: a pile of children's toys, nothing but a game. Father Dagon and Mother Hydra wrapped me in tentacles, and whispered, *"This is Enough,"* but "enough" was a compromise I was not willing to make.

I know Alunijo died without me. I know the alliances broke and the hybrids disappeared into the mainland and the Wong Jeru slipped back into the ocean and Father Dagon produced no more gold, and eventually, the tiny ships of Europe came whistling around the Cape and enslaved everything that had been mine. When I see Java floating on that glassy sea, I do worry that I have disappointed my parents—my birth-mother Dyah, that is, and my birth-father Sora. They loved that island so, wanted only greatness for it, and now look. But Truth was waiting for me in the South Pacific and I had to heed that call.

"Homesick" my mother was and I am, too, sometimes. I'm sure the pain gnaws because I haven't found R'lyeh. The High Priest is not ready. The stars don't yet align. Every now and then, while I float on still waters and wait for Cthulhu's call, I go to my old southern shore and walk amongst the ruins. The brick split gate still stands, and although my banyans died, new banyans grew in their place. I haunt whatever kingdom has taken root on my mother's bones. The Muslim sultans gave me new names; that is probably how you know me. Nyai Roro Kidul. Queen of the South Sea. Spirit-Queen.

When the light is right, I can see in their eyes the awed devotion of my very first legion, but they claim to worship other gods now. Everything is veiled. I know you feel it, too. Only the humming promise of Cthulhu remains, a final signal of Truth emitted from some deep crevasse of the world. Listen.

ABSOLUTE ZERO

When Max Beecham was eight years old, his mother Deena (delirious from antihypertensives) gave him a Polaroid and then lay down on the carpet behind him. Inside the white border of this photograph lurked a thing with the naked body of a gaunt man and the head of a dark, decayed stag. It sat on a tree stump the way neighborhood men sat on bar stools, surrounded by a cavalry of thin, burned trees. Max almost recognized this nightmare place as Digby Forest, a festering infection of wild land on the edge of Cripple Creek. In the dusk the image was shadowless and tense, as if that black-eyed Stag-Man meant to lunge out of its frame. As if it was only waiting for Max to look away.

"What is it?" Max asked.

"That's your father," said Deena. She had her back to him. Her thin cotton dress stretched to translucency across her long torso. He could see the shape of her vertebrae. "You're always asking, so there he is."

He thought she was joking and he turned to prod her, but she had fallen asleep. He put the Polaroid face down on the carpet and pressed his fingers against his eyeballs. It was the first thing in his life that he wished he could unsee. He would hear later that time heals all wounds, but the deep slice in his heart that this picture created never got any better. The next summer Max tried to walk Fallspur Bridge for the right to join the Petrinos on the other side, but halfway across and already wobbling, he looked up and saw the Stag-Man crouched in the trees behind the Petrinos. And the bastard never left him alone; the Stag-Man watched him try to impress the slouching upperclassmen, the tall blonde girls in athletic shorts and shirts that claimed them as the property of Jesus. He might win himself a little respite—when he was concentrating on a math exam, for example—but as soon as his mind unclenched, the Stag-Man would be there: looking in the window, waiting behind the fence.

During this time, his mother went on disability. She nearly drowned in the bathtub twice—when he pulled her out she said she was trying to "get back to herself." This was a lie. He knew that she was trying to get back to that thing, that Stag-Man.

"Why did you tell me?" he'd shout at her when he got older. By that time she had confined herself to her rocking chair, with her gaze fixed on their lopsided black locust tree. No, it was not their tree—it was older than he was, and he knew she wouldn't have planted it. It was no one's tree, and maybe that was why it had grown up crooked. "Why didn't you just keep this shit to yourself? You could have lied to me, you know. It's not like I would've known."

Max flapped the Polaroid in her face—his mother did not respond. He had tried to destroy the photo but every time he took it to the backyard with a lighter, some bony inner feeling stopped him. So it lived in his closet in a taped-up shoebox, supposedly contained.

"Why did you tell me!" he shouted. "Come on, Mom!" The urge swelled to seize her and wrestle her to the floor—anything to break her out of the stasis that had closed in around her like a hard coat of amber. He grabbed the chair instead, swung it around so that she couldn't look at the tree anymore.

He immediately wished he hadn't. Her miserable, time-eaten gaze felt like the swing of an iron bar.

"You didn't like what you saw?" She was breathing shallowly. When she sighed it sounded like wind rushing through a pipe. "Bummer."

She and the tree died that winter. The end was very hard. Deena fought the hospital staff with long-dormant claws whenever they rolled into her room with needles and droopy bags of liquid medicine. "Fuck your poison," she would say. The hospital was two hours away from Cripple Creek, and the neighbor who drove Max in and out of the city always fish-tailed on the icy roads. The flat white landscape would spin past with no beginning and no end; the neighbor would mumble obscenities, and Max would think ecstatically about dying. At first the tree went on without her, its branches twisting round its trunk, but Max burned it down.

Max's grandmother, Rowena, came down from Vertigo to see him through high school. She shed no tears for the one she called her lost child. "She was gone by the time she walked out of those woods pregnant with you," said Grandma Ro. "So I've been mourning your whole life."

***

Years later, after Grandma Ro had passed on (she died in her daughter's bedroom; Max taped the door shut afterwards, designating the room "condemned"), Tom Lowell caught something large and alarming on the edge of his property. By then Max was twenty-six and working at Ticonderoga Mills, buying wheat from the ragged, leftover farms of Cripple Creek.

Whenever prices dropped, Max would see them leaning heavy against their trucks, eyes to the dirt. Sometimes they cussed him out. Max reasoned that they shouldn't have been clinging to their backwards lifestyle anyway. He hated their excuses: their fathers' fathers had cultivated that land for generations, and now the grains were in their blood. "What if your fathers' fathers have been killing for generations," he would mutter to himself. "What then?"

Then you strip yourself down to the smallest, purest molecules and rebuild yourself up to something better, that's what. Max thought that he had pretty well succeeded at this—at least he did not see those eyes in the mirror anymore, at least he had a job and a girl and a house (his mother's house, but still)—but then Tom Lowell started running around town saying that he was charging twenty dollars to see the Meanest Looking Thing on Earth, this Devil's Child. Max began to feel the Polaroid staring at him from inside the shoebox again.

Nothing very strange had happened in Cripple Creek in the years between Max's birth and the capture of what Tom Lowell christened The Creeker—aside from the woman who ran the plant nursery, Chastity Dawes, getting pregnant out of nowhere and giving birth to a small fawn. The hospital had the creature euthanized, despite the mother's objections. But other than that, life in Cripple Creek had been normal. Progress continued apace. The racetrack, the shopping mall, the microbrewery. They were on track to match Grand Island in annual revenue. God knew theirs was a community on the rise.

Kevin from work wanted to see The Creeker. He wanted to see it so he could laugh at it, and at Tom Lowell. "It's probably just some two-headed cow," Kevin said. "Lowell's a nut, you know. I heard he went hunting for some Demon Razorback of Arkansas once."

Of course Max knew what this Creeker was, in the bowels of his soul. It was the Stag-Man. It was his...

And then he would have to go to the rest room and cradle his head between his knees. Maybe he shouldn't have gone. On the drive over, his stomach was flipping so badly that he couldn't talk. But it would have looked strange if he'd bowed out—he'd gone to mock the "crop circles" out at Rookshire, after all—and besides, his depraved subconscious just couldn't let go of the image of Tom Lowell's farm and the captive creature behind its fence. In the days before they finally went to the farm his world had warped into a tunnel, a vortex like the one at Rapid City, with all furniture and foliage blurring together and everything hurtling toward a pair of eyes like lumps of coal.

Caridee Lowell, sixteen years old with eyes sunken from methamphetamine, sold red tickets out of a tin lunchbox. "To your left," she hissed after taking their bills. There was no need for directions; the bright yellow fireworks tent was visible all the way down Cahokia Drive.

The tent was surprisingly quiet. The dozen people gathered inside would knock heads to whisper to each other, but all their eyes were fixed upon one location: a metal crate on the far side of the tent, large enough to shuttle a cow. "It's one of Murray's old transport cages," Tom Lowell said. Several years ago there had been a short, ugly attempt at a town zoo—both the Ag Department and Fish and Wildlife had to get involved. The surviving animals had all been taken away, supposedly, but one reasonable theory argued that this Creeker was some mutated, mutilated escapee. Angry with man. Hungry for revenge. An old story. "It's for handling wild animals, so don't worry. He won't getcha."

And there, in the cage, was the Stag-Man. After years of staring at a three-inch image in a palm-sized Polaroid, its immense size overwhelmed Max. He would have needed to stoop to get inside that cage, but the Stag-Man had to sit, cramped, its knees to its chin. Its four-foot antlers flared out from its cervine head like skeleton-wings. Max could see immediately that it was too big for this cage, too big for this tent. Its skin was loose—it was not feeding enough. His slow-burning father, the monster. The captive. Why was it just sitting there? What was it thinking? Dread crawled up his throat. He felt fear, yes, but also the early twinges of sympathy.

Max and Kevin heard the nervous mumbling as they pushed to the front—"Where the hell did that thing come from?" "What's it doing here?"—but no one wanted to answer, because no one really wanted to know. Sometimes after they asked these questions they would cough and pat their chests, as if they had accidentally invited themselves down some terrible internal rabbit hole. The ones that simply said, "I don't know what to say" fared better. Kevin whispered "No fucking way" with his eyes glazed, and Max was thinking, *"Father."*

Up close the scent of rank earth nearly knocked them down. Max could barely believe the Stag-Man was real and tangible and capable of bleeding—it had made so much more sense as a dream-spirit, his mother's Boogeyman. He stared at the beast for fifteen minutes, helpless, trapped like a rabbit in a snare. He thought it was because the Stag-Man knew him as a son but post-tent conversation would reveal that everyone in the Creeker's presence thought it was staring them in the eye, holding them rapt.

A little girl standing beside Max clutched the bars as if she was the one imprisoned. She was watching the Creeker breathe, so it seemed, and sobbing quietly the entire time.

***

There were casualties. Unlike the Big Eats Barbecue, Tom Lowell's show did not spread joy. People left the tent either stone silent or pissing mad, bickering about "that one night in Reno" and "what you did with my father's money."

The biggest casualty that night was Pastor Connor from the Good Shepherd Lutheran Church. He had come to pressure Tom Lowell into closing down the show, but of course had to look at the exhibit first. It was a mistake. After staring at the Creeker for several minutes he ran out of the tent, shoving his own parishioners aside, and collapsed on the grass with his hands to his heart. Kevin called an ambulance and Elise Buckley fed him aspirin, but it was too late.

"Ah, geez," said the kid in the paramedic uniform. "I *told* him not to go."

"You've seen the Creeker?" asked Kevin.

"I went opening night," said the paramedic-kid. "I was freaking out for a whole week. Kept thinking about all the squirrels I shot coming back rabid and biting me in my sleep." He tried to laugh. "Fucking weird, right?"

After Pastor Connor was lifted into the back of the ambulance the rest of them stood in a circle with their hands in their pockets. They were more distressed by the Creeker than by Pastor Connor's death, which seemed like a just response to that monstrous aberration. A small child screamed from some parked car—they glanced up, but dropped their chins when they heard the stern voice of a disciplinarian-father. Finally Elise Buckley lit a cigarette and started to talk.

"I guess it was a bad summer, if that thing's wandering out of Digby this time of year. Isn't that what happens with bears? If they're scavenging in October, you gotta figure it's because they didn't get to feed enough in the summer. Feeding on what, I don't know. People's lost dogs, I guess."

After this little burst they fell quiet again, thinking about dogs they had lost, and horses that had supposedly run away, and then the really unpleasant stuff: the missing people. There had been no more than a handful in the past ten years, but how the news stations had dwelled upon those unlucky few. Everyone around for the last census remembered at least one. Even the missing migrant workers were considered tragedies. *They must be cold out there,* people said.

"That thing's not ours," Kevin mumbled into his gloved hands. "It's not our problem."

Elise shook her head, took a big drag, and walked away. "I really hate all of you people."

Then it was just Max and Kevin watching for shadows on the darkened grass. "I saw a chupacabra once," whispered Kevin. "I was visiting my grandparents in Texas. It was the middle of the night when I heard it howling. It killed my favorite goat."

The Stag-Man was some kind of witch, Max decided. In all the years that he had known these people, nothing else had warped them so. He knew what Kevin and Elise and everyone else was feeling—like they were wobbling on the lip of a great dark funnel—because he had suffered the power of the Stag-Man's gaze every night since he was eight. Max wanted to tell them this, but like hell would he admit to his friends and neighbors that he shared any blood with that thing in Tom Lowell's cage. He had a brief moment of panic: what if Kevin saw some familial resemblance between his long features and that of the Stag-Man? He frantically rubbed his face. He was feeling for rough fur and a soft wet snout, but all he got was dry human skin. When he was twelve he had asked his mother if he had anything in common with the Stag-Man, and now he heard her reply: "Believe me," she'd said, with a snort, "you're nothing alike."

***

Mallory Jablonski taught fifth grade at Cripple Creek Elementary. It was the same school Max had attended, but they were not schoolyard sweethearts—she grew up in Lincoln, and she had the straight teeth and designer jeans to prove it. She'd been on a school dance squad, which Max understood to be a mythical troupe of hot girls in black leotards that would never be permitted at Cripple Creek High, where even the cheerleaders wore turtlenecks and chastity rings. Mallory had been on a class trip to New York. She liked sushi. All sorts of things, and still she radiated that earthy glow of harvest corn. Mallory was cultured; Mallory was genuine. He drove her around town slowly, with the windows down, because damn if his classmates wouldn't be surprised that he managed to catch a girl like that. Mallory always laughed when they stopped at intersections. "Traffic's real bad today," she'd say. It was funny because there was no such thing as traffic in Cripple Creek.

When the Creeker became the talk of the town she asked him to take her to see it. "All my students are talking about it," she said. "Have you seen it?"

He thought of the Polaroid. The slow-burning eyes. "Yeah."

"And? Is it scary?" She bit her nails, grinning. She probably thought it was some pathetic artifact of rural Americana, a cousin of cow-tipping and haystack rides. "No, don't tell me. I want to see it myself."

Max took her to the Lowell farm that Friday. The carnival tent was fraying now that the first of the cold fronts were moving in. Mallory had been talkative as they crossed the pesticide-yellow grass, but in the presence of the Stag-Man, she approached the cage as if in a trance. She knelt down at the bars the way she did at Mass and looked soulfully, silently into the Stag-Man's eyes. Max felt acid bubble into his throat. They were exchanging secrets and truths, he could just tell. She was in communion with the same incubus that had seduced his mother. He would have yanked her out of that deferential pose by her hair, but Mallory stood up just as he was reaching down. She stuffed her hands in her sweatshirt pockets.

"Let's go, I want to go," she mumbled. "I don't feel well."

A throng of preteens that had set up a devotional camp outside the Stag-Man's cage leered up at them. They looked like jackals in black clothes. "Ooh, yeah," said one of them. "Run along and hi-i-ide." Max sharply told them to go home—trying to sound like a responsible man, even though his own father was a freak in a cage—but they sang back, "This *is* home."

He and Mallory walked back to his truck with his arm around her shoulders. He could feel her trembling. It was a cold sort of relief to see that she was suffering instead of enraptured. She was nothing like his mother, he told himself. She was an innocent. Virtuous. Competent. "I shouldn't have brought you here. This stuff's no good." He bit his lips, in guilt. Mallory shook her head absently but didn't speak until they were in the muscular safety of the Chevrolet Colorado, barreling down Cahokia Drive, listening to Doctor Touchdown on KMKO Radio.

"I used to have an imaginary friend."

He turned the volume down. "Huh?"

"But I don't know if she was really imaginary. She came out at night, from the wetlands. She would tap on my window. Glowing like a gravestone. No one else saw her but I... saw her more and more after my sister died." Max hadn't known about this sister. "I think she wanted me to go away with her. She said there was a castle under the water at Napoleon Pond. Oh, God." She slumped forward in the passenger seat as if something had punched her in the stomach. Max wondered if this was why she could not sleep facing any windows, why she slept in the pitch-black dark with the sheets over her head.

"I never told anybody. But I guess seeing that thing on the farm… brought it all back." She looked over at him plaintively. "You think I'm a freak, don't you? Just say it. I know that's what you're thinking."

It was a strange moment. He would dwell upon it later to try to determine what had possessed him to tell her the truth. Maybe he was shocked that a girl as presentable as Mallory could feel his bewildered shame. Maybe he thought shared alienation would deepen their bond. "I don't think you're a freak," he said. "Something even stranger happened to me."

She raised a pale brown eyebrow.

"You know that… thing on the farm?" She nodded. "Well, that's my father." He immediately exploded in terrified laughter. The sensible, screaming part of him wanted to backtrack before things got any worse—tack on a quick "Holy shit, just kidding!"—but when he opened his mouth only nonsense dribbled out. "My mother was a strange lady. She was the kind of person that chased tornadoes, you know? No jeep or cameras or nothing, she'd just head out the door and run after them. She's dead now. Died a long time ago."

Mallory was trying to smile. But she was waiting for that "just kidding!" and when it didn't come—when every word that rolled down his chin was a confirmation of the wretched truth—Mallory gathered up the handles of her purse and said to take her home. She looked like she was about to jump out of the truck. "I have a lot of quizzes to grade," she said.

He reached over, teeming with concern, but Mallory recoiled from his hand. It was as if she was saying, *No—I never touched you. I disown you. I don't know who you even are.*

The road dwindled. Her driveway was covered in fallen leaves. "Mallory," he said, hoping to remind her of what they had been sharing for the past six months. "It doesn't change anything."

Mallory's eyes widened; she was probably remembering the same six months in retrospective horror. "I can't do this, Max." The passenger door swung open and the cold rushed in. "I can't do this now."

And then she was gone. He had wanted to marry her. He had visualized himself walking into her parents' house in the old part of Lincoln, all brick walls and roundabouts and leafy trees, and introducing himself to her father the banker. *"My name is Max,"* he would have said, and there would have been no doubt.

***

He started dreaming about hurting Mallory. He didn't enjoy these dreams, but they satisfied the same ache in his belly that years earlier made him want to shake his mother until her head popped off. The Stag-Man was there too, watching and waiting, and after the floor swallowed Mallory's ruined body, the Stag-Man would remain: bright and powerful and merciless. A fire in the woods, an old whispered force. Sometimes the Stag-Man called him "son."

Sometimes Max would curl around the creature's feet because in the dark the Stag-Man was all there was to the world. With its crown of antlers it looked like some wise and wizened tree. And sometimes when Max woke up he would go to the bathroom mirror and rub his forehead to see if his own velvet-covered antlers were growing in.

Tom Lowell had cut the entrance fee in half. Word had spread of the Creeker's negative side effects—*nausea, heartburn, indigestion*—and now the farmer stood alone in the middle of his driveway, hands on his hips, watching for vehicles on Cahokia Drive. "You think it makes 'em feel better to think this stuff doesn't exist?" he asked Max, cocking his head, chicken-like. "Hey, isn't this your third time?" Like the Stag-Man was some ride at Worlds of Fun.

Three drunks in Husker windbreakers were tossing peanut shells at the Stag-Man. They were giving themselves points for contact: five for the body, ten for the head. They did not deign to speak to it even in the way they spoke to their dogs, even though the body they shot at was just a taller, stronger version of their own. Max felt a pang of defensive anger and shame, but the Stag-Man seemed to be smiling back at them. Not that its deer mouth could grin, but its eyes were gleeful.

Max crept up to the cage. It was filthy, and swarming with bronze cockroaches. He sensed the Stag-Man watching him and his legs wobbled—the last two times he'd been in the tent he'd been able to hold steady, but not now. Moving his center of gravity closer to the earth quelled a little bit of nausea, but still he had to ask the question. "Do you know me?"

A peanut shell hit the back of his head. "That's ten for me!" shouted one drunk; "Get out of the way!" said another. Max hissed at them and did not move. Instead he eased his hands between the bars, gingerly laying them on the floor of the cage. A cockroach ran over his empty ring finger and down his sleeve, but the Stag-Man was silent. Max swallowed. Of course it didn't know him from Adam—God knew how many women from Cripple Creek had gone running into its forest on summer nights. He took out his wallet, and a small secret photo he kept behind his ID. A woman with coiffed black hair and a red Christmas sweater gazed up and out with gorgeous cat-eyes. She was a little drunk but still healthy then, surrounded by cheap tinsel.

"This is my mother. Twenty-seven years ago, you…"

The Stag-Man looked at the photo and curled its lips back, showing its teeth. Those teeth were pointed. Max shuddered, and one of the drunks started to retch. At first the man spat bile and beer, but upon reaching into the back of his throat, began to pull out a long and thin industrial wire.

Max should have gotten fired that week—not that he would have cared—because he couldn't focus on his paperwork. The window behind his desk let in too much light and too much landscape. Cripple Creek seemed filled with broken pre-war churches and painted-over signs: the skeletons of older towns. No matter where he went—the Kwik Shop, the liquor store— these battered, ghostly layers peeked through the concrete he walked upon. "You remember that lady Chastity Dawes?"

Kevin glanced at him over the crest of a golden taco. Max had tried to bring up the chupacabra, but Kevin would always pretend to be choking on something or getting a phone call. "The one that gave birth to a deer?"

"Yeah. Whatever happened to her? I know the Gordons own the nursery now."

"She killed herself, man. Well, 'died of exposure.' But when you ditch your car off Highway 2 in the middle of a snow storm so you can go walking through a cornfield, I don't know how you call it anything else." Kevin shrugged. "I guess once you've given birth to a monster, what the fuck else are you going to do?"

Max tried to picture those cornfields. They were a grim sight in winter—the stalks either pale and withered or draped with silent, crushing snow. "Isn't that right by Digby Forest?"

"Hell if I know. I haven't been *there* since elementary school."

"Field trip," said Max. He remembered his own school-sponsored foray into Digby Forest—or rather, he remembered being terrified that he would see the Stag-Man. He was so frightened, so attuned to any blur of movement and any sound of breaking twigs, that he learned nothing at all about Nebraska's native forests. And here Chastity Dawes had gone running *toward* this doom, just like his mother sinking in the bathtub. At the time he had thought, *Is this world so bad?* but maybe they were onto something. "She was going on a field trip."

"What?" The taco muffled Kevin's words. "You know, Beecham, sometimes you freak me out." He kept talking, but Max was looking out the window. Clouds had swooped in from the south in violent formation, armies of fists against armies of hammers. Something was on its way. Judging by the speed of his heartbeat, it was probably his fate.

***

Tom Lowell and his daughter Caridee were found murdered in their living room on Tuesday the 20th. Tom on the couch, Caridee on the floor, the television broadcasting an episode of the soap opera *Coming Up Roses.* To say murdered was to put it kindly: they had been disemboweled. The Creeker was gone, its cage bent open like a soup can. Relief washed over Cripple Creek, because people assumed that the malformed beast that shared their name had gone back to Digby Forest. They were duly sorry about Caridee, but at least nobody would have to see that damn thing again. Max alone knew that it was still in town, hiding in collapsed barns and hobbled school buses, and he lay awake at night waiting for it to come crawling through his window. The thought still made his skin crawl, but it was oddly reassuring to feel that he still belonged to someone, something. It was nice to know that he was still someone's son.

At Cabela's, he looked at the Deer Head Mounts. There was a

whole wall of them, right beside the Buffalo Mounts and European Mounts. Some had shoulders, some only necks. The replicas were cheaper, but the originals looked at Max with soft and sad fraternal recognition. They were kin to the Stag-Man, his father—only smaller, with fair and innocent faces. They did not look like monsters spat out of hell. They looked like the deer that the Deer Crossing signs warned of, the deer that lived in the narrow strips of woodland between the farms and the roads. He briefly imagined the heads of all the world's beasts mounted upon a giant fortress wall. His own head was among them, bolted to a wooden slab.

The sales clerk was rambling statistics. "That rack's a 17-pointer, with a 30-inch spread. Came off an early season northern whitetail…"

"Can you take the skin off?" Max asked.

The sales clerk looked shocked. "No… but we've got deer skin rugs."

They had grizzly skin rugs too, as well as wolf skin rugs and cougar skin rugs and muskox skin rugs and child-sized lynx and badger and beaver skin rugs. All had heads attached to their flat and floppy puppet bodies. Unlike the snarling predators—still fighting even in this state of preserved death—the buck's mouth was stitched closed. "It's got a canvas backing. Professionally taxidermied."

"I'll take it," Max said.

That evening he sat on the couch and wrapped himself with the deer skin rug. The buck's head sat upon his own—he had to slouch to keep it from falling down his back. His new skin was so suffocatingly warm that he turned off the heater. Then he exhaled, trying to feel comfortable. He dug his nails into the hide and imagined it to be his own. What were the odds, he wondered, of having been born into a human body? Maybe it was the wrong one. Maybe he should have been a ruminant all along, just like Chastity Dawes' fawn.

A door opened—judging by the hard slap of metal on wood, it was the screen door in the kitchen. He looked up. The Stag-Man, bloody-mouthed, stood in the doorway. Its antlers were scraping the ceiling. At first it was just breathing, staring; then it came gliding forward, never raising its hooves off the fake wood-paneled floor.

"Father," mumbled Max, hoping that it would see him in his deer form.

The Stag-Man did look into the false glass eyes of the dead buck, but quickly lowered its gaze to Max's real eyes, all hazel and watery and bursting with nerves. That gaze reached right inside his head and rummaged around.

Within this visual stranglehold the house changed and decomposed. Filth rose to the surface. He saw his mother creeping down the stairs out of the corner of his eye. Neither she nor his father saw each other. Her bloated lips called his name. After ten seconds, Max had to look away.

The Stag-Man hovered above him, sniffing deeply, then withdrew with a grunt. It paused at the doorway. It was waiting, Max realized. It grunted again and Max got to his feet. They were sharing a floor now, father and son.

It was like sharing an earth.

How new this night-world was. A man with a flashlight could only point out the random human signposts that survived nightfall in the country—the gravel of a driveway, the lawn chairs on a porch. All else was lost in the dark and gnarly mass: the pulsing, growing *stuff* that flashlights could not bear to focus on. Max was in the thick of it now, this world without property fences (only land), without cars (only lights), without houses (only wood). He was not sure if he was running or drowning, and he had lost the deer skin somewhere back on 10th Street. Sometimes he could throw himself fully into this night-run, lose himself in the muscle-searing pursuit of his Stag-Man father who did not run but madly leapt from things that used to be mailboxes to things that used to be trash cans.

And then he would look down at his hands and see his pale, chilled human skin. It made his stomach fold. He was pushing so fast that the ground seemed to roll beneath him, so fast his mind tumbled like a whirligig. And all the while, deep welts grew on his skin where trees had clawed him. With blood in the air, the Stag-Man let out a trembling, hungry, open-throated howl. Max felt it in his spine, as deep and familiar as a knife in a wound. He almost stopped. The boy inside him wanted to crawl home. *This is home,* he told himself. *The others would have found you out eventually. You would have started to stink. So don't mourn. Don't mourn.*

***

Bill MacAtee was dead, but he was not the one the Stag-Man wanted. The Stag-Man had killed him with a teacher's patience, lingering over the precise angle and depth of the slice across Bill's stomach, encouraging Max to scoop out the viscera. Bill was the kind of asshole that used to drive around town calling quiet men fags, and Max (having been Bill's target once or twice) tried to be glad that Bill was dead. And maybe he was, but not like that, not with long swaths of Bill hanging out and inviting flies, not so Bill could stare up at the clouds like a middleschooler rolling his eyes. The Stag-Man had already moved onto the true object of its desire: the MacAtees' sheepdog, groomed and collared with hair the color of a Holstein cow. It had come running after Bill, barking indignantly, but when the Stag-Man turned toward the dog with its branch-like arms outstretched and its dirty claws dripping with the master's blood, the domesticated little creature buckled down, whimpering.

At least the Stag-Man killed it quickly. Max wasn't sure why—some hint of tenderness, or pity? The dog might have been wild, in another life time. After it collapsed, blood soaking its blue collar black, the Stag-Man squatted down and dug a hole beneath the dog's ribs. Liquid gushed out along with a twitch and a squeak as if the little life was not quite gone. Max pressed his hands against his own belly. The Stag-Man pulled tendons and muscles and gelatinous organs out of this cavity like they were the treasures of the damn Sierra Madre, but all Max saw when the Stag-Man's hands opened was inside-out-dog, all the wet under-the-skin shit that he didn't want to see. And then the smell—putrid, sour, like drowned flowers—hit him.

Max retched. He slapped his hand over his mouth so that when the salt bubbled up his throat he could chase it back down. When he looked up the Stag-Man was standing at full height. The burnt black eyes drilled down into him as if from the pinnacle of a grotesque tower. The steaming, dripping hand was still available; God only knew he tried to take it. His father was grunting at him, thrusting the hand forward, snorting. He had flashbacks of walking across Fallspur Bridge, and the sunburned children on the other side who screamed at him to hurry and cross. The plank wobbled. The world beneath, the great bottomless funnel, rocked and churned. His body failed him now as it had failed him then. The Stag-Man threw the innards at his heart and Max compulsively shuddered, trying to shake the wetness off without getting it under his nails. Maybe it was this final twitch that ruined it, because the Stag-Man turned then, growling: away from Max, back toward the wild tree line. Max hurried after, mewling like a lost animal. He had not realized until then how warm he had felt in his father's presence.

And then his father had him by the neck in a bristling, rough embrace. His ribs were groaning, but Max tried not to struggle. His mother had sometimes held him this way. *"Come here. Oh God. Don't cry."* A bark-skin hand clenched the roots of his hair—so tightly that he could feel his scalp peeling off his skull, tears shooting into his eyes, so tightly that he forgot all but this pain and an incomprehensible fear—and ripped Max away. Like a man pulling off a leech. A human would have been disemboweled and a fawn would have been taken along, but Max was just tossed into the winter grass, a formless mess not even a mother could love. It came down like an iron gate between them: *you are nothing of mine.*

Max flinched and curled his muscles, trying to turn his trembling body into a fist. The Stag-Man was gliding away toward the foggy pines. "Don't you dare walk away!" Max shouted. "Hey, you look at me!"

There was no response. He remembered his mother sitting in her rocking chair, staring unshaken at the black locust tree. He could have set himself on fire and not drawn her eye—not until she coughed on his ashes would she realize that the skinny thing she sometimes called her child was gone. He grabbed Bill MacAtee's shotgun, pulling back the cold, thick fingers one by one, and after another warning—another *"Look at me!"*—he fired it at his father. The cartridge opened a hole in the tawny hide of his father's back. Blood-petals sprayed into the frosted dawn like a bridal bouquet, but for a full thirty seconds, the Stag-Man kept walking. What call could be higher than its own survival? Max's eyes began to water and when he looked back after wiping his face, the Stag-Man was gone. A deflated lump so unlike the striking figure in his mother's Polaroid lay in its place. The pines shook and Max hunched over, shivering.

"Bill?" Caroline MacAtee stood on the back porch. Her trembling fingers rose to touch her mouth. Max could not tell—simply could not determine—whether she was staring at him or at the dead things gathered at his feet.

"Everything's okay!" Max shouted, raising the rifle. "It's gone now, I took care of it!"

Caroline MacAtee didn't thank him—she backed into her house and slammed the door. But maybe he couldn't blame her, because here it was starting to snow.

***

The wild had been tamed, and now they were losing visibility. Max was too busy clenching his teeth and the steering wheel to manipulate the windshield wipers, and he drifted toward what looked like a glory-white horizon before recalling fear and slamming on the brakes. He slid to a stop half-on, half-off the shoulder. "A fire out in Digby Forest..." KMKO Radio was starting to cut out. "Not sure if they're going to send the Fire Department on account of... hope it doesn't come near us..." On the other side of the road, a pudgy man in a green Parks and Recreation jacket stood next to a blinking truck. He was trying to shovel the remains of a very large piece of road kill into the truck's open bed. Black tarp was whipping in the wind.

Max rolled down his window. "What is that?" he shouted.

"Hell if I know," the Parks and Recreation man shouted back. "Guy said it just showed up in the middle of the road, didn't even try to get out of the way."

The corpse was the size of a small horse and covered with icy fur, but elephantine tusks protruded from the garbled carcass.

"Sixth call we've had this hour. I didn't even know we had these many animals to run down." The Parks and Recreation man started laughing, then coughing. "You know there's birds falling out of the sky by the racetrack? Something in the weather, I guess."

Deena used to say that animals could tell when it was time to get the hell out of Dodge. "You'll know when bad times are coming," she whispered, "Because you'll hear them *howling.*" Max closed his eyes. He never wanted to think of that name again. Never wanted to see that bewitched smile again. *Stay dead,* he thought. *Stay dead.*

"You hear that Digby's burning down?"

Suddenly tired, Max rested his arms against the steering wheel. "Yeah, I heard."

"I hope they let it burn. That no-good place." The man's lower lip was trembling. "It's just a breeding ground for monsters."

Burning the black locust tree had cauterized some of the wounds in his young heart. Maybe that was all Cripple Creek needed: a good cleansing burn, some scar tissue to seal away the unpleasantness. He nodded. "Get rid of it," he said. "Nothing else you can do." With growing anger, the Parks and Recreation man smashed his shovel against the unknown animal. The creature was fixed to the ice, more figurine than entity, too ugly and beaten to be mounted on somebody's wall. Max looked away.

Both eastbound and westward, cars were diving off the edge of the road into the white expanse. Max counted eight in all. Their doors were open, their seats were empty. He didn't know where those drivers thought they were going—did they really think there was anything left to run away to? The world was smothered with ash and snow.

Mallory's fluorescent windows glared like the beacon of an arctic outpost, so harsh he had to squint. He rang the door bell and listened to her slippered feet approach from the other side. Was she looking through the peep hole? Did she see spatters of blood, any antler stubs? No—she was unlocking the dead bolt, unhooking the security chain. She opened the door, and he was surprised by how empty and sterile her home looked, like a hollow egg. Bare as the sky and the buried fields. *No, not empty,* he told himself. *Safe from monsters.* "Max?" She leaned her listless head against the door. "What are you doing here?"

"I cleaned myself up," he said. "I bashed in those demons. I dropped that baggage... feel lighter already. I'm good as new." He realized that he could not feel his lips. But after all these years of feeling, he could use a little numbness. It was a small price to pay for the capacity to forget. "I want to start over. Please, Mallory. We can be happy, I know it."

Mallory's sleepy blue eyes looked him up and down. She smiled faintly. As she parted her lips to speak the wind rose to an ear-splitting shriek, and all the sound in the world went out.

NO GODS, NO MASTERS

Lily was praying for a crash. Not a bad one. Just a fender bender. Something that would force them to pull over, to wait for the highway patrol, to stop. To not go to Sparta. But the demon was the only one listening, so nothing happened.

She watched the wretched snake of traffic twitching and glitching on the other side of the highway divider—wiser people trying to squeeze into the city—and was riled with a resentment that started when the first sign came up for I-52. She didn't even really know Salome. She hadn't seen the girl since she was twelve years old—all spider arms and legs and a thick mermaid braid that she would whip over her shoulder whenever she lost patience, which was often. She was not surprised Salome ended up in this bind. Salome never seemed to be much into listening.

And now Lily was trapped in a car with a cousin who was carving her arm like a tree and a mother who wouldn't stop asking about grandchildren. No, not children. Grand-*daughters*. She clenched her fist so hard that her nails left little crescent-moons in her palms. She didn't know how they didn't see it: that every girl born to their clan was just another extension on the very

201

long and very large loan that the Juggernaut had extended them, centuries ago.

"Hey. Babe. Try not to kill your family," Dez said before she left that morning, on their shit-stained front stoop in their fortified neighborhood. Lily had rolled her eyes at him; he was chuckling, more than even he knew he should have been. Sometimes he forgot about the weight they lived under. Then he added, "Be careful," with a pointed lift of the eyebrows, because most of the time, he remembered. She made him swear to call her the moment he heard from Hopeview—even if it was bad news—and then wrapped her scarf around her neck like a protective brace and went to her mother's waiting, growling Cadillac.

"You know I'm not getting any younger," said MJ, tapping her cigarette against the lip of the cracked-open window.

Lily sighed. "I told you, Mom. Dez and I are not taking that chance. We've got a good feeling about the new adoption agency, we think they could come through."

"But what about your amazing Twining blood?" Jada said from the backseat. Lily craned her neck to look back at her. Jada was twenty-five now, with singed black tips on the fringes of her tortured corn-yellow hair. Her arm was purple and pulsing from Jada's carving with the scratchy end of a ballpoint pen: *I Only Fuck G.* A boyfriend, Lily assumed.

"That blood can die with me," Lily replied. She could feel MJ's eyes burning a hole through the back of her head—this was why she wouldn't come over for dinner anymore.

"That's a fool's errand," said MJ. Her voice dropped by an octave, as it always did when she talked about the demon. MJ was now Artistic Director of *BarBarElla* and still this was true. The demon dwarfed all possible measures of human power. "It's never going to let you adopt some Chinese baby while you're still fertile. Are you kidding me?"

"Better than risking it," Lily muttered.

"Honey, there are ways to make sure you have a daughter. I told you, there's a way. You drink nothing but chamomile for the first month. You stay away from dogs…"

"That's just old wives' bullshit, Mom."

MJ had raised her voice again. "It worked with you!"

"It didn't work for Aunt Tess, did it?" It was a shitty thing to say to MJ and she knew it—knew that the punch had landed as soon as MJ's weather-beaten lips collapsed around her cigarette—but it was the easiest way to get out of a conversation she was utterly tired of.

"Sick burn," said Jada. She could be snide about it; she'd never known Tess, and certainly wasn't there when MJ and Caroline forced her into a bloody, panicked third-term abortion. Aunt Caroline had shielded her from all such unpleasantness—*don't want her to feel like a victim of her fate,* she said. And so after her annunciation rite first exposed Jada to violence, she had quickly, fervently reenacted the whole thing with her Barbie and Ken dolls, trying to get on the right side of power. Sixteen-year-old Lily had walked in on seven-year-old Jada smashing plastic against plastic, growling, "You're mine forever, you bitch!"

"Tess got lazy," said MJ. "Just like Salome. But I know *you'd* never let your guard down. You're smart."

Lily shrugged and turned up the radio. "It still wouldn't do anything for Dez's demon. Even if it's a girl, it might turn out like Bat Boy."

On their third date at Pho 25, Dez told her that a "horrible disease" ran in his family, and it wasn't safe for him to have biological children. By the halting way he said "safe," Lily knew he had a demon swimming in his blood too—perversely, this shared burden only made them fall in love faster. Like the Twinings, the Fishers of St. John's were born with a fifty-fifty chance of carrying their demon's strand—in their case, a feverish, red-eyed hunger and a full set of tiny shark teeth—but unlike the Juggernaut, the Fisher demon didn't care about sex. And un-like the Juggernaut, the Fisher demon had already been born—manifested, replicated, and then killed by a tearful family—a hundred meaningless times. All it wanted—so Dez said—was to remind the Fishers of the price of freedom, to chain them to its yoke forever; to make a mockery out of their slavery, because it was a goddamn *demon,* and awful that way.

"That's the funny thing," Dez said one night while they were drinking cheap beer on the roof of his apartment and contem-plating the terror of an incomprehensible universe where dead stars ate other dead stars. Lily used to wonder if there were de-mons like the Juggernaut in outer space, and eventually con-cluded that demons simply shadowed life, that there was a hell-plane that stretched as far as the intelligent could go. "We sign these pacts because we think there's no other way out. And only after do we realize what *no way out* really means."

"Well, that's not our responsibility," MJ sniffed. She had never liked Dez's family. She was too similar, Lily suspected, to Dez's own mother. The two women had passed each other at the wed-ding like a pair of crashing icebergs. "Don't those people have their own ways?"

And Dez's mother had never really liked Lily either. She had taken one glance at her and known that her womb was cursed. Lily didn't need to be psychic to read the look Mrs. Fisher gave her son across the table at Sunday brunch: *you couldn't have picked one that wasn't already busted up?*

"Don't worry about it, Lily. I'm pretty sure Jug would tear Dez's demon in half anyway." Jada sounded so proud of this possibility. Jada, and even MJ, had always found something *impressive* and *singular* about the Juggernaut that Lily couldn't understand. She couldn't derive pleasure from being associated with something apocalyptic. *No wonder you don't like nukes,* Dez said the first time she explained this. MJ said she was too up-tight; scared that power would bite her. Her jealous co-workers at Knox Gilbert would have a good laugh at that. "I just don't get why Jug needs to be born into a boy. Why does his vessel need to have a dick? Like, ugh. Why?"

"Probably the same reason Cady Twining had to make a deal with a monster in the first place," Lily snapped.

She heard Jada chortle deviously and she twisted in her seat to glare at the girl she used to babysit when Aunt Caroline need-ed to go on a bender; the girl who once pushed a bitch in her seventh-grade class down a flight of stairs using only her will, or so she claimed. Jada lifted her arm to show off what she had finished carving: *I Only Fuck God.*

"You both," MJ said with a nicotine-kissed sigh, "need to be grateful for what you got."

***

On the night before her seventh birthday, Lily was washed, dressed in a scratchy beige shift that smelled like moth balls and patchouli, and left alone in her grandmother's attic overnight. "Why can't I stay down here with you?" she asked her mother, who tensely smiled and petted her hair and said, "Because this is for big, brave girls." Lily assumed she was tense because she'd been fighting with Daddy.

Aunt Tess said that everybody would be just downstairs and then opened her mouth again as if to say something else, but then caught herself and didn't. Aunt Tess was so kind, so quiet. Then Aunt Caroline came down from the attic with a cigarette lighter in her hand and said, "Everything's ready," and her mother got a strange, mournful crinkle in her eye.

Lily knew, by then, about the Juggernaut—she had learned about him on her sixth birthday. He was like the Tooth Fairy, or Santa Claus, except he only visited their family and he could be very, very mean so she had to be very, very careful. But he did bring gifts. Invisible gifts, gifts you didn't know you'd received until after everything worked out. *What does he look like?* Lily remembered asking. *He's a shadow,* her mother said, and used her fingers to make a bunny head appear on the wall. And Lily reminded herself of *bunny ears* as she walked up the stairs, her heart threatening to burst out from her ribs, *just bunny ears on the wall.* But every step she took was a step closer to the thick anchor that she felt tethered around her waist, to the great pulsing darkness that lived in empty rooms and just beyond the porch light, the poisoned darkness that she sometimes saw overwhelm her mother and Aunt Tess and Aunt Caroline, the never-sleeping darkness that she now understood would drown her, too.

They sat her down in the center of a giant pentagram and closed the door and left her there, just as she was realizing that those "empty rooms" that she'd always been pulled back from had never been empty in the first place. He had been there. She recognized the feeling now. And the darkness wasn't really *dark,* either, not dark like the fragrant, animal-filled night. Dark like the abyss at the bottom of your stomach. Dark like bloodstains on carpet, like rotted teeth. Dark like she had never even imagined before.

A shadow floated up from behind an old dollhouse and got bigger and bigger as it circled the attic and finally settled on the broken wood planks straight across from her, as if the man casting the shadow—because it was a man, a very tall man, it had her father's broad shoulders—was standing right behind her. *"Hello, Lily,"* a deep voice like fresh hot candlewax whispered in her ear. She jerked uneasily, and she felt the air thicken up like mud around her, holding her still. Everyone had been very clear on this point: she wasn't to put up a fight. Some little girl that would have been her Great-Aunt Somebody had fought, way back when, and the demon had broken her the way concrete breaks a falling body. *"My, my, aren't you a pretty little girl."*

She thought she was going to die, and that was the truth. She didn't even have the strength to cry. The pain felt world-ending, the pressure so intense that she was sure she was going to break apart. The demon pulled her eyelids open and forced her to look at hell, though the only thing she would remember from the tour was the barren eternity of burning plains. At one point she realized she had a nosebleed, and then fainted; when she woke up the demon was gone, and she was in her grandmother's canopy bed. Bathed in a daylight that felt oddly false instead of reassuring, like those old photographs of dead people posed to look like they were just sleeping. She had the suspicion that she'd never feel alive again.

"I'm bleeding," was the first thing she said to her mother, who burst into tears and left the room. Aunt Tess came in with a bowl of ice cream and *Beauty and the Beast* on video. It had been her favorite movie—clever Belle, the dancing cutlery—but she had hated it ever since.

"Listen, sweetheart," said Aunt Tess, while Belle dodged the terrible Gaston, "there is a curtain around you. A big red theater curtain." She closed her eyes and thought of the Community Playhouse where they saw *A Christmas Carol* the year before. How excited she'd been to see those curtains billowing as if in giddy anticipation. "It's protecting you from him. If everyone follows the rules... that curtain will never be pulled. Do you understand?"

And so she told herself there was no end to that velvet

heaviness, no opening, no door. Just a sea of gently rippling red on which she could lay down her buoyant head, and rest.

***

Salome and her husband lived in a modest bungalow on the outskirts of a small town outside Sparta that never adjusted to the end of mining. Salome and Jesse met online when she was sixteen and got married as soon as it was legal. None of the Twinings had been invited to the wedding, neither the women nor their husbands, but they understood from Salome's extraordinarily weak-willed mother that it had taken place in a small country church, under the oversight of a real pastor and everything. Now they lived in a house decked with American flag pinwheels and red geraniums and for a moment Lily felt sorry that they were there at all. Maybe Salome just wanted to forget she was a Twining. Maybe she found religion. Maybe she thought the Abrahamic God—unlike the Juggernaut—would let her live the American dream.

"Look at this place," MJ said, snorting derisively at the tender woodcut welcome sign: God Bless This House. She rang the doorbell and the house responded with a tinny round of "Take Me Out to the Ball Game." "The gift's been clearly wasted on this girl."

"It's not a *gift,*" Lily hissed.

MJ opened her mouth to respond—they'd had enough fights on the subject, Lily could already choreograph the entire argument—but then the boy who had to be Jesse came to the front door and glared at them with the suspicion of a thrice-beaten dog. He was handsome, sullen, with tempest clouds in his blue eyes. No surprise that he would be Salome's type; he had probably done a tour in the war.

They weaseled their way in with a candy gift basket and the soothing promise of heartfelt congratulations. Jesse was protective but stupid, and he let them in. Just like he had let the demon bed down under his roof. He probably didn't even know it was there, though they felt it from the moment they stepped inside: the air was oily, and smelled of rotten eggs.

In the living room, an old man who Jesse identified as his father was watching the Cherokees game, nearly welded to his chair. A speckled mutt curled around his feet perked up when the Twining women entered. MJ shot Lily a look—*See? Didn't stay away from dogs*—and Lily had to suppress a groan. "It's all right, boy," said the old man, with a serrated edge to his voice that indicated All Right was the last thing this was.

Jesse took them upstairs and Lily held her breath. The whole drive down, she had imagined this moment—Salome standing by the window, stroking her newly rounded belly, a beam of sunshine crowning the new mother and the innocent life she carried with the angelic, dull-witted purity of a shy Madonna in a Flemish painting. Salome would beg, like Aunt Tess had begged, that maybe the baby would turn out all right, even if it was a boy. Doubt and guilt and naked envy would rear up and prevent her from doing what needed to be done. Instead the desire to throw caution to the wind—not just for Salome, but for herself—would roll in like a West Coast fog. And then, the world would end.

But she needn't have worried. There were no cherubs to crush, no bluebirds to shoot. Salome was knitting a tiny yellow something but that yarn was the only light in the room. The expectant mother herself was engulfed in a cloud that was not new, not tender, not full of possibility, but ancient. Rancid. She was so pale and thin under the weight of that quaking boulder in her stomach that it was unbelievable she hadn't been hospitalized.

When she saw her estranged family, she hissed out a labored breath and clenched her knitting needles in warning.

Jesse went to prop her up, mumbling that she'd had a difficult pregnancy, so the doctors had put her on bedrest. "Poor thing," said MJ, showing off her teeth. "Say, Jesse. You don't mind if we girls talk alone for a moment, do you? I'm sure your pops could use some company."

Jesse swallowed and a little frown grazed his jaw, probably because he hadn't been holed up here in this coffin-for-a-room in the first place. And who could blame him? *Men never stay,* MJ used to say, usually with a bottle of Merlot and Billie Holiday. *It's because they can all sense when there's a bigger dog in the house.* Lily chewed the inside of her cheek, thinking of the exceptions—her father, Dez (she believed, she trusted, she had to)—and meanwhile, Jesse kissed his little demon-possessed wife on the forehead and left with his tail tucked between his legs.

Jada kicked the door shut after him and said, "You look like shit, Salome."

And so Salome did, for a lot of reasons. After generations of Twining women had become pilots, computer engineers, lawyers—even one groundbreaking deep-sea diver—pallid Salome did seem to have wasted the gifts that the demon had first promised Cady Twining. Salome bared her teeth—her gums were bleeding, no doubt decaying under the pressure of the incinerator she was incubating. "I don't want to see any of you. Get the fuck out. Right now!"

MJ held up one carefully manicured finger, peeling her eyelids back in a primitive, vulpine scare tactic that probably would have worked on Jesse or Bryce, but barely affected Salome. She was still a Twining girl after all. And pregnant with the Juggernaut, at that. "You know why we're here. To deal with this little situation you've gotten yourself into. That *thing* in your stom-

ach. Now don't worry, I've got some special pills doctored up…"
Lily winced as MJ rifled around in her purse, thinking again of
Aunt Tess—the blood, the knife, the flailing legs held down by
white knuckles, MJ screaming, *There's no time!*—"But you need
to take them right away. No more dilly-dallying."

Salome immediately slapped the pills out of her hand. Sighing,
Lily sank to the floor and grappled for them under the bowed
marital bed—grimacing when her fingers came away coated in
a cold, grimy, tangible malice—like a thousand ghostly baby
hands pressing through a fragile womb. She put the two pink
triangles back in MJ's palm and said, "This isn't a joke, Salome."

"Who's laughing?" Salome's veiny bug eyes turned to her, as
if she wasn't sure—who *was* that ashy blonde in the blue trench
coat? "You're the ones trying to kill my son." She laid a protective clamp of a hand over her stomach and softened her voice to
the sing-song trill of a younger girl hosting a tea party. "But he'll
never let you. Now that he's so close to being born."

Inside her belly, the baby—the Juggernaut's long-delayed human vessel, the only thing he had asked Cady Twining for all
those years ago when he swam across Spirit Lake and into her
desperate, destitute arms—seemed to buck up in approval. Salome let out a small grunt of pain that she tried to disguise, and
Lily thought she saw an opening. She dove for Salome's clammy
wrist and tried to squeeze some life into it, some blood. Some
resistance. "You have no idea what harm he would do to the
world if he had a vessel," she whispered, shaking the limp hand.
She was trying to impart to her compassion, and empathy, trying to make that lumbering heart beat for something outside of
herself and the Juggernaut. "But you know what he can do to us,
and that's from behind the veil."

"So what? I don't care." Salome's wrist slipped away. "He won't
hurt *me*. He chose *me*."

Envy in the form of a different arrow struck Jada, who shrieked, "You dumb bitch! He didn't choose you! He's being forced into your stupid baby because nobody else was dumb enough to have a boy!" And before anyone knew it, Jada had scraped the pills out of MJ's hand and was trying to force them down Salome's throat. MJ pushed her weight onto the girl as soon as she realized what was happening, and screamed at Lily, *"Hold her down!"* Just like MJ and Aunt Caroline had held Aunt Tess down and sliced her and the baby open with a—

Lily flinched. She froze. And it wasn't fifteen seconds later that Jesse came bounding into the room like a big loyal labrador and practically threw Jada into a dresser.

Pills went bouncing across the carpet and eagle-eyed Jesse— no doubt he'd grown up shooting, him and Big Daddy Bryce— was the first to spot them. He didn't wait for an explanation. He didn't have to. He threw the women a stormy look and then marched out of the room, taking the pills with him. Jada and MJ went hurrying after him. All three were yelling, violently grappling with each other with a familiarity that other families would have reserved for maybe twenty years down the line.

Lily stayed behind. That bathroom was too small for three, she told herself, although a niggling possibility scratched at the back of her mind that perhaps she was just too weak. Too passive. Cooper and Steve certainly said so when she was named Managing Partner: *she has no leadership skills, she's not a doer.* She heard the toilet flush and a string of profanities erupt from MJ, and when she looked back at Salome, the devil's surrogate was panting and staring at the ceiling with eyes glazed over with rapt admiration. Love. A trickle of saliva dribbled down her pale neck. Then a shadow moved across the ceiling, like a roof closing over the world, and the door whipped shut.

"Fuck," Lily whispered, and the red theater curtain that had kept the Juggernaut at bay started to move. Of course some-times in years past it had trembled—when she was coaxed into playing with a Ouija board in high school, when she tried to sever her familial bond in college, when she met Dez—but now it was *moving*, spinning on its track… opening, Lily realized.

Beyond the cage of the bedroom, they could hear Jesse shout-ing, his meek voice barely able to worm through both wood and Juggernaut: "Honey? You okay? I can't get the door open!"

Tears of joy streamed down Salome's face as she reached up to the shadow that was reaching back down to her, saying *La-La-Love You!* "I told you, he loves me!"

"What? Sal?"

As Salome tilted her face up for a kiss from the bending shad-ow that was pouring like molasses out of the ceiling, Lily tried to say, "She's not talking to you," but with the curtains rushing open for the world's most special opening night, no sound es-caped her at all.

***

Lily's parents fought a lot. Over breakfast, on car rides, through-out Christmas. Lily became very good at picking a distant point on the horizon and focusing on it so intently that she could block out everything else. But while other sixth-graders' parents fought over dishes and secretaries and vacations taken and not-taken, Lily's parents fought over the Juggernaut: the great grinning shadow that loomed over their lives like a circling vulture. Her father hated the Juggernaut. That, Lily remembered. It always boiled down to the fact that he didn't understand.

"I don't understand how you can live with yourself knowing what that *thing* has done to her."

Lily curled into herself on the couch, wishing he hadn't brought that up. *Satan's Brides,* the neighbor lady had called them, and when her mother sneered Lily knew the neighbor lady was right. Like that horrible movie she'd accidentally watched with the blonde lady who couldn't stop stabbing herself in the stomach while a chorus of people in animal masks danced around her. *Satan's Bride in The House of Sin!* She closed her eyes and willed herself to think of Aunt Tess's curtain, the big red gapless theater curtain like a pacific, silent sea of blood.

"How can *I* live with myself? Oh, I don't know. Maybe the same way my mother and my sister and every other goddamn Twining woman has lived with it since 1679!" Her mother was holding a wine glass like it was a butcher knife, and flailing it vaguely at her father. "Maybe you should ask how *you* can live with yourself, because you knew full well what you were getting into! So spare me the self-righteous Puritan bullshit!"

Her father scoffed and slammed the dishwasher shut. "I thought you were part of a New Age thing, Marjorie. Like a prosperity religion or something. Not a goddamn demonic harem!"

Her mother jerked back as if that word *harem* had smacked her in the face. Her voice sank to an awful, razor-wire whisper. "You think this is the life I want for myself? For her?"

"I don't know, Marjorie. You don't seem to put up much of a fight against that filth."

For a second, everything went dark—the lights, the television, the clock on the stove that marked the time as 9:28 PM. After the length of a half-breath, it all came back to life—the ring-a-ding-ding of the game show she'd been watching, the hum of the refrigerator. And then Lily looked down at *The Crucible* to see that the page she'd been reading had been torn nearly out of its spine. She shouted, "Mom!" but both her parents were frozen like ceramic lawn-deer, glancing from one ceiling corner to the other. "Shush," her mother was whispering. "Wait."

They waited, barely breathing, for about two minutes. And then her father took a big breath and said, "No." Lily widened her eyes; no one had ever said *no* to the demon. "I've had it. We are not going to waste one more second of our lives enslaved by a demon. Period." He started walking toward the couch, reaching out his hand to her, even while her mother stayed paralyzed near the cupboards, screaming, *"John, wait!"* Lily looked up into her father's soft cow-eyes, his trembling brow, and reasoned that she had never seen him look so frightened. "Come on, baby. We're getting out of here."

She did reach out her hand. To comfort him, if nothing else. But before their fingers could touch, her father suddenly went flying backward, skyward, like a trapeze artist swinging away into the peak of a circus tent. He slammed into the ceiling and just stayed there—*poor Daddy!*—arms outstretched like a butterfly in a spider's web with his face somehow dark, veiled.

Lily screamed. Her mother fell to the ground and begged, "Please don't hurt him! He didn't mean anything by it! He's sorry, I promise he's sorry!"

The television screen distorted with a buzz of static and Lily screamed again as the top of the game show host's head disappeared, leaving only a flickering, gaping mouth. "He's had it, Marjorie!" the game show host growled, but his jaw flapped like he was laughing. "And I've just about had it with this punk too! And now for the million-dollar question..."

Her mother kept screaming, *"He's sorry!"* and Lily was screaming it too, trying to help, but the Juggernaut didn't care. Of course he didn't care. He dropped her father from the ceiling with such force that Lily could hear every bone break—with such force that the tile floor caved.

***

All night, her dreams had been bad. She had stayed up the night
before talking to Dez—no word from the adoption agency, but
he wasn't worried, no!—and as she crossed the upstairs landing
on her way to the house's only bathroom, she had overheard
Bryce and Jesse whispering downstairs, under the drone of the
post-game report:

"They're witches. They're here for the baby. Probably to sacrifice it to the Devil."

"Then what the hell do we do? Call the reverend?"

"Hell, no. They'd eat Reverend Foley alive."

And so all night she had burned at the stake, hung by a noose,
drowned in a river; died again and again at the hands of her
neighbors. And each time, the Juggernaut—two feet taller than
her tormentors, cloaked, and crowned with a shining halo of
spines—had come weaving through the jeering crowd like an eel
and purred, "Let me in, *bay-bee.*"

She woke up exhausted and angry, boxed in by walls pa-
pered with laughing babies and watering cans. She checked her
phone—no new messages—and went downstairs to try to convince Jesse that his sweet little jailbait wife was pregnant with—
what, now? *Antichrist* was what MJ settled on last night, saying
they had to use terms Jesse would understand.

"I still say you should help me channel Jug," Jada whispered.
She was hovering by the stairs, on the borderlands of the living
room where MJ and Jesse were trying, supposedly, to talk. Her
big raccoon eyes were blinking nervously, like a scavenger caught
in the trash. "I know I can control him. Better than some stupid
baby, anyway. Come on, Lily. Aunt MJ won't listen to me."

For just a moment, Lily allowed herself to imagine it. Jada
would take the Juggernaut into herself, her psychic skeleton
being strong enough to cage him, and free them all from his

terrible weight. She might turn into the strongest witch in the modern era—she might transcend the mortal plane. MJ would never have to do another intervention. And as for Lily... she closed her eyes and saw herself with Dez, walking a heavily-bundled toddler under Whistler Park's maple trees in the fall, their own beautiful curly-haired, blue-eyed child. Longing filled her, stretched her out like a medieval rack. She squeezed a few tears away and saw Jada smiling with an anticipation that felt fiendish. All that girl had ever wanted was to ride the dragon. No, to steer him. Her monster, her *Jug*. The insanity of the desire quickly reminded Lily of its futility. Jada was a matador who'd been gored by a bull and promptly decided to join the rodeo. But that bull, that cosmic minotaur, would never be ridden.

"*Jug*' doesn't want you," Lily snapped. For a second Jada looked like a little girl in her mother's makeup—unwanted, clownish, lost. "You're nothing to him. You're just an incubator." A dull phantom pain shot up where the Juggernaut had first branded her. She wanted to say that this was the true reason she had to adopt: that even though she'd forgiven MJ for having her, she would never forgive herself if she imposed this pain upon some other innocent little girl. But she saw the curtains swishing like the sly wagging of the Devil's tail, and didn't.

"I've been practicing..."

"How? Thumb-wrestling Bloody Mary?"

"Ugh. You know what your problem is?" Neurosis, her therapist would have said. Fear of intimacy. High levels of anxiety. Common among trauma victims. *Are you sure you don't want to talk about it? Yes.* "You're too scared to even try to change anything!"

Lily thought about pleading her case—she graduated Summa Cum Laude, she was Managing Partner, she was *accomplished!*— but the little punk went running upstairs in her clunky hightops and slammed a door. Lily sighed.

Under a lamp covered with folksy roosters and wheelbarrows, the woman from the city and the boy from the country stared at each other over the still sky of a dormant snow globe. Lily recognized her mother's body language—the arched eyebrows, the tilted head, the leisurely crossed legs—it was her mastery of that look, as if she was in total control of the moon and the tides, that crowned her queen of the coven after Great Aunt Nance died. The fact that it was pretense—a tight lid to cover a pot that was always at full boil—used to drive Lily crazy. "You're so full of bullshit!" she would scream. "Everything about you is a lie!" But looking at her now, intently pushing and prodding at Jesse's eyes, somehow it wasn't so bad.

"Just think about it, Jesse." The words poured out of her mouth like liquid silk, and Jesse—eyes to the electrical bill—didn't see MJ raise her eyebrow conspiratorially at Lily. Despite the pressure of their situation—the pregnant jackal upstairs, the burden of life in a glimmering soap bubble—Lily had to smile. "That thing Salome is carrying is putting her life in danger. It's a monster. I know you feel it when you're near her. You know there's something very wrong."

Jesse paused, and Lily could see his gaze bounce from table to doorway to popcorn ceiling, where a large muddy stain was spreading under the weight of the marital bed. "Where's your proof," Jesse said, his voice crackling. "The doctor says every-thing's fine."

"There hasn't been a boy born to our family since before the Revolution."

"Salome always wanted a boy," whispered Jesse. "Said she wanted to give me a son."

"She's afflicted," MJ said. "She doesn't know what she's saying. What she's... *invited.*"

But Lily remembered young Salome. She remembered finding

twelve-year-old Salome listlessly smoking a Marlboro as a boy who had to be old enough to join the military pushed her in a park swing. *Creak creak* by the half-light. Salome had stared absently at the darkening sky as the grown boy delicately pulled her long fishtail braid, tilting her head back toward his belt buckle. On the walk back to Aunt Dorothy's house, Lily asked her if she was all right, and what had Salome said? "Just thinking about plane crashes. The fireball. The fall." A little smile had played at her glossy, fuchsia lips. "Humans are so proud of themselves, but they're nothing. I can't wait for them to see just how small they are, when the world ends."

Her phone beeped. It was Dez. *L, can you talk?* "Fucking damn it," Lily whispered, because she knew it couldn't be good. She knew Dez. If it was good news, he'd have sent her a bunch of baby emoticons. Jesse was still protesting, protecting his wife and what he thought was his unborn child, when she hurried through the kitchen and stepped out into the humid, cicada-infested warmth, letting the half-broken, cobwebbed screen door bang shut behind her.

"What happened?" she asked, before he could even say "Hello." She heard a deep sigh from the other end. "Hopeview called." "And?"

"I'm sorry, babe. They denied our application."

This time, they hadn't even bothered to give them an explanation. And they had heard it all: from bullshit concerns about giving a baby to an interracial couple, to legitimate concerns about her father's violent death, and the seeming prevalence of SIDS in his family.

"My mom's right," she said, crossing her arm against her suddenly knotted stomach. "He'll never let us have this."

"We'll keep trying," he insisted, but he sounded tired. "Is everything okay there?"

Birds flew overhead; dogs barked in the distance. A thousand insects burrowed through a thousand holes, constantly consuming. "Okay as they'll ever be."

She walked back into the house feeling sorry for herself, contemplating telling her mother that they should just leave Salome and Jesse and *the world* to their fate—and then froze, because Jesse was standing now and whaling on something with a signed Cherokees baseball bat. Something dressed in black. Something blonde. Her mother. Marjorie. Before she could think about how much blood was leaking onto the hardwood floors, before she could even scream, Lily had grabbed the snow globe and hit Jesse with it, right between the exposed tag of his T-shirt and his mop of dirty blond hair. She hadn't been trying to hurt him, not really. She'd just been trying to stop that up-down swing of the baseball bat. But by the crack that rattled through him and the suddenness with which he dropped the bat, she knew she had.

Jesse fell on top of her mother, his forehead hitting the floor with a loud, unsettling thump. She heard a grunt and then a familiar voice, right in her ear, like a wasp digging in search of a host: *I always liked the taste of you.*

She jolted as if tasered and dropped the bloody snow globe. Instead she crumpled down toward her mother, mumbling "Mom?" to the eyes that were now open and oxidizing and filled with blood, hoping violently that she was still somehow alive. But the nest of hair that her mother always kept diligently dyed—ColorCharm 40, Gentlemen Prefer Blondes—was soaked through. Wet crimson. And a blackness beneath it. The same color seeping slowly from her lips. "Mom?" Lily's hands hovered over the body, held back by the prickle of a psychic force field: that barrier all animals know, between the living and the dead. "Mom?"

Then there was the sound of keys struggling in a lock, and the front door being pushed open, and someone shouting into the house, "Jesse? You home?"

Lily couldn't move as Jesse's father, the one who said the Twining witches would eat Reverend Foley alive, shambled his way into the kitchen and laid eyes on the still lump of flesh that was now his son. Old man Bryce's stone face melted for just a second as Lily saw him remember his boy's first steps, first words, first home run in Little League under an unseasonably warm April sun. And then that softness firmed up again as the old man realized, as we all do, that the only salvation for pain is anger. He started yelling with tears in his eyes, asking her just what she thought she had done, reaching for something on his belt—oh, a gun.

"He was attacking..."—*killing killing killing*—"my mother."

But Bryce was mad with sorrow. He didn't need eyes to see as he pointed the gun at her face, his mouth dribbling, *"what did you do what did you do"* like a broken cuckoo clock. Lily bent her head toward the congealing crater in her mother's head, then shut her eyes. She was waiting for the end, but instead of a bang there was only his breathing: unsteady, belabored. Had Bryce changed his mind? Seen her kneeling like a devout supplicant on the floor and realized killing her wouldn't bring his boy back? She opened her eyes and saw Bryce pointing the gun at the kitchen lamp, at the roosters and wheelbarrows. Big globules of sweat were seeping out of his skin. His eyelids were pulled back in shock though his eyes themselves were dead, flat, slammed against something they couldn't comprehend. That absolute fear superseded any sadness for his son, even any anger toward Lily. Truly, it superseded old man Bryce himself.

Jada was behind him, fingers stretched wide, big raccoon eyes staring not at the little piece of black phallic metal but at his head—at the little fleshy part of his brain that was trying, and failing, to resist her silent shout. Her eyelashes flickered, her jaw twitched from side to side. Whimpering slightly, Bryce started turning his wrist, barrel of the gun now peeking shyly at his own receding hairline.

Lily whispered, *"Jada, no!"* because she could feel everything unraveling, the whole living room tipping toward a cliff that would leave her and Jada covered in blood and howling at the moon, digging through the dirt on all fours—succumbing to the demon's madness was only ever one slice away, and the Juggernaut's silent shout was always the loudest of them all.

Jada huffed and nodded hard, like a child trying to tug a tooth loose. Bryce brought the butt of the gun crashing down against his temple and fell on the floor, moaning as he kept hitting himself—right between the eyes, both hands now, with feeling!—tears coming now from pain. Jada was making a whinnying noise between a laugh and a sob, staring at her murderous hands. But Lily could only lean down toward her mother Marjorie and softly, very softly stroke her hair.

***

Lily's mother was single for four years after her father died. She was focusing on her child, she told her friends, focusing on the career she needed to provide for that child. But really she just didn't want to bury anyone else. "You I can protect," she'd whisper when she thought Lily was asleep. "Just you." But then she met Bill Blythe at the Crystal Hare and decided that maybe Bill would be able to take care of himself. He was part of the local Pagan community, but like Lily's mother he hovered on the fringes, a quiet eclectic. He was self-trained, composed, educated. Lily wanted to hate him, but didn't. He'd call her "young lady." He'd shake her hand.

Their apartment was waging a losing battle against a rat infestation so they moved in with Bill, whose house was very clean and covered in masks. Then one afternoon Lily came down from her new room that always, somehow, smelled of warm, moist earth, and saw only Bill sitting on the couch, watching a red candle burn. "Your mother went out for groceries," he said, and patted the cushion. "Come here. I want to talk to you."

She came over. He had always been nice to her. A few weird comments here and there about how her awkward short skirts weren't very classy. But on the couch that afternoon his eyes were lit with a flame that could kill. His hand landed on her denim-wrapped thigh and she barely heard him as he said, "You know you're very special, don't you?"

Of course she knew, by then, that she was special. "Lily Twining's just so special," this girl Sara Hofstein used to say, because their English teacher always picked her essays to read aloud, because she always got A's in Physics. She felt bad about it, especially since it was all the demon's doing. Her mother tried to tell her that wasn't so, that she was smart all on her own and the demon just cleared the path for her—but then she thought of Justin Cho's model rocket blowing up in his face during the outdoor science fair, blinding him for life, and wanted to die.

Then he asked her if she had ever had sex. No. Did she want to? No. Then he smirked, said, "Don't you know how powerful you are?" and lunged at her. Lily scrambled away, throwing everything she could at him—a magazine, a coaster, one of his horrible pouting wooden masks—and when he followed her into the kitchen, saying he just wanted her to reach her full glorious potential, didn't she want to help bring a *God* into the world?—she threw a bottle of extra virgin olive oil. It hit him right in the head but he didn't even register it; barely grimaced. Then her mother came home and went crazy and after trying to kill Bill they packed their stuff and left. The whole drive to the highway-side motel, Lily silently worried that the demon had found a way through the curtain by conducting Bill like a marionette, or at least helping him along, laying out a path of breadcrumbs, saying *here, here, right here.*

While her mother yelled on the phone—not at Bill, who she'd never speak to again, but at Aunt Caroline, Aunt Beth, Great-Aunt Shelby, the other women who weren't technically Lily's aunts but may as well have been—Lily went out to the empty motel pool and fiddled with her phone, trying to care about her classmates' cafeteria drama but unable to think about anything other than the trigger-happy Juggernaut, who crouched in empty rooms.

She typed in *help cursed by demon* and scrolled past most of the suggestions—One Prayer to Cast Out All Demons, and How to Know If You've Been Hoodooed. She clicked on Understanding Generational Curses but it was all about the Bible. But then finally, she found the thing she hadn't known she was looking for: MysticXOXO, a "support community for those suffering from paranormal and psychic afflictions—XX only!" There was a lot of purple font on black backgrounds, a lot of gothic angels crying glitter-blood, and there was a forum.

She watched one of the intro videos. A scrawny purple-haired girl in a brightly-lit bedroom pulled aside the collar of her band T-shirt to show what looked like choke marks on her neck. *"My name is Tori. I'm fourteen. I'm from Tampa. Every day I wake up like this. Sometimes I feel like I'm on the very edge of losing my sanity. And I'm afraid it's only gonna get worse."*

An Asian girl kept her eyes fixed on something hidden, something off-camera. *"My name is Caitlin. I'm fifteen years old. There's a black shadow that follows me. I see him everywhere."*

There were other girls, she realized. Other girls like her. Which meant there were other Juggernauts, or things that had become Juggernauts, and the thought might have sent her into a psych ward if not for the fact that those other girls were surviving. They were, somehow, alive.

Please post a video introduction so we can get to know you.

She opened her camera app and clicked the video function. She saw herself, distorted, eye sockets swollen with lack of sleep, drugstore mascara smeared. She tried to smudge the residue away before hitting the red record button. "My name is Lily. I'm sixteen. I'm... I'm from outside Herrod City." That was all going to change soon. Her mother said they had to move. Somewhere quieter. "A woman in my family made a bargain with a demon, hundreds of years ago. I'm terrified that he's going to come and collect what we owe him, after all this time."

After she posted it, an influx of messages came pouring in: hearts and XOXOs and lipstick kisses. *Stay strong, girl. Believe in yourself. There is a light inside you that he can NEVER put out.* There was a real strength amid their mania, a real self-assuredness that couldn't possibly have come from anything other than their own rituals and mythologies and the cold hard fact that they were still breathing, despite the flying dishware. Maybe it made her cocky. Maybe sleep deprivation had finally cost her all reason. Whatever it was, she ended up screaming into the night, "You are not going to hurt me! Do you hear me? You are not going to hurt me!"

The stars were silent. She heard cars and her heartbeat and something else—coyotes?—in the distance but not the Juggernaut's deep breaths like blacksmith bellows. Surely he would have responded by now to such a taunt. She turned, thinking for one audacious second, then another, that perhaps this act of defiance had set her free. "Mom?" she called. "Mom, come out here!"

And then a wind—a minor hurricane—rose up beneath her feet and threw her into the pool. Water rushed into her and held her down on the turquoise tiles, musing softly as it churned into her ear, *you said you'd do anything for me Lily so open up buttercup*. The dull perimeter lights above started to fade as pressure closed around her head like a vise and she imagined them to be distant planets of the solar system, not traveling in orbit but hanging dead like Christmas ornaments, captured by a crooked unseen force. I really am dying, she thought. Oh well.

And then she saw her mother. Leaning over the warbling edge, her face shadowed but her lion's mane glowing golden. Crashing through the water. Prying under the Juggernaut's hold… finger by finger. Making the planets spin again.

***

They tied up Bryce and shoved him in the bed of his truck. Then they buried MJ and Jesse in the backyard with a shovel they pried out of a weather-beaten shed. Lily kept insisting on digging deeper, wider, so it took all afternoon. Luckily the backyard was hemmed in by hedges of untamed boxwood, and the neighbors all seemed to be out, or perhaps just dead. Afterward they sat overlooking the two rectangles of dirt that they'd tried to sloppily cover with patches of lawn, Jada weaving together three blades of grass, Lily picking at her cuticles.

"You got good at that telekinesis thing. Last I saw you were just knocking over coffee cups to make your mom mad."

Jada snorted. "Well, you got good at your fancy Wall Street thing, too."

The sudden unbidden vision of MJ smirking with pride leapt into Lily's head. All the women of her mother's generation—Aunt Caroline, even Aunt Tess—saw a measure of worldly redemption in the mess they were in. They were the sort of women who forced stone lemons to yield blood lemonade. They were used to tying things together to make them whole: half-assed, duct-taped, good enough. *Be grateful for what you've got,* MJ snarled when Lily fantasized about dropping out of college, and though she never spelled out what that "what" was, she didn't have to. It was the Juggernaut. If nothing else, they had the Juggernaut.

"Why did Salome do this?" she couldn't help asking. "Why is she trying to bring him into the world?"

Jada shrugged. "Because she wants the world to end."

"But why does she want the world to end?"

"I don't know. Because the world sucks."

For a long minute, they watched a small drone rise above a distant tree-line, whirring noisily, tilting unevenly, as neighborhood boys yelled for control. Finally, Jada said: "She was obsessed with footage of the Challenger going down, you know. Soaring, and then... falling. I think he showed it to her. While he was..." She trailed off briefly; a sharp pain welled up behind Lily's eyes. Sometimes glimpses of hell still smacked her consciousness, always at the strangest of times—just this flash of a red lunar crater and an enormous black volcano vomiting a sky of endless ash, while waiting at a crosswalk with a thousand other well-dressed corporate ants. "She asked me about it when she was seven. I found a video online. She must have played it twenty times. She probably figures, if you're going down, hey. May as well be in the driver's seat."

Under Jada's stare, the drone started sputtering. Its lights blinked out and it went careening toward the trees with a mechanical moan—the boys manning it screamed in anguish. *Man proposes, Witch disposes,* as MJ would have said. She glanced at Jada, who truly was powerful—one of the most impressive wielders of psychic energy Lily had ever met—and who'd make a formidable host for the Juggernaut, if the Juggernaut would have her. She expected Jada to be grinning like a mischievous fox after the drone's defeat, but her gaze was blank.

"Come on," Jada said, brushing off her jeans. "Let's go see how that bitch is doing."

That bitch was half-dead in the bedroom, staring dully at the ceiling and whispering strings of poisonous little words—consume, she was saying, consume me—as her mountainous stomach shifted back and forth. Lily put a cold cloth on her forehead and Salome started to sing, though her tissue-paper-thin voice kept breaking, tearing into fragments: "Look upon me... all day... with... thine eyes..."

"Lily. Look."

Jada was standing by the window, having pulled back the faded curtain to reveal a suddenly-darkened world. Ashen storm clouds had moved in at visible speed from over the mountain and brought fists-full of lightning with them. "He's here," Jada said. A look of adrenaline-crazed excitement worked its way like a spasm across her face—she was an Amazon, a Valkyrie. With a rare wild grin, Jada squeezed the window sill and said, "Let me try this."

Cold horror slid down Lily's throat. She nearly tripped following Jada down the stairs, but the whole house seemed to be folding and creasing like an origami crane. Afraid to let go of the wall, she stumbled through the kitchen and saw Jada in the backyard, holding her hands up to the lightning storm as if daring it to choose her, to enter her, to live through her. She heard Salome's triumphant voice shrieking in the brittle, breaking leaves—"He loves me!"

White lights lit up the dark tent that shrouded them like the strobe flashes on Saturday nights at The Cobweb, that downtown club with the vampire-themed drinks. She reached the open back door. Loose dirt was levitating in the air. The grass was a roiling vortex around Jada. "Jada, get back here!"

"I can do this, Lily!" As if they were still talking about shooting down drones. But this was how they had always fought: insistent, ugly, right-to-the-gut. *I know Jada's a bit of a pill,* MJ said after their third consecutive knock-down-drag-out over Thanksgiving dinner when Jada wouldn't stop quoting The Exorcist. Lily snapped at her that this wasn't a game and the Juggernaut killed innocent people, and Aunt Caroline hissed for everyone to please stop saying his name. *But she's young. She doesn't understand what all this really is. She needs your help.*

"It isn't safe!" Bad move, Jada didn't care about safe. She tried again: "He's already chosen a host!"

"My Lord!" Jada shouted. "See me, your servant, as I see you! Live in me! Sheath me in your glory!"

No guts, no glory. Five whip-snap lightning snakes raced across the sky, rushing toward a central point of convergence above the crown of Jada's head. Jada spread her fingers and braced her high-tops to absorb the force, but this was not a gift. There would be no coronation. Lightning burst less like a snake and more like a spear, bypassing Jada's waiting hands and blasting straight through her head. Through the thunder the Juggernaut roared, *Burn! The! Witch!* and Lily thought she could hear Jada screaming but really, it was her own throat that was raw.

The smell of burned flesh was so thick that Lily had to retreat into the house and retch into her hand, flecks of saliva mixing with tears. For several minutes she stayed slumped in the dark breakfast nook that still reeked, despite the Lysol, of blood and death. Then she heard an anguished cry from the upstairs bedroom.

What could she hope to do against the Juggernaut's machinations? Nothing. She should have gotten in MJ's car and driven away. But there was a human plea in Salome's voice that she couldn't ignore. And there was a blood-beat in her veins drumming that someone had to witness this moment. Someone had to watch as the terms of Cady Twining's ancient contract—made under duress, yes, but a promise made with the Devil is a promise kept—were finally fulfilled.

Lily forced herself to move. She'd make a good mother. She knew it.

Salome was sitting up in bed, straining against the baby. As soon as Lily laid eyes on her she wanted to scream the foulest curses in the canon, because Salome was finally lucid. Her eyes were glimmering, her chin warbling, her cheeks flushed with fever. She looked not a day older than her nineteen years, and she was scared. She was showing it. Of course—the baby, *Juggernaut Junior,* was now digging its way out. Expelling itself. Letting her go. But judging by the red flood between her legs, it was going to be too late.

Lily crept up to her, trying not to look at her imploding belly. "Salome," she whispered, but would Salome even remember her? Prudish, prissy Cousin Lily, who went away to the East Coast for college and then became a corporate slave? "It's gonna be okay."

"Where's Jesse?" Shit. Lily glanced at the wedding picture on the bedside table—the couple was leaning against a hay bale, Jesse resting his forehead against his wife's temple in deference, in love, in gratitude, as Salome's pretty red mouth dropped open in mid-laugh—and her head started to pound. *Bang bang* as she raised the snow globe and brought it down on Jesse's brainstem, *bang bang* as Jesse raised the baseball bat and brought it down on her mother's skull, *bang bang* as the Space Shuttle Challenger launched from Cape Canaveral and then fell, to the cries of the crowd, into the Atlantic Ocean.

"He had to go get something." Lily tried to smile. "For the baby. He'll be right back."

Salome nodded, still weeping, and then threw her head back and screamed again. Screamed like she was being taken apart. Lily could think of nothing else to do but kneel, her face against the mattress, and let Salome squeeze her hand. Eventually both the squeezing and the screaming stopped, and Lily looked up and saw that Salome was no longer breathing. Her eyes were half-open, her gentle gaze cast forever downward and her lips forever parted—at last, she was a Madonna.

And from the end of the bed there came the most terrible sound, like a baby's cry spliced with a death rattle, and then the wet noise of flesh sliding against flesh. Lily searched for the red curtains that had encased her since she was seven and did not find them—there was only the empty stage now, waiting impatiently for the main act to arrive. In this moment the demon's mark became an anchor inside her womb that forced her to look—*Look upon me all day with thine eyes!*—with Cady's eyes, shared by all Twining women: blue and sad and questioning.

From between Salome's dead knees, a toddler-sized baby—if that monster could be called a baby—crawled of its own volition out of Salome's body, heaving itself up by tiny-muscled arms and ripping forcefully through her skin. It looked up at her mid-howl and grinned with a creeping, complex malice that even childless Lily knew would have been beyond any normal infant of any species. It was the Juggernaut made flesh, and as she saw when it wiggled forward, definitely a boy.

"Hi Lily," the Juggernaut said, sounding like a baby with advanced smoker's lung, "I've been waiting so long to meet you." An infernal, cackle-like giggle as a thin, serpentine tongue reached out to lap up the natal blood cloaking its face. She could tell he was going to be beautiful when he grew up—which was probably going to be in the next few days, if not hours. "You look just like Cady. Your meat is very pretty."

Lily ran. She thought about starting a fire, but panic won out, and besides, she didn't know if the Juggernaut might not just lick up the flames like mother's milk. As she grabbed her mother's purse she heard a thump from upstairs. Something had fallen to the floor. By the time she peeled out of the gravel driveway in her mother's Cadillac and glanced in the rearview mirror, the Juggernaut was standing in the middle of the road, as tall as young bluestem grass. Eyes glowing golden like an animal in the dark. Watching her go.

***

Lily hated The Cobweb, but Dez thought it was a fun place—anything that involved "normies" playing with "the dark side" amused him—and his friends wanted to go out on Friday night and she was trying to be a chill girlfriend, four months into their relationship, so there they were. Dez was drinking a Count Orlok. She was drinking a Carmilla. She'd almost ordered it virgin, but remembered at the last minute that *that*, at least, was not a problem anymore.

Dez was in a bad mood and trying to disguise it because he had no excuse—his team had just won a case on which he'd had the privilege of serving as second chair. She was in a bad mood because she had a positive pregnancy test on Wednesday and an abortion on Thursday, and while she was hurrying past the protesters at the Planned Parenthood on 27th street, one pretty teen in a Life Warrior shirt jumped out from behind the tiny coffined fetus dolls and God Hates You signs and shrieked straight at Lily, eyes on fire, "Congratulations! It's a boy!"

So they were both short-tempered as a pair of snippy chihuahuas to begin with, but as usual, Lily was showing it more—interrupting his friends' assholish assessments of various women, mocking the waitresses' vampire fangs, saying vampires were so last decade anyway. At one point his law school friend Henry widened his eyes and muttered, "Some breeds just have *bad* temperaments," and Lily was about to claw him a new one when Dez pulled her aside and said, "What is *with* you tonight?" As if she was the one instigating everything. A catapult of snub-nosed anger and guilt snapped inside her, the distant desire to bring the enormous chandelier down onto her head and just put everyone out of the misery of dealing with her.

"I had an abortion yesterday," she said, at last.

"*What?*" He couldn't hear over the club remix of "My Boyfriend's Back."

"I *had* to *have* an *abortion!*" she screamed.

They staggered down two flights of stairs without saying goodbye to his friends and stood on the sidewalk with the armed bouncers and the unlicensed murder cabs and the crying twenty-somethings realizing, just now, that the Earth they were going to inherit was dying.

Dez was so concerned, so frustrated that she hadn't told him as soon as she counted the days since her last period and found the number to be too high—certainly as soon as she fainted in the Knox Gilbert bathroom before her 9 AM presentation. He thought it meant she didn't trust him, but what it really meant was that she didn't want to lose him. "I could have been there for you!" he said, gesturing wildly at the world's abortion clinics, but all she could tell him was the truth: "He would have killed you. He would have killed you if you had helped me."

His eyes bulged, no doubt imagining a jealous ex. He didn't know how right he was. "Who?"

But they had already talked about this, over the course of an entire painful weekend, and Lily almost hailed a cab then and there. "Dez, I wasn't joking about the curse I told you about. It's real. This isn't like those... those fucking waitresses with their plastic fangs and their terrible Eastern European accents. This isn't a costume. Everything I am, everything I've ever done, is because of this *thing*, this *monster*. I'm cursed, Dez, I'm broken."

Of course the standing assumption at work was that she'd slept with the CEO, even though as Cooper said, "Hard to imagine Ice Queen giving a blow job worth more than a buck."

Dez was shaking his head, making cautious little movements toward her as if trying to approach her for a cha-cha. "L. It is *not* everything you are."

She scoffed in disbelief as a police car wailed past.

"Listen to me, listen. You know what I heard as soon as we won that case? I heard *my* demon saying, 'You shouldn't even be here. You're only here cuz your ancestors cheated their way out of slavery. You're trash dressed up in your master's clothes. I gave you all this and I can take it away.' That fucker was ready and waiting for the jury to say Guilty just so it could step in and ruin everything. But I gotta remind myself, and you gotta remind yourself, that the demon's just this ugly thing that bashes heads in and waits to get born. It's got jack shit to do with who you are, what you can do."

He was holding her. She asked, "How do you get past the guilt? Knowing you cheated?"

She felt him sigh deeply. "My mother always said... life's not fair. You gotta do what you gotta do to survive." He pulled back a little to look at her as a blast of sweet, cold air made his shirt collar ripple slightly—but it was nothing, just the bouncer opening the door to let another gilded couple in. "Anyway, we didn't cheat. We pay the price. Every damn day."

***

Witch proposes, God disposes.

Cady Twining had been climbing all night—through the wild and the wood, through witch-hazel and elderberry, over branches and animals both dead and alive. The more tears in her skin and dress, the faster she scrambled. Running from her fate, so Hannah Bolton said, running from the true and just wrath of God. Hannah Bolton and her husband John wanted Cady hung for witchcraft, even though she was sure that the Boltons and the Downings and the Hills were the ones who had been crippling her family's livestock ever since her father died. They also said her poor broken mother had died of drink; an unchaste witch just like your mother, Merwyn Downing said. It was burning her to give up her father's land; she knew that without it, the world would kill her. But she would rather die by nature's hands than her neighbors', she had already decided. She was just going to have to find a hole somewhere, so she could bury herself in the dirt like a broken-winged sparrow and die.

She slept all night on the pebbled shore of Spirit Lake, ready to embrace the howl of the wind but hearing only silence. She dreamt of being dragged away by an enormous wolf, and then of a tall man in a heavy cloak and crown hovering over the water. She thought there was a chance she wouldn't wake, but her eyes were open at dawn, and something unseen was racing across the glassy lake toward her—something that was slicing off the top inch of water like a knife. Perhaps she could have started running. Perhaps she could have prayed. But she did not. She waited until the knife rested against her neck, until the offer was made, and then she said yes.

She climbed back down the hill to see the Boltons dead, the Downings chased out of town, the Hills on trial for witchcraft.

In the years that followed she slipped back unnoticed onto her father's neglected land and tilled its earth alone until she married a quiet, peaceable newcomer and had twin daughters, each of whom were dragged from their beds and into the trees on the night of their seventh birthday. After that Cady cocooned; she found the psychic nest she wanted to die in and curled up within it, yet no long sleep came. So she cupped her daughters Mary and Martha each by the cheek and told them everything. "You must never give him a son," she said to them, and then she walked to the massive drop of Swallows Ledge and jumped to her death. She had considered taking them with her, but hadn't had the heart. *Weakling,* she thought on the way down.

And many years that followed after that, Lily Twining woke up on the side of the highway, having buckled under the weight of her newfound freedom on her way home, and realized that the wail coming from under the glove compartment was her husband calling.

"L?" He sounded very far away, lodged in a world that was now gone. "What the hell happened? I've called three times! Have you seen the shit that's coming out of Sparta?"

She silently shook her head, hoping he wouldn't tell her. The radio was off, and she didn't want to know the numbers of the dead. She had already seen it, anyway—she understood now, at long last, that the Juggernaut had foretold it years ago. When he first held her in his grip and turned her body inside out, he had shown her how simple and ultimate true barrenness was.

"It's over now, Dez." She wiped a few insistent tears away and tried to think of him. She had broken up with him once, and drunkenly printed out a photo of them arm-in-arm in the Virgin Islands just to write in permanent marker across his face: *BETTER OFF ALONE.* Now all at once every time she thought of his face all she could see were black "X"s over his eyes, the tilted crosses steadily reverberating to the beat of something much older than the two of them. She quickly resumed talking. Tried again to make everything all right. "We can have our baby now. Boy or girl, doesn't matter. We just need to find a way around your demon but we can do it, I know we can. We'll pray."

She could tell by the fast pace of his breathing and the hush in his throat that he was incredulous. An unbeliever. But Lily was laughing, laughing like a small child with her head banging against the head rest, laughing because the great dark volcano was rising fast over the horizon, swelling like a metastasizing heart against the ribs of the world. The blind engine. The master and subduer. Their eternal unbreakable God.

ACKNOWLEDGMENTS

Thank you to writers and editors who have supported me over the years, including Paul Tremblay, Gemma Files, Silvia Moreno-Garcia, Nick Mamatas, John Langan, Brett Savory, Simon Strantzas, Jesse Bullington, Paula Guran. Thank you to my English teachers and political science professors, including Anne Cognard, Alexander Cooley, Mona El-Ghobashy, and the late Nicholas Spencer.

Thank you to Ross Lockhart and the Word Horde team for taking on *She Said Destroy*.

Thank you to my best friend Lindsey Allen for suffering through my early stories and tragedies and always calling me on my shit. "Girl, I Love You" is for her.

Finally, I want to thank my parents, Farchan Bulkin and Jan Hostetler, for letting me read at the dinner table and buying blank notebooks by the crate. "Endless Life" is for my dad. "No Gods, No Masters" is for my mom.

PUBLICATION HISTORY

"Intertropical Convergence Zone." *ChiZine*, ed. Brett Savory, 2008. Reprinted in *Million Writers Award: The Best Online Science Fiction and Fantasy*, ed. Jason Sanford, 2012.

"The Five Stages of Grief." *Three-lobed Burning Eye*, ed. Andrew Fuller, 2008.

"And When She Was Bad." *Nossa Morte*, ed. Melissa De Kler, 2009.

"Only Unity Saves the Damned." *Letters to Lovecraft*, ed. Jesse Bullington, 2014. Reprinted in *Year's Best Dark Fantasy & Horror: 2015*, ed. Paula Guran.

"Pugelbone." *ChiZine*, ed. Brett Savory, 2010.

"Red Goat, Black Goat." *Innsmouth Free Press*, ed. Silvia Moreno-Garcia and Paula Stiles, 2010. Reprinted in *Lovecraft's Monsters*, ed. Ellen Datlow, 2014.

"Seven Minutes in Heaven." *Aickman's Heirs*, ed. Simon Strantzas, 2015. Reprinted in *Year's Best Dark Fantasy & Horror: 2016*, ed. Paula Guran.

"Girl, I Love You." *Phantasm Japan*, ed. Nick Mamatas and Masumi Washington, 2014.

"Endless Life." *Phantasmagorium*, ed. Laird Barron, 2012.

"Violet Is the Color of Your Energy." *She Walks in Shadows*, ed. Silvia Moreno-Garcia and Paula Stiles, 2015. Reprinted in *Year's Best Weird Fiction*, Volume 3, ed. Simon Strantzas and Michael Kelly, 2016.

"Truth Is Order and Order Is Truth." *Sword & Mythos*, ed. Silvia Moreno-Garcia and Paula Stiles, 2014.

"Absolute Zero." *Creatures: Thirty Years of Monsters*, ed. John Langan and Paul Tremblay, 2011. Reprinted in *Fantasy Magazine*, ed. John Joseph Adams, 2011.

"No Gods, No Masters." (original to this publication).

"…a brilliant Cthonic horror fantasia full of creepy religion, grief, pain, sorrow and snakes." –Gemma Files, author of *Experimental Film*

When reporter Cora Mayburn is assigned to cover a story about a snake-handling cult in rural Appalachia, she is dismayed, for the world of cruel fundamentalist stricture, repression, glossolalia, and abuse is something she has long since put behind her in favor of a more tolerant urban existence.

As Cora begins to uncover the secrets concealed by a veneer of faith and tradition, something ancient and long concealed begins to awaken. What secrets do the townsfolk know? What might the handsome young pastor be hiding? What will happen when occulted horrors writhe to the surface, when pallid and forgotten things rise to reclaim the Earth?

Will Cora–and the earth–survive? The answers–and pure terror–can only be found in one place: *Beneath*.

Trade Paperback, 314 pp, $16.99

ISBN-13: 978-1-939905-29-1

http://www.wordhorde.com

"...an excellent read for those who enjoy myths and legends of all kinds." —*Publishers Weekly* (starred review)

For a decade, author Christine Morgan's Viking stories have delighted readers and critics alike, standing apart from the anthologies they appeared in. Now, Word Horde brings you *The Raven's Table*, the first-ever collection of Christine Morgan's Vikings, from "The Barrow-Maid" to "Aerkheim's Horror" and beyond. These tales of adventure, fantasy, and horror will rouse your inner Viking.

"...stories that will make you want to don your helm, sword and shield before riding off into battle." —*The Grim Reader*

Format: Trade Paperback, 306 pp, $15.99

ISBN-13: 978-1-939905-27-7

http://www.wordhorde.com

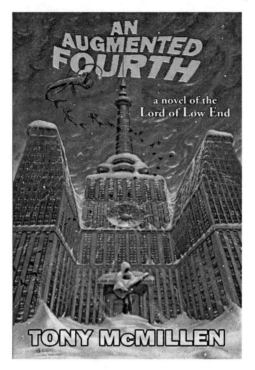

Codger Burton, bassist and lyricist for Frivolous Black, the heaviest heavy metal band to ever come out of the UK, awakens to find his hotel snowed in, his band mates evacuated, and monsters roaming the halls. Looks like Codger picked the wrong week to quit using cocaine. From the twisted mind of Tony McMillen comes the hilarious rock and roll horror of *An Augmented Fourth*, a novel of the Lord of Low End.

Trade Paperback, 314 pp, $15.99
ISBN-13: 978-1-939905-31-4
http://www.wordhorde.com

Can we speak with the spirits of the dead? Is it possible to know the future? Are our dreams harbingers of things to come? Do auspicious omens and cautionary portents effect our lives?

Edited by Ross E. Lockhart, *Tales from a Talking Board* examines these questions—and more—with tales of auguries, divination, and fortune telling, through devices like Ouija boards, tarot cards, and stranger things.

So dim the lights, place your hands upon the planchette, and ask the spirits to guide you as we present fourteen stories of the strange and supernatural by Matthew M. Bartlett, Nadia Bulkin, Nathan Carson, Kristi DeMeester, Orrin Grey, Scott R. Jones, David James Keaton, Anya Martin, J. M. McDermott, S. P. Miskowski, Amber-Rose Reed, Tiffany Scandal, David Templeton, and Wendy N. Wagner.

Format: Trade Paperback, 228 pp, $15.99

ISBN-13: 978-1-939905 35 2

http://www.wordhorde.com

ABOUT THE AUTHOR

Nadia Bulkin writes scary stories about the scary world we live in, three of which have been nominated for a Shirley Jackson Award. Her stories have been included in volumes of *The Year's Best Horror* (Datlow), *The Year's Best Dark Fantasy and Horror* (Guran) and *The Year's Best Weird Fiction*; in venues such as *Nightmare*, *Fantasy*, *The Dark*, and *ChiZine*; and in anthologies such as *She Walks in Shadows* (winner of the World Fantasy Award) and *Aickman's Heirs* (winner of the Shirley Jackson Award). She spent her childhood in Indonesia with a Javanese father and an American mother, then relocated to Nebraska. She now has a B.A. in political science, an M.A. in international affairs, and lives in Washington, D.C.